PAUL DIFILIPPO
brings us just the fax, as a pair of kids prove the pen is still
mightier than the sword, even in the electronic age.

JOSEPHA SHERMAN
shows us a princess who is out to prove to her father and people that
women have equal rites, especially when it comes to demon hunting.

TOM PICCIRILLI
illustrates just how deadly greed can be, as one man returns home
to revisit the dark past he thought he had left behind.

MIKE RESNICK
takes us full circle for a very unique take on the history of
science fiction.

ALLEN M. STEELE
shares a vision of a family lost and in danger on the
first human voyage into space.

PATRICK THOMAS
takes us to Bulfinche's Pub where a woman trying to get away with
murder attracts some unwanted attention from Death himself.

THE 2ND COMING

The Best of Pirate Writings, Vol. 2

EDITED BY
EDWARD J. MCFADDEN

PADWOLF
PUBLISHING

PADWOLF PUBLISHING INC.
457 Main Street, #384
Farmingdale, NY 11735

WWW.PADWOLF.COM

THE 2nd COMING: The Best Of Pirate Writings, Vol. 2
Edited by Edward J. McFadden III

Cover art © 1997 Brian Durfee
Copyedited & proofread by Ian Randal Strock

ISBN: 1-890096-13-X
Printed in the USA
First Printing

For my daughter, Samantha Paige McFadden, whose pending arrival pushed me to complete this project.

Special thanks: to Kathie Golden for typing much of this book from the original printings--this book would not exist if it had not been for her help and dedication; to my wife, Dawn; to my mother, Carol; to Patrick Thomas; to Diane Raetz, Stuart Weinberg and everyone at Padwolf Publishing, Inc. for believing in me; to Warren Lapine; to Tom Piccirilli; and to all the authors who were kind enough to allow their works to appear in this book.

<u>CONTENTS</u>

INTRODUCTION
THE 2ND COMING –
THE BEST OF PIRATE WRITINGS VOL. 2
BY
EDWARD J. MCFADDEN III

Well, here we are again. (If you're here for the first time, that's OK, just know you've entered Volume Two, and Volume One awaits you.)

As with Volume One, this introduction will try to relate some information about myself, **Pirate Writings** and why this book exists. The main reason **The 2nd Coming: The Best of Pirate Writings Vol. 2** was published was to find a new audience, folks who had never seen or heard of the magazine. Hopefully, Volume Two will accomplish this goal in much the same way Volume One did.

It was 1998 when Padwolf Publishing, Inc. and I began discussions about the final version of **The Best of Pirate Writings: Tales of Fantasy, Mystery & Science Fiction**. The final draft of the book, per my bean, was approximately 160,000 words. Padwolf, an up-and-coming publishing company that was succeeding due to smart budgeting and extreme dedication, had their own thoughts. Hence, it was agreed, pretty much from the outset, that the revised first edition of **The Best of Pirate Writings: Tales of Fantasy, Mystery & Science fiction** would bear a Volume One label upon it's cover and I would turn in a manuscript that reflected the most commercially viable version of the book, with the broadest editorial scope, not to exceed 80,000 words. The understanding was that if and when sales justified it, Volume Two would be published. I consider Vol. One a success. Though there are still copies available of Vol. One's First Printing, I believe Padwolf agrees with me. It is a strange dance that leads one person, or company, to expend time, energy and money on another person to deliver a product that people want to buy. I'm not talking about the 1,000th rehash of Dickens or Bradbury, but something different, irreverent, funny and moving. As with all things analyzed after the fact, Padwolf and I recognize some missteps in the first volume, starting with the biggest printer error of the century, to a cover that was a little too over the edge, even with it's pun-like blurb from

Dean Koontz proudly displayed on the cover. Live and learn.

That's where this whole crazy thing started anyway…live and learn.

The Lord of the Rings, as I've written before, was the start of my literary life and hence symbolically played a large role in the creation of **Pirate Writings**. Seeing LOTR on plastic cups at fast food restaurants was a bit much for me to take, however. *Star Wars*, *The Matrix* and the like are somewhat different--they were children of the media blitz--LOTR had been around for over 50 years (long before the "Happy Meal".) A story known by many, studied by few, I pride myself on being somewhat of a Tolkien historian. When I first started writing and editing, I wanted to pay homage to Tolkien, and in a very public way. Writing a story using his characters or material is not legal; stories in tribute had been tried, and failed, in my opinion. Poetry seemed to somehow slip under the radar. *Minas Tirith Evening-Star*, a Tolkien fanzine that has been published since 1962, printed poetry featuring Tolkien's characters, and had had no reprisals, no cease and desists. So, in tribute to Tolkien, I submitted the following as a "poetry" submission, and they printed it in their 25th anniversary issue.

THE TRAVELER

It was September 22, S.R. 1446, and I had been three days out from Bree when I crossed the Brandywine Bridge and headed for Stock. As I walked, the Brandywine River flowed noisily by, its currents exceedingly strong for a Fall night in The Shire. A chill wind blew faintly across the land, whispering of times and places long gone, whispering of the sea, of the Grey Havens.

The need to taste the best beer in the East Farthing, as well as my craving for companionship were, perhaps, the main reasons I stopped at the Golden Perch. Its rustic exterior, its homelike surroundings, a place where friends came to meet, a perfect place.

Upon entering, I had been treated to a surprise beyond my reckoning; Master Samwise was in town on business. He sat in a corner surrounded by many hobbits. His age-worn face gray and drab, yet his eyes still gleamed with adventure and poetry. The group of over-zealous Hobbits were pestering the more-than-delighted old hobbit to recite a piece of his verse, which over the years had become quite refined.

"Very well! I daresay most of you have heard this one before, yet tonight…it seems fitting, if you understand me," he said as silence fell about the inn. Then standing up, with his hands behind his back, as if he were addressing a group of hobbit children, he began.

Evening fell, and stars shown bright,
  the ripple of the sea forever white.
Songs of elves and men echoed long and fair,
  carried softly on the night air.
The hemlock stood still, the beasts silent,
  a place of peace, a place of alleviation.

Galadriel stood waiting there,
  the moonlight shown in her golden hair.
Nenya shined with power and might,
  its single white stone, frosty and bright.
Elrond in a mantle of gray,
  of the age gone by, he had naught to say.
Vilya he wore, the mightiest of the three,
  its tacit puissance none could see.
Bilbo rode atop his small gray steed,
  his mind, his life, free from burden.
On they rode, through the midst of The Shire,
  through the Far Downs and down to the sea,
  to Mithlond, to the Grey Havens.

A white ship lay waiting there,
  its sails and bow strong and fair.
Narya shown on Gandalf's hand,
  as he waited and looked out upon the land.
There many farewells were said,
  to Sam, Peregrin and Meriadoc,
  without whom all would have fallen.

Frodo sailed away on the white ship,
  his mind filled with memories,
  'The road goes ever on and on . . .'

The road endeth at the sea.

        Sam's voice trailed away into silence, his face glowing red as
he looked around at the faces staring at him in wonder. I'll never forget
that night. Even as I sit in the kingly Citadel of Minas Tirith, my heart is
in The Shire.

Understand, *Minas Tirith Evening-Star* openly advertised and sold magazines…so chances are it went across the desk of someone monitoring the family's rights to Tolkien's work, just like Star Trek fanzines are reviewed and dismissed at Paramount.

Know as you read this book that Tolkien is here. From the poem *Caradhras*, to the story *The Mines of Moria*, and many more subtle references. I have known Tolkien a long time, and am happy millions more have discovered his vision.

And so things change. ***Pirate Writings*** is no more. This second, and final, volume effectively seals ***Pirate Writings*** history. When I sold the magazine to DNA Publications, it was always understood that at some point the vagueness of the name would hold the magazine back…and it is a commercial product after all. So when DNA acquired the rights to publish ***Fantastic Stories of the Imagination***, a fiction title that had been around more than 30 years, we decided it was time to fold ***Pirate Writings*** into ***Fantastic Stories*** with me as the editor. So, like the dark lord, ***Pirate Writings*** lives on in the legal text of ***Fantastic Stories***, which is now a full-color, slick, commercial fiction magazine. The future will undoubtedly hold a "best of" ***Fantastic Stories***, but under what guise, in what shape and size, none yet knows. Hopefully it will be as rewarding as ***The Best of Pirate Writings: Tales of Fantasy, Mystery & Science Fiction***. Read on and enjoy....

WARNING, WARNING
ALLEN M. STEELE

The first interstellar expedition was doomed from the beginning.

Not because of inadequate technology—the starship itself, an elegantly designed saucer-shaped craft, used a revolutionary hyperdrive as its main propulsion system—but because of lack of forethought. Yet the mission planners were so intent upon colonizing an Earth-like planet that lunar-based telescopes had discovered, against all odds, in orbit around Alpha Centauri, that they didn't take into consideration all the variables.

First, there was the foolishness of sending forth a single family. Some-one failed to read J.B. Birdsell's paper, "Biological Dimensions of Small, Founding Populations" (*Interstellar Migration and the Human Experience*, University of California Press, 1985) which postulated, with considerable evidence gained from the observation of isolated third-world populations, that a group of at least one hundred people was necessary for the formation of a healthy, self-sustaining colony. Yet the starship had been built to carry only six passengers, who would be sealed within cryogenic freezing tubes during the four-and-a-half years it would take the vessel to reach its desti-nation. Budget cutbacks were cited as reason for the fact the ship wasn't made bigger, yet the mission planners could have selected a biologically diverse crew. Three single men and three single women, perhaps, or even three married couples. A family of five, plus one unattached male, may have been psychologically stable, yet it also severely limited the available gene pool. A lot of crude jokes were made about the possible pairings among the three children and the ship's pilot.

But that wasn't the worst of it. A saboteur hired by a hostile nation—Iraq? North Korea? Libya? To this day, no one knows for sure—had man-aged to become a member of the launch support team; indeed, he was the doctor who gave the crew its preflight physical just before launch. Shortly before the starship left Earth, the doctor successfully penetrated the secu-rity cordon surrounding the launch pad and entered the spacecraft. A guard discovered him within the ship, but the doctor killed him; his body was later discovered in a dumpster near the pad. The doctor then reprogrammed the ship's environmental control robot to destroy its major systems six hours after launch.

It should have been a perfect crime, yet the saboteur's luck ran out when he was caught aboard at liftoff. Panic-stricken, he revived the family and the pilot from suspended animation, but not before the robot severely damaged the inertial guidance system and destroyed the radio transmitter. The starship's hyperdrive, now wildly out of control, propelled the vessel out of the solar system; no one aboard was sure what happened next, but somehow the vessel caused a wormhole to form, and suddenly they found themselves in another part of the galaxy.

It was only merciful intervention on the part of the family matriarch which prevented the pilot from jettisoning the doctor from the airlock, yet the saboteur—clearly mentally unstable from the beginning, and now a full-blown paranoid-schizophrenic—attempted twice to kill members of the crew before the ship was forced to crash-land on a desert planet.

The members of the expedition tried to make the best of their dire situation. The youngest child, who was something of a prodigy despite his youth, restored the robot's original programming so that it was no longer homicidal. Meanwhile his father and the pilot explored the area surrounding the crash site, and his mother and two older sisters successfully set up a base camp. For a time, they gained the semblance of a model nuclear family, and soon they undertook the task of making their ship flightworthy once more.

Yet the doctor had become increasingly psychotic. When he wasn't talking aloud to the robot or hoarding food rations, he was still scheming to murder various members of the expedition (save for the boy, upon whom he seemed to have an unhealthy fixation). Soon it became too much for them to bear. After a whispered conference with the father, the pilot drew a laser pistol from the ship's weapons locker, escorted their unwanted guest a couple of miles from the base camp and, behind the shelter of a large boulder, shot him dead. The doctor was buried in a shallow, unmarked grave; to the end, no one knew if the name he had given them was his real one.

The execution of the doctor, albeit necessary, nonetheless had a bad effect upon morale. Until this point, the older daughter had been attracted to the pilot, which had been anticipated by the mission planners and condoned by her parents. Afterwards, she became increasingly aloof, not only from the pilot (who in turn became frustrated when his advances were coldly rebuffed) but also her family. She was the next to die, when a sudden earthquake dislodged a massive boulder and caused it to roll down a steep escarpment beneath which she happened to be standing.

The pilot was the sole witness to her death; in the weeks that followed, he fell into a state of acute depression which left him sullen and unwary. Nearly a month later, one of the sixty-foot-tall cyclopean giants who prowled a nearby valley found him while he was tending to a remote weather platform. His remains were discovered the following day, or at least those which hadn't been devoured.

Struggling against shock and grief, the rest of the family redoubled their efforts to repair the starship, yet the odds had turned against them. The alien world, so Earth-like at first glance, had gradually revealed itself to be unrelentingly hostile, and they were woefully unprepared for its abrupt climatic shifts and bizarre life forms.

Yet it was human error that killed the younger daughter. Her brother hand-built a SOS rocket that he planned to launch into space. Just whom it was supposed to attract is an unfathomable question, considering that the planet lay some uncalculated distance from Earth; the fact that his father allowed him to proceed with this project in the first place is an indication of their desperation. Yet shortly after launch, the rocket exploded in the high atmosphere and fell back into the camp as a fireball; although the boy survived its impact, his sister was incinerated.

The boy went into catatonic shock; refusing to speak, refusing to eat, he could only stare straight ahead with blank, dead eyes. His parents decided to return him to cryogenic suspension. Two of his siblings had perished already, and now they feared for the life of their youngest child. So they dressed him again in his silver-foil spacesuit, and placed him in one of the freezing tubes within the ship.

This was a wise decision, for it was only three days later that they were caught in a freak electrical storm caused by the planet's erratic climate. They were attempting to cover the small hydroponic farm when lightning struck the metal tarp pole the father happened to be holding at that moment. He was killed instantly.

In the end, the mother fought a solitary battle to preserve what little was left of her family. With the assistance of the robot, she managed to get the starship back to operational condition; although the hyperdrive was never completely restored to warp capability, it could attain a maximum velocity of .75 light speed. Yet when the time came for her to leave the nameless planet upon which she had been marooned, she found herself unwilling to leave her husband and two daughters. Perhaps this was misplaced loyalty, or perhaps she had simply gone insane herself. Most likely she believed that the expedition had been jinxed from the beginning, and that by remaining behind she would remove the curse.

Whatever the reason, she programmed the robot to launch the starship back into space. When the starship lifted off, she was huddled beneath a flimsy tent near the family graveyard, watching as the saucer rose into the monochrome sky. A brave, strong-willed woman, she managed to survive for three more months before she succumbed to starvation.

Once the ship was in space once more, the robot plotted a return trajectory to Earth, based upon star charts and data from the ship's onboard computers. That task took nearly two hours; it's possible that the robot could have done the same job earlier, while the ship was still near Earth, had the doctor not fouled its programming. Yet a job done late is better than a job never done, and once the return course was set, the robot returned to its bay on the vessel lower level, from which it would periodically emerge, once every six months, to check the ship's status during its voyage home.

It was destined to be a long trip. The starship had crashed on a planet in orbit around 70 Virginis, located nearly 59 light-years from Earth. Even at maximum velocity, it would take the ship nearly a century for it to complete its journey.

Within a cryogenic tube on the ship's upper level, the sole surviving member of Earth's first interstellar expedition remained an eternal child. In a perpetual state of REM dream-sleep, his subconscious mind evoked surreal fantasies in which his family, along with the pilot and the doctor, were not only alive and well, but also having spectacular adventures. Locked in suspended animation, he encountered extraterrestrial circuses and intergalactic traders, space hippies and space bikers, frog-headed princes and carrot men and mouthless invaders from the fifth dimension, all utterly strange yet comforting in their simplicity. And through all this, his family was always with him: his sisters ageless and beautiful, his mother kindly and forgiving, and his father handsome and brave. The robot sang and cracked jokes, and the doctor became his guardian and best friend.

The dreams of a young boy, lost in space.

<u>CARADHRAS</u>

Sunlight shimmers off the
new fallen snow
My small window is frosted,
covered with memories of Smaug

In my mind's eye I see them,
burrowing like ants through
the evil snow

I feel the ring pulling, searching
its malevolence stretching out its arm
calling the Dark Lord

The chill wind bites the fellowship,
pushing them toward the dark
On they move, slowly,
until they are free

I can feel the ring's anger
a cold hatred
The company is weak, yet determined
I know they will go on
even though Caradhras has defeated them

-Translated into modern English by Edward J. McFadden
(Written by Bilbo Baggins and first read in The Hall of Fire, S.R. 1419)

FAX
PAUL DIFILIPPO

Garth Barth weighed ninety-eight and one-half pounds. And that was counting a dozen pens in a plastic pocket protector, a pair of Hush Puppies and eyeglasses with lenses thick as geological strata. He wore chinos and madras shirts buttoned to the neck. His hair sported a cowlick that resembled the ass-plumage of a certain species of South American quetzal. In short, Garth looked like a quintessential member of that much-maligned class known far and wide across the nation, a class which boasted members in every high school, college, and large corporation.

A techno-dweeb-hacker-nerd-bookworm-pointdexter-putz.

The only difference between Garth and other members of his class—and a large difference it was—was that his look was a conscious effort, a deliberate disguise. Protective camouflage, if you will.

At age thirteen, just as he was preparing to enter the violent Darwinian social arena of high school, Garth had come to the conclusion that there was no one in his peer group who could share his particular interests and concerns, these ranging from the history of altered states of consciousness to artificial intelligence, from comix to industrial music, from biology to theology.

Moreover, there existed certain individuals who were downright inimical and hostile to this point of view, people who actively resented his opinions and would defend to Garth's death his right to be beaten up for trying to use his freedom of speech.

Having reached this conclusion, based solidly on the facts available to him, Garth decided he would strive to become as invisible as possible, hiding his true subversive nature beneath a mask of acceptable weirdness. Making a survey of all possible socio-cultural roles, Garth settled upon his current disguise as providing the best cover. Not only did most parental adults look approvingly on such inbred scholastic types, but to Garth's peers the nerd somatotype had become almost transparent, due to overexposure in the media. Even the most brutish jock nowadays could hardly be bothered to torment such a nonentity—especially if the nerd in questionscould be counted on to supply written-to-order term papers.

Three years after coming to this decision, Garth was still somewhat surprised at how well his scheme had worked. No one had ever noticed that his Hush Puppies were cleverly crafted foam shells concealing Adidas, nor that the tee-shirt under his madras advertised a Captain Beefheart album, nor that his lenses were plain glass, nor that half of his breast-pocket pens concealed tightly twisted joints in their barrels.

Still, despite the success of Garth's disguise and the freedom it gave him to pursue his own interests, it was a lonely life Garth led. Sometimes he wished there was at least one person he could open up to and be himself…

One fine spring day during gym period Garth found himself sneaking off the playing field of Xerox Inc. High. (The school had renamed itself in gratitude after receiving a large corporate grant.) A coed field hockey game was in progress, and Garth had no desire to have his shins bashed to flinders. Some of those girls were really vicious… No, such subliminated warfare was not for him. Instead, he would sit peacefully in his usual hiding place until it was time to get dressed. He would peacefully smoke a joint and contemplate his latest experiments.

Around the side of the building, a set of wide concrete stairs led from the ground to a second-floor emergency exit. The stairs were open on either side. Beneath the cement structure, set back in the thickest shadows, was an old plastic milk crate someone had lifted from the cafeteria. Here Garth could sit and, by occasionally craning his neck, still maintain a view of the game, so that he would know when to rejoin his classmates.

The bare dirt beneath the steps smelled of urine from a hundred drunken extracurricular pissings. Garth was anxious to light up and dispel the aroma. He had just taken his seat and removed a pen from his pocket (he still wore his buttoned-tight madras with his gym shorts) when he became aware of a subdued sobbing directly at his elbow.

"Uh, who's that?" asked Garth warily.

The sobbing stopped. Through sniffles, an accented voice said, "It's me, Reba. Who're you?"

Reba Amoeba was a recent arrival to Xerox Inc. High. Her family had moved here from Texas, fleeing that state's economic depression. Reba's real last name was Tupple. Everyone called her Reba Amoeba cuz she was kinda fat. She probably weighed twice as much as Garth, but she was tall too. Garth didn't think she looked so bad. She had a sweet, albeit blotchy face and dressed nice. In addition, she had the biggest, most awesome tits Garth had ever seen. He suspected that half of the enmity she incurred from other girls stemmed from unacknowledged jealousy. Garth also thought her accent was charming.

"It's Garth. From math class."

Reba snorted. "Humph. Mister Brain."

Garth felt hurt. His self-devised image and reputation had never seemed so cumbersome. Perhaps he could let it drop just this once.

"Maybe," Garth replied mysteriously. "And maybe not. What're you doing here anyway?"

"I hate all those smug dudes and bitches and they hate me. I don't need to get whopped upside the head with a stick to make it sink in."

Garth nodded in the darkness. His eyes had adjusted, and he could make out the silhouette of Reba sitting on the grungy dirt. Her hunched shoulders made her look pretty miserable. Garth felt bad for her. "That's more or less my situation too. But listen, I got something to make you feel better. Here, hold this a second."

Passing the pen to Reba, Garth fumbled for some matches.

"Oh, great, a pen. What're we gonna do—write some equations?"

Garth just smiled. "Let us not prejudge things, shall we?" Garth took back the pen, unscrewed the barrel and removed a fine joint. He held it toward Reba so she could see.

"Wow," she exclaimed appreciatively. "I haven't smoked anything since I left home."

"Uh, care to share my seat...?"

Garth shifted, and Reba quickly settled half her large butt onto the milk crate, leaving a little corner for Garth. It was enough. Her big old warm hip felt like heaven. Garth lit up, and passed the joint to Reba; in between tokes, they soon began dissing representative local shitheads. Before they knew it, they were laughing and hanging on each other like forever best friends. When they stumbled out from beneath the steps at the end of the period to head back to the locker-rooms, they saw that each had one bare thigh whose back was imprinted with a waffle pattern. This really cracked them up, and they could barely walk.

Meeting afterwards in the corridor outside the gym, Reba and Garth looked somewhat shyly at each other. Things seemed a little different in the light of day, on the downside of their shared high.

"Uh, you won't tell anyone about my pens, will you?"

"Not if you don't tell 'bout how you found me crying."

"Oh, no, not a word, I promise."

"Me too."

They were silent a moment. Then Garth said, "Wanna come home with me after school and see what I've got in my basement?"

"Why, sure."

Garth smiled broadly up into Reba's face. She lit up too. He tried to think of something suitably impressive to say, but nothing came to him. Finally, he took off his glasses and whispered, "They're fake."

"Oh," said Reba. She seemed to understand. At least Garth hoped so.

After school Garth found Reba waiting with a fatalistic look that betokened many previous disappointments. When she saw Garth, she broke into a huge smile. He had been half hoping she wouldn't be there. This sharing stuff was tricky, and took more thought and work than being alone all the time. He hoped he was up to it, after such a long solitary existence.

At the door of Garth's house, Reba paused.

"Won't your Mom think it's funny, you bringing me down the basement?"

Funny? Garth felt a quiver. What did this girl have in mind? God, she was big….He tentatively took Reba's hand. She squeezed it. Garth was moved. "I don't know. I never had anyone over before. Let's see."

Mrs. Barth was skiing. Dressed in Rossignol boots, red spandex tights and a leotard, she shuffled on a Nordic trainer in front of a wall-sized rear-projection television screen which Garth had constructed from scratch. Synched with the trainer, the visuals on the screen zipped through Alpine slopes glistening with fresh powder.

"Hi, Ma. Listen, I've got a friend with me. We're gonna look at my hardware, okay?"

Mrs. Barth was intent on her cross-country pilgrimage, and didn't look up. "Uh-huh, fine, dear. Oh, could you turn up the heat before you go? It's a little chilly in here."

"Sure, Ma."

After notching up the thermostat, Garth brought Reba to the cellar door. He flipped on the basement light and they went downstairs.

"Your mother seems nice," said Reba

"She's heavily into fitness."

"I thought so."

Garth unlocked the door of his basement headquarters and motioned for Reba to enter first.

Half of Garth's secret hideaway looked like an electronics retailer. There were racks of stereo equipment, VCRs and monitors, and computers. Piles of CDs and tapes spilled from shelves. The other half looked like James Watson's wet dream. There were pocket gene-sequencers and peptide-linkers, ribosomal simulators and enzymatic baths. There was also a couch and a dorm-sized fridge.

"This place is so cool!" Reba said. Garth felt proud. "Where did you get all this stuff? And how did you ever afford it?"

"Oh, I do a little work for a few companies. Programming and stuff. It pays pretty good."

"Don't they mind how young you are?"

"They never see me. It's all done over the net."

By the way of illustration, Garth powered up a Pentium machine. Then, remembering his manners, he went to the fridge and removed a beaker containing a yellow liquid. "Want a drink?"

Reba looked slightly suspicious. "What is it?"

"It's just a mildly psychoactive relaxant and stimulant that will uncoil your DNA, ream out your cholesterol and refresh your long-term memory. And best of all, it doesn't taste like anything gross. I usually cut it with orange juice."

"In that case, I don't mind if I do."

Garth poured the drinks, and they toasted, then sipped.

"Mind if I get out of this stupid disguise?" asked Garth.

"Go right ahead."

Garth took off his glasses and combed his cowlick down. He stripped off his button-down to reveal a John Zorn tee-shirt. He unlaced his foam Hush Puppies and cast them aside. He put on a CD and turned around. Reba was sitting on the couch.

"This DNA stuff is great. I feel like I'm floating above all my problems."

"I thought you'd like it."

"Come sit down with me."

"Okay."

They sat quietly for a while, listening to the music. It was Talking Heads.

I got a girlfriend that's better than that
She has the smoke in her eyes
She's moving up, going right through my heart
She's gonna give me surprise

Reba had finished her drink. Her eyes were full of smoke.

"Do you want to see my tits? I noticed you're always looking at them."

Garth nodded wordlessly.

Reba peeled off her shirt.

She wasn't even wearing a bra. She didn't need one. Reba's boobs were the largest unsupported domes this side of Saint Peter's in Rome.

Garth jumped up. "I—I've got to digitize those."

"Say what?"

Garth was already scanning Reba's chest with a video camera. In thirty-seconds, her magnificent equipment had been transferred as pixels to the screen of Garth's computer.

"Is that all you want to do with them?"

Garth mentally kicked himself. Where was his head at? He had been pretending to be a nerd for too long.

"No. I mean yes. I mean—oh, you know."

It was time to stop making sense. Garth threw himself on Reba.

Pretty soon they were making flippy-floppy.

Garth stared at the full-color image of Reba's tits on his monitor. Thank God for high resolution!

It was the next afternoon, Reba had to help her mother with grocery shopping, and couldn't come to Garth's house. In a way, beneath his disap-pointment, Garth had been grateful. He needed a little time alone to collect his thoughts and try to figure out what he was feeling.

Basically, he guessed, he was very proud to have Reba as his girlfriend. They had talked a lot yesterday, and she seemed like a really smart and sensible person. Plus she was really sexy. At least Garth thought so. And who wouldn't, looking at those breasts?

Studying Reba's digitized physiology, Garth was overcome by a sudden feeling of benevolent pride. He wanted the whole world to realize what a great body Reba had. He wanted to broadcast this picture to every television in the country.

Garth's thoughts jarred to a stop. Wait just one second. He could do something almost as good.

Garth's computer had a fax board in it, effectively transforming it into a fax machine. It also had a database containing thousands of public-access fax-machine numbers. Garth had obtained these from a paperback book sold in any well-stocked bookstore. They were the numbers of many major corporations, retailers and government organizations. In addition, Garth had added any further fax numbers he had happened to run across, from local delis to foreign embassies.

These numbers, he supposed, represented a sufficient cross-section of the populace to appreciate Reba's tits.

Garth brought up the fax program. He instructed it to send a fax of Reba's tits to every number in the database, first routing the messages through a circuitous path that would prevent it being traced back to him.

Garth hit the ENTER key and sat back. The first black-and-white fax was already on its way.

Twenty-four hours later, as Garth opened the door of his den and ushered Reba in, the last fax was just going out.

Garth proudly explained to Reba what he had done.

She was silent for a moment. Then, very calmly, she said, "You sent a picture of my boobs to every bank, every newspaper, every television station you could find?"

"Yup."

"Every realtor, every architect, every lawyer?"

"Uh-huh."

Reba's lips were compressed to a thin line. Garth began to grow a bit nervous. "Every Kinko's, every Staples, every Seven-Eleven with a three-hundred dollar fax machine?"

"Well, I didn't—in fact, that's exactly—"

Garth was on his back on the floor. Reba was kneeling and choking him and screaming.

"If you wanted to ruin me, why didn't you just drag me naked through the town behind a bus! I've heard of guys who kiss and tell, but you're a monster! This is the worst thing I've every been involved in!"

Garth croaked pitifully. Reba slightly relaxed her hold on his throat.

"Your face wasn't in the shot! And no one will ever trace it back here. I swear it! I'd never do anything to intentionally hurt you, Reba. Never!"

Reba started to cry. Garth got painfully up and put his arms around her. After a while she stopped.

"You know what I should do?" said Reba.

"What?"

"I should digitize your stupid willy and send it out after my boobs."

"Well, go ahead, I deserve it. But the disparity in size will make for a big anticlimax."

Reba managed to laugh. "Well, you know, I can see what appealed to you about this idea. It's kinda neat to think you can hit all these people with any message you want, and they just have to take it."

Grateful for an exit to the incident and also intrigued by where Reba was leading, Garth said, "Oh yeah? What kind of faxes would you send?"

"Well now, I don't rightly know offhand. Let's have a drink of that DNA stuff and talk about it."

Reba entered Garth's basement workroom. She was now such a fixture around the Barth household now that she let herself in and out.

"Your Mom yelled from the living room to me as I was going through the kitchen. She wanted me to turn on the water in the kitchen sink and splash it a little. I did, but I didn't ask why."

"She's got a rowing machine now."

Garth spotted a rolled-up magazine in Reba's hand. "More visual fodder?"

Reba grew excited. "You bet. Look at this. Can you believe it?"

She opened up the magazine, which was a copy of *Time*. Inside was a picture of Vice President Gore holding a little girl on his lap. The caption said she was this year's Easter Seals poster child.

Garth eagerly grabbed the magazine. "If we had asked him to pose for us, it couldn't be better! You're obviously thinking of that image we were wondering what to do with last week—"

"Exactly."

"Okay, let's see how they fit."

Garth digitized the Vice President. He erased the little girl from his lap. Then he loaded an image previously extracted from a recent hit movie: a naked woman in a sitting position. He pasted her into Gore's lap. The Vice President's face remained plainly visible; his hands now rested in the woman's snatch. His wooden expression assumed new dimensions. A little fill concealed the seams between the two images.

"Perfect," said Reba.

Garth switched to typing mode and signed the image:

THE MAX PLANCK-MAX ERNST BRIGADE. Then he sent it out over the phone lines.

"I wonder if this one will get as much publicity as the one we did about the Pope?" speculated Reba.

"It would be hard to top the Pope bowling with Mother Teresa. But this one might do it."

"I'm already thinking about the next one."

"Me too."

It hadn't taken Reba long that day a month ago to convince Garth that he was missing out on the true potential of his fax scheme. Sure, sending out an image of her boobs had been a cute start. But he could hardly continue in that mode. If he was going to go to the trouble of flooding the unsuspecting public with images, he should make sure they were suitably subversive ones. The spontaneously formed, unplanned and unregulated network of fax machines around the world had the potential to function as a kind of guerrilla anti-media. And Garth and Reba could be the schedulers.

Since that decision, they had sent out one fax daily.

They had rudely abused dozens of public figures, but realized they had still merely scratched the surface. They had portrayed Yeltsin screwing Maggie Thatcher. They had depicted Billy Graham rolling for high stakes in Vegas, surrounded by chorus girls. They had shown Jesse Jackson shaking hands with the head of the Aryan Nations. They had rigged improbable couplings of various stars: Cher and James Earl Jones, Eddie Murphy and Meryl Streep, Mick Jagger and Dolly Parton. They had done collages without human figures illustrative of various world problems. Tractors emptying grain into missile silos, an anthropomorphic mosque duking it out with an animated cathedral, an elephant drowning in a sea of human junk.

The reaction among the recipients of these images had been bigger and better than Garth and Reba could ever had hoped. For the most part, of course, the collages had not been taken as "real," whatever that meant. (Although there had been one small Midwestern paper which had run the image of the Pope bowling with the caption: POINTIFF ENJOYS DAY OFF.) Instead, the images had entered that amorphous netherworld of office humor and rumor, previously populated with crudely drawn sketches of outhouses with funny signs, big-busted secretaries fending off the advances of their bosses, and vaguely anti-authoritarian or cynical slogans. The quality of the work done by Garth and Reba was so superior, the conceptions so funny and radical, that their images drove the weaker ones out of the urban mythological ecosystem.

The output from Garth and Reba was Xeroxed and circulated far beyond its initial outlets. Within hours of its initial dissemination, it was multiplied a hundred fold and disbursed across miles.

The two kids found out about all this a week or two after starting the transmissions. Feeling down about the apparent lack of response to their work, they had been hanging around watching television. The six o'clock news came on. There on the screen was that day's image: Tipper Gore attending a drag-queens' ball, looking right at home.

Garth and Reba perked up and listened.

"The President has vowed to bring to justice the perpetrators of what he called 'this libelous and scurrilous semi-scandal-type aggravation.' He added, 'Not that I feel that so-called gay or homosexual individuals necessarily de-connote a less-than-positive image in my administration."

After that, things really took off. Several alternative weekly newspapers began running a week's worth of faxes on their comix pages. Anarchistic individuals began blowing them up to poster size and hanging them around their neighborhoods. Anti-American foreign governments began using certain images as propaganda. The CIA printed up millions of the fax that depicted Gadhafi humping a camel and showered them over Libya.

When other unknown co-conspirators began issuing similar faxes, Garth and Reba decided to label theirs, to distinguish them from inferior imitations.

Garth had become Max Planck, Reba Max Ernst.

The outer life of the two Maxes had not changed a whit. Still shunned and reviled by their peers at school, they silently smiled through everything, aware of their true stature and mission, secure in their comradeship.

Now Reba said, "I wonder what the President will have to say about today's shot?"

"Something incomprehensible, no doubt. Whadda ya say we go out for a soda?"

"Sounds good."

Garth and Reba walked to a local deli that featured quiet booths. The deli had a fax machine so that office-workers could send their lunch orders in. One wall formed a gallery for all of Garth and Reba's faxes. They were secretly proud.

While they were drinking their ice cream floats, up walked someone they knew: Burt Lowdermilk, the captain of the school basketball team.

"Well, if it's not the geek and the freak," said Lowdermilk. "What a pair of lovebirds. Jesus, I hate to imagine what would happen if you two ever had kids. Not that that's a possibility."

Garth had begun a slow burn that was threatening to ignite fusion. Reba's lips were turning white around her straw.

"Nothing to say? Oh, well, that's okay. I don't understand no scientific shit, and your girl talks like a hillbilly."

Laughing, Lowdermilk departed.

"Boy, I hate that guy," said Garth.

"I'd like to rip his balls off—if I could find them."

The next day, still smarting, Garth lifted Lowdermilk's face out of the yearbook and pasted it into a crowd scene. The hapless citizens were waiting to be smashed under the enormous ass of the chairman of the Fed.

Two days later, while Garth and Reba were downstairs, the doorbell rang.

"Mom's out," said Garth. "Would you get it, Reba?"

"Sure."

Garth went back to his work. After a while, he realized how long Reba had been gone. Curious, he went upstairs.

The house was full of men with guns. Reba was arguing with a guy with a dour face and five-o'clock shadow. The guy spotted Garth.

"I thought you told me Mister Barth wasn't home, ma'am."

"I—he—that's not—"

The man held up his hand. "No excuses, please. Just the fax, ma'am."

The penalty for unsolicited electronic distribution of obscene materials was a year in prison and fifty thousand dollars fine. As minors, Garth and Reba got probation. Their fine was paid by donations from millions of supporters.

A Hollywood mogul had received the very first fax, the simple love-struck one depicting Reba's tits. Every since then, he had been searching for their owner. In the publicity surrounding the kids' trial, he found her.

Five years after the trial, Garth sat in a lounge chair by the side of his swimming pool. His hair was immaculately styled. He wore two-hundred-dollar sunglasses, sandals and a Euro-cut bathing suit. He had gained a few inches and pounds.

Reba stuck her head out the patio door. She had shed the few pounds Garth had gained, and more than grown into what remained. She wore a bikini and heels.

"Another drink, dear?"

"Sure. Make it two scoops."

A cordless phone kept Garth in touch with the movie studio he owned. As he slurped up the last of his soda, it rang.

"Speaking. Oh, Sid. Hi. What've you got? Two million and a share of the gross? How many? What percent? Listen, Sid, slow down, I can't keep up with you. Listen, write everything down, draw me the big picture so I can study it and send it right over. Messenger? What century are you living in?

"Fax it poolside."

SHANI
JOSEPHA SHERMAN

Sultan Ozirakh sat alone in the council chamber of his mud brick palace, brooding. Outside the chamber window mountains rimmed the horizon, jagged and fierce as so many fangs sheltering Ifrana, his oasis land, shining green and fertile in the hot desert sun. So much green should have gladdened any desert man's heart, but Ozirakh only groaned at the sight and buried his face in his hands.

It was all the fault of those hundred-times-accursed *efriti*, those demons who'd decided the one good trading route through the mountains, the one pass that kept Ifrana from stifling in isolation, was just the place to lodge. Ozirakh groaned again. At least there were only three of the demons, or so the wild-eyed soldier who'd been the only one to escape them had insisted. But those three were evil enough for three hundred! Bad enough that they preyed on caravans; bandits did that. But when the word got out that they ate those they caught, that put a stop to travel into Ifrana.

We can't survive on our wells alone, the sultan thought in misery. We've grown too vast in numbers for that. We must trade with other lands.

Ozirakh had sent his bravest soldiers after the *efriti*. But arrows shattered against those evil, scaly skins; swords broke like twigs. Only that one shattered man had returned to him.

Who is left? Who can I possibly send?

"Father?"

Ozirakh looked up with a start, staring at the small, slim figure with her straight black hair and startlingly yellow eyes, for one ridiculous moment thinking, Mera . . . But of course it wasn't his once-upon-a-warlike-time wife. "Shani."

Shani was his daughter, to Ozirakh's utter shame his only child, his heir by default, the issue from his marriage to Mera, a tribeswoman of the fiery, wandering Zhan. What a mistake—a wild, glorious, terrifying mistake— that marriage had been! Ah, the fights they'd had (and oh, the ferocious reconciliations!). Mera had never had the vaguest idea of the submissiveness proper to a woman. And at last she had run off with her nomadic tribesfolk, and only Ozirakh's pleading that Ifrana couldn't be deprived of its only heir had persuaded her to leave Shani with him.

Mera surely must have loved him, Ozirakh told himself wryly, because at least she hadn't tried to knife him before leaving Shani. Shani had enough of her mother in her for Ozirakh to long ago have despaired of instilling that womanly submissiveness in her. Instead, he'd settled for having the wildness tempered by regal lessons in history, geography and statecraft. If she had to be his heir, he would at least see her trained like one!

The lessons obviously hadn't included tact. "Father, you can't just sit here and brood! You have to do something about the *efriti*!"

"And what do you think I've done?" he snapped. "Have you forgotten about all those soldiers who've lost their lives?"

Shani signed. "The poor men. No, of course not, but—"

"What more do you want of me? Do you want me to go riding boldly out there?"

"I don't—"

"Believe me, girl, if I thought it would make a difference, I'd sacrifice myself in a moment; let those damned demons chew on my bones!"

"But, surely there's another way, something besides warfare."

"Against demons? You're not a fool, Shani! Don't talk like one! No. Everything that could have been done has been done."

"But it hasn't!" she insisted. "I could—"

"You!" Ozirakh thundered. "Do you think yourself a hero? Do you dare? Go back to your quarters, girl! Remember that! Now leave me."

He could practically feel her frustrated rage scorch him, but Ozirakh sternly ignored her. And of course Shani at last had no choice but to obey him. Alone once more, Ozirakh sank back to his chair, and his brooding.

The little fool. All had been done that could be done. Of course all had been done.

Shani stormed down the palace corridors, too angry with her father to be still. How could he talk like that? How could he just up and abandon his people? And how, oh how, could he patronize her like that?

Ah, gently, gently. She could remember what her mother would have said: she who keeps her head wins her war.

Aie, Mother! Why did you have to leave?

Never mind. She knew why. Mera had been slowly stifled by living within palace walls. Shani couldn't quite understand that; there was too much of her father in her for her not to enjoy settled comfort. Besides, Ifrana was her land, her home, as it never could have been for her nomadic mother.

But, I'm my mother's daughter, too, and damned if I'm going to turn into a meek little slave!

Particularly not when Ifrana's safety, its very existence, was at stake. Shani thought of her father's people, *her* people slowly dying if the trading route could not be reopened, and bit her lip. That couldn't be allowed to happen! There *must* be a way to rid the land of the demons. Shani turned abruptly and headed down a flight of stairs for the palace library.

Sure enough, old Haruch was there, his back to her. Too eager to wait, Shani called out, "Haruch, I—oh. Sorry. I didn't mean to startle you."

She hurriedly knelt to help the old scholar gather up the books he'd dropped. "Haruch, I want you to be honest with me this time."

He blinked. "About what, Princess Shani?

"Those *efriti* didn't just happen to appear where they did, did they?"

"Princess Shani . . ."

"Haruch, please! I have to know. My father had something to do with it, didn't he?"

The old man sagged. "Yes," he murmured wearily.

"But how? Why?"

"It was an accident. You see, he was down here in the palace library when I chanced to find an ancient scroll. Would that I'd destroyed the thing before he could see it! You see, on that scroll someone had inscribed a spell . . ." The tired old eyes blinked at her. "He meant only good for Ifrana, you must believe it."

"Of course I do. Go on, please."

The scholar sighed. "The magic was only supposed to guard the pass. Who would ever have thought the spell would turn out to be so horribly literal? When your father had finished, the pass was guarded, indeed— guarded from every living human soul!"

"It summoned the *efriti*."

"It . . . alerted them to a fine, safe lair," Haruch corrected, "and a plentitude of prey."

"I don't know very much about magic," Shani admitted. "But if my father set the spell, doesn't that mean only one of his blood can undo it by destroying the *efriti*?

The scholar nodded, and Shani bit her lip. "So," she murmured. "I was afraid of that. Still . . . come, tell me everything you know about *efriti*, everything."

He eyed her doubtfully. "Well, they're evil beings, no shadings of nice- ness at all, huge and cruel just for the sake of cruelty. They are magical in essence, of course, though they have no innate spells of their own . . ."

As the old man droned on and on, Shani had to bite back a smile. She loved her father dearly, even when he was at his most maddening, but even she had to admit he never was one to look at the obvious. It used to infuri- ate her mother. Shani could remember the woman shouting at him that because he'd once been a warrior, he always let his sword do his thinking.

Well, maybe that wasn't quite fair, Shani thought. Ozirakh was normally a good, strong, honest ruler. But he did hold Haruch in a sort of gentle contempt for being a mere scholar who'd never once held a sword. He never would have suspected that ever so slightly despised scholar might have the information needed to—

Shani straightened as Haruch broke sharply off, staring at her in sudden horror. "Why do you need to know all this?" he asked.

"Oh . . . I was . . . curious, that's all."

He wasn't believing that. Voice shrill with alarm, Haruch stammered, "Princess Shani, you can't be thinking of—you mustn't—you can't!"

"Hush, now."

"But you're not a trained warrior! Yes, yes, I know you can handle a dagger and even a sword, but—I'll stop you. I'll tell His Majesty and—"

"No, you won't. You know the *efriti* must be destroyed, and the spell with them."

"But, I—you . . ."

His voice trailed into silence at Shani's smile.

"I think I have a plan," the Princess told him. "In fact, I know I do. And it's not going to need force of arms at all, not really. Oh no, my good, kind Haruch, all I ask of you is a carpet, a coil of rope, and three jugs of wine!"

Shani stole quietly down the palace corridors, her slim form shrouded in a servant woman's drab brown cloak, her face hidden behind a scratchy veil. Lashes downcast to hide her telltale yellow eyes, feigning proper humility even though it chafed at her spirit, the Princess slipped past courtier and guard alike, with not a one of them so much as glancing her way.

Ha, now for the stables! I only hope Haruch hasn't failed me.

He hadn't. For all that the old scholar was blatantly miserable about the whole thing, he had left a camel laden with the requisite rug, rope, and wine jars standing half-hidden in shadow. Grinning, Shani shed the constricting servant's robe and veil, revealing the hooded cloak and loose white robes of a desert traveler. The Princess fastened a sword belt about her waist, staggering a bit at the weight of the blade, then reveled for a moment in the sudden free rush of air (admittedly camel-scented air) on her now bare face, then swung into the saddle, glad her mother had taught her the fine art of camel handling. Not a soul stopped her as she rode slowly, seemingly totally at ease, out across Ifrana, heading for the mountain pass. And the *efriti*.

This was the caravan route down which the *efriti* loved to rush to the attack, this narrow, lonely pass between two rugged cliffs that towered up to all but shut out the sun. Shani looked about, all at once sure she could hear the death cries of her father's soldiers, and of the poor, doomed travelers on whom the *efriti* had fed when—

No! Stop that! Only children let their fancies run wild. She was not going to let this gloomy place frighten her, not when not a thing had hurt her.

So far.

Stop that! Shani snapped at herself again, and slid to the ground. For a moment she stood stretching stiff muscles, then led her camel some distance away, hobbling it, hidden, among a jumble of great fallen rocks. Staggering under the weight of the carpet, the Princess carried it back into the open and spread it out right in the middle of the pass, then returned for the equally heavy wine jugs. Shani placed these on the carpet, then straightened in a sudden surge of panic. Aie, aie, what did she think she was doing? Her father was right, she was only a girl—

And a Princess. And the heir to the throne of Ifrana. Its people were her responsibility as much as they were her father's, and if what Haruch said about the spell was true, only she could protect them now.

"Enough," Shani told herself softly, and settled herself on the carpet to wait.

With a sudden rush and a swoop, the *efriti* were before her. Shani bit the inside of her cheek till it bled to keep from screaming at the horrible sight of them; all claws and fangs and eyes like orange flame. Their skin glinted with grey-green scales, and they reeked of blood and cruelty and hungry death.

"Look, brothers!" one croaked harshly, plainly meaning to frighten her. Its fanged mouth was clearly never shaped for human speech. "See what a fine woman-gift is before us!"

"Hardly a gift," Shani said, and amazed herself at how calm she sounded. Too frightened to be afraid!"

The three demons started at her words, then circled her in a dizzying rush of stale wind. Their words rained down on her from all sides. "Who are you? Who?"

Shani only smiled.

"A woman," one *efrit* hissed.

"A girl," spat another, "only a girl."

"A human!" the third *efrit* mocked. "A meal!"

"Are you so sure?" Shani asked, and the efriti froze, staring down at her.

"So calm," one said.

"So quiet," said another.

"She does not scream. She does not fear us," said the third. "Why does she not fear us?"

"Why not ask me?" Shani said.

Three pairs of flaming eyes glared into her own. "Speak!"

For a moment, staring into the terrible, empty cruelty in those eyes, Shani was terrified she'd never be able to answer. "Perhaps," she forced out at last, hand toying with the fringe of the carpet, "one has heard of you, oh mighty *efriti*." She wasn't going to lie, not if she could help it. Shani suspected such perilous things as spells—particularly spells to be broken— would not allow for falsehood. But that didn't mean she had to actually tell the truth, either.

"A sorceress," they hissed, and the faintest flicker of alarm was in those terrible eyes.

"Who else would be sitting here in the middle of nowhere?" Shani asked.

"Who else would be waiting for you?"

She looked up at the *efriti*, forcing herself not to flinch. "Are you mere beasts?" the Princess asked. "Are you mere mindless things that hunt and kill and eat?"

Insulted, they drew themselves up to their full, horrific height. "No! No! Of course we are not!"

"And yet you waste time and power hiding here in the mountains like such beasts."

"The prey is good!" one insisted.

"But boring," Shani cut in. "If you were to ally yourself with a sorceress, a human sorceress, just think of the mighty deeds you could perform! With your strength and her knowledge of the human kind, you could rule a land!" That was the wrong thing to say; the efriti were too alien to care about ruling. "Humans would cringe before you," the Princess continued hastily. "Think of their fear! Think of the joy of feeding it, enhancing it!" I can't go on like this, I—I can't! But Shani forced herself grimly on, "Think of the feeding then, on prey that is intelligent enough to know and fear its master! Is that not far, far better than this stupid hiding in the mountains, this pouncing on whatever passes, like a cat on a mouse?"

"Yesss." It was a savage hiss. "Ah, yessss."

If they asked her why a human would want to betray her own kind, she'd be lost. But Haruch had been correct, bless him, the *efriti* really did seem to be near-mindless cruelty personified. It never even seemed to occur to them to ask. Now, if only . . .

"Do you agree?" Shani asked. "Will you seal the pact? Will you let me take you right to human lands?"

"Yes!" they snarled, and Shani hastily looked down at the carpet rather than see the demonic fury in their eyes.

"T-then," she said, and swallowed hard to stop the tremor in her voice. "Then why not do this once as humans do? Drink with me as humans do." That clearly puzzled them. Haruch, Haruch, you were right about this, too: the *efriti* don't even know what wine is!

Hastily she broached the three wine jugs. The *efriti* brushed her aside, their casual strength horrifying her, and raised the jugs as though they were weightless. As Shani watched, hardly daring to hope, hardly daring even to breathe, the *efriti* drank the strong, unwatered wine as though it were water, drank it to the very dregs and hurled the jars aside to smash against the rocks.

Oh Powers, it isn't having any effect on them.

But then one *efrit* staggered, blinking in bewilderment. "Funny . . ." it muttered. "Funny . . . nice drink!"

A taloned hand big as half her body gave Shani what was probably supposed to be a friendly tap. The girl went sprawling, breath knocked out of her, and the *efriti* stared down at her in surprise.

"Good just, human! Do it again!"

A second hand came smashing down at her. Shani twisted desperately aside, but even so the impact was enough to send her flying against a rock. She struggled to her knees, gasping, aching, seeing the laughing *efriti* coming at her again.

Drunk, they're even worse! They're going to kill me, and laugh while they do it!

But without warning, one *efrit* swayed and fell headlong. The other two blinked down at the first, gnashing their long fangs in befuddlement. And without warning, they, too, crumpled to the ground. For what seemed an eternity, they lay like upturned turtles, clawing the air, muttering, "Kill all the humans . . . eat all the humans . . ."

And then they lay still, snoring heavily. Shani forced her aching body to its feet. Fortunately nothing seemed to be broken, though she didn't doubt she would be bruised over every bit of her.

But now one last ordeal lay before her. Gritting her teeth, Shani drew the heavy sword and started forward.

It had been a long, weary ride back to Ifrana and the royal palace. At first, swaying in the saddle, Shani didn't even notice her father standing in the doorway.

"Shani! What—where—"

He came running to catch her, royal dignity forgotten for the moment as she slid from the saddle, so worn with fatigue she nearly fell. Ozirakh's hands closed with bruising force about her already sore shoulders, and she winced.

"Father, please."

"What? Are you hurt? Look at you! You're filthy! Where in the name of all the Powers have you been? How dare you—"

She was far too tired to argue with him. "I kept my promise," Shani said wearily. "I said I would bring the *efriti* to Ifrana, and so I did. At least part of them."

As servants opened the carpet roped to the camel's back and cried out in horror at the sight of three hacked-off *efriti* heads, Shani smiled faintly to see her father stare at her in wonder. "Nothing but a girl, oh Father?" But she was past the point of caring about pretty triumphs. "The spell is broken," the Princess said. "The *efriti* are dead. And I beg for only two things."

"Name them, daughter! Anything!"

Shani burst into weak laughter. Tomorrow, the terror of what she'd undergone was probably going to hit her, but for now all she could do was tell the sultan:

"First, I desire, with all my heart, a bath. And second, I want never, never to smell the smell of wine again!"

SEEMS LIKE OLD TIMES
TOM PICCIRILLI

Santa must have been reading my Christmas list back to front because the last thing in the world I needed was a tear-streaked blonde pulling at my elbow.

After twenty hours of driving I'd made it to the Dry Falls county line. My '68 Mustang finally gave up its 170,000-mile ghost and I'd walked the last hour through the winding back roads heading towards main street in the light rain. Only in Dry Falls could you still kick up dust in a shower.

The Drop-Out Inn used to be Harlsey's Sunshine Diner when I was a boy. Except for the sign out front nothing else seemed to have changed much: the patrons were the same, the dog-eared photocopied menus still offered such delicacies as a *Hound Dog Chili Burger Special*, and, if you were inclined to do so, you could find the same sights of distant lands in the grease stains on the floor and ceiling. It was better than staring at the two slumping, mascara-smeared waitresses or the toothless drunk gumming toast at the end of the counter.

And then she rushed in.

Without a doubt she was the most beautiful woman I'd seen in the last fourteen hundred miles. Maybe eighteen years old at the outside, her lips were made to pout, and the wind had swept her long, honey-colored hair in a tousle around her freckled neck. She dressed like Daisy May, with cut-off jeans riding way too high, short white blouse tied at midriff, showing off the perfect tan of her smooth belly. Worst of all—depending on how you think—she was crying harsh real tears. After you've been betrayed by the lying sobs a couple of times you learn the difference. Honest weeping affects any man who had a soul, and Dry Falls tends to crush souls from those who possess them and breeds guffawing morons who are without.

Having foregone sleep for twenty-eight hours, with only beer and beef jerky in my stomach, legs tight and the shoulder holster cutting a wide arching welt over my shoulder, I didn't want to even talk to another person, much less get involved in something I knew would be bad from the start and only become much worse.

"Please, mister, you gotta help me," she said. Her fingernails were short and dirty; for some reason, I liked that about her. She twisted a handful of my jacket and tried to yank me to my feet.

I turned in my seat the same moment my Hound Dog burger arrived. Her lips looked infinitely more edible than what lay on the plate. I sighed and asked, "What's the trouble?"

"My brothers, they're coming for me."

In most of the country someone might ask *Why are you afraid of your own brothers*? In this town it became a question loaded with ridiculous answers like, *Maybe she didn't feed the chickens* or *Maybe their gene pool is just a little too shallow.*

"Please!" she shouted, terrified, pulling me by the arm and scratching me along the welt. I winced and shoved her away, and nobody else—not the kids in the back, the truck driver slurping his coffee next to the pay phone, or the waitress—took any notice of her.

"Okay," I said. "What do you want me to do?"

That stopped her. Eyes that might be described as "limpid" in another age widened, and the corner of her mouth turned down. She did a nervous jib and hugged her arms, smoothing the sweat into a sheen. I looked out the plate glass window and saw nobody in the parking lot, nothing out of the ordinary.

There are times you go with your guts no matter how tired, hungry, broke, and on edge you are. I'd traveled across the country from New York to see my father one last time, to get what was deserved and pay what was owed. It would be just about the worst meeting in my life, second only to the one I'd had with a Colombian hitman named Throat on the night that ended my career on the force.

The fly-specked phone in the corner was rotary. I picked up the receiver and reached into my back pocket for change. A meaty guy with a FRED'S TRUCKING insignia on his cap shoved back his seat and stood, came forward and pressed his chest at me. "I'm waitin' for a call," he said.

"I need the sheriff."

"Six blocks up, past the church, make a right."

They'd either moved the police station or he was lying. "Look, it will only take a second. The girl over there is in trouble."

"You will be, too, if you don't put down the phone."

His tone had a completely inoffensive lilt, as if he didn't really want to break my arms but would do so in a friendly effort to teach me proper etiquette. It had been a long time since I'd heard anyone with that self-assured, mudkicker timbre. The sediment in my veins stirred. I was waking up a little, and it felt pretty good. Fred smiled beatifically. I could count all his teeth on my fingers. One halfway decent shot to the jaw would take out the rest of them.

The girl wheeled in close to me, doing her best to hide under my arm. Fred gently took the receiver out of my hand and hung it up. The phone rang instantly and he answered by saying, "Ma? Zat you?"

"I need your help," she told me again. "Get me outta here, please, I swear I'll make it worth your while."

I doubted if her seductions were always so inept, but I gave her credit for at least thinking of rewarding me. We went out into the parking lot, and she gave a short moan, looking around as if expecting her brothers to leap down from the roof. At the far end of the lot was a pickup with FRED'S TRUCKING on the side. I led her to it and she whispered, "This yours?"

We got in and I found his keys under the seat. It's amazingly infantile to steal something from a man who mouthed off a bit, but for the first time in days I smiled. I started the truck and began backing out. Fred came sprinting across the parking lot when he heard the guttural pop of his engine, and I pulled away slowly, just ahead of him as he ran. I rolled down the window and shouted, "Tell Ma I said hello!"

The girl laughed, a nice giggle, a little wild but still in control. If I'd gone this far for her, she no doubt decided I'd be along for the next part of the trip. Her eyes remained fixed and haunted but some of the tension eased. She'd gotten out of the frying pan, and now had to decide just where burned the fire. "I'm Holly," she said.

"Where to, Holly?"

"You from around here, Mister?"

"No."

"Figured. You got that moody Northeastern breeze to your voice. There's a house, about seven, eight miles up ahead off county route fourteen. It hasn't been lived in for years, all boarded up and mice filthy, but it'll do for now until I catch my breath."

"Won't your brothers think to look for you there?"

She stared at me. "No, nobody goes there anymore."

The drizzle ended. Here, it never came down more than ten minutes at a time. We drove the wooden bridge passing over Sutter's creek, which had once been a river and had now gone to dry bed. She pointed occasionally, telling me, "Turn here," leading me further into the dark, highback ridges. The scenery caused a flood of memory to reel back inside my mind faster and faster like shards of a mirror coming together, but it still took me a while to realize where we were headed.

"Left," she said.

I pulled the truck left and we rose into a clearing across a dead field of sunburned crabgrass and dust. The house there fell back into a mass of overgrown thistle brush, dormers rising against the full moon and liquid starscape of the night sky. This country was littered with abandoned houses, but unlike New York where the homeless found every empty cranny, here the mighty clapboard traps lay empty for decades.

Holly discovered the flashlight under her seat, checked it against her palm and grunted in satisfaction. "Moon's so bright we almost don't need it." We got out and she navigated me among the ruts of the wasted lawn and rotted steps of the front porch. The field mice scurried and bolted at our sounds.

Inside, she'd made a lean-to for herself in the center of the living room, complete with clothes, blankets and an oil-burning lamp. The room was torn up from top to bottom: the floor looked like a mine field had gone off. Smashed wood and tile, mangled plumbing and ancient wiring lay exposed in the broken walls. I knew the rest of the house would be the same. Holly struck a match and lit the lamp. The fireplace had fresh ash within.

"How long have you been shacked here?"

"Just a couple nights."

Humming to herself now, either as a defense or a disarming maneuver, she settled onto her sleeping bag. I leaned against the slate at the base of the fireplace.

"Okay, Holly," I said. "Spill."

Now would either come the further seduction, more weeping, or else outright deception. She didn't trust me, but at the moment required my help and figured I could be handled later as need be. Now that the tears were gone, I could see she had the same lying eyes as most of the Dry Falls populace. Nobody was any good at real trickery, only idiots bought into trusting their neighbors, yet they all thought they could pull craftiness on one another.

Those lips turned into a smile that tightened my abdomen, and she unbuttoned another button on her tied-off blouse. "You haven't told me your name."

My best New York cop glare didn't cut much in bramble country, but she understood I wasn't about to pass out at her feet, despite how much her mouth made my own water. "You got all night to waste? Forgotten already what it felt like back in the diner?"

The pout returned and she sized me up again, searching for chinks. It was starting to become irritating. "All right," she told me, "here it is. I took some money from them and now they're after me."

"Try again," I said, moving closer until I stood over her. "First off, nobody in Dry Falls has any money, and you weren't hysterical because of a little stolen beer cash."

Quickly, yet lithely, without any sudden moves, she slid her hand towards her purse on the floor. I kicked out and knocked the bag aside, reached down and dumped it. Wadded up tissue fell out, along with two opened packs of cigarettes, Vaseline for the lips, and the torn, singed, mouse-chewed remainder of a hundred dollar bill.

"That's mine," she said.

I handed it to her. "It's not worth anything. You've got less than a quarter of the entire bill." The lamp threw haphazard shadows and yellow tongues of light over her face. I watched her cheeks grow tinged with crimson.

"All right," she said, "the truth. An East Texas lawyer was around these parts early this month. My brothers think any lawyer walks about with a thousand or more dollars in his wallet. They think I stole a wad of his bundle and won't let me alone until I give it up, but I ain't got any. I found that hundred dollar bill in this house, this very room, part of a mouse nest in the far wall. It don't mean nothing, but try telling that to Shad and Timber Haskell. You ain't from around here, so you don't know. They're gonna bloody me."

In the spring of '75, the sheriff's daughter was kidnapped by a redneck named, of all lovable names, Barney, and sent a ransom demand for ten thousand dollars. Redneck child-snatchers aren't as greedy as their New York counterparts, they have a more banal view of the value of the dollar. Throat had been paid a hefty quarter million to take me out after his boss learned I'd been sleeping with his wife.

But the sheriff didn't have ten grand and begged the money from the town's affluent mayor, Casper Crofty. Crofty agreed and came back with a hefty satchel that was soon left at the appropriate place. However, Crofty had been too afraid to chance losing ten thousand, and the satchel had been stuffed with a rich man's bricks backed in dirty socks. Two days later, the girl was found in Sutter's creek without half her head. The sheriff took ten thousand from Crofty at gunpoint, blasted him with a shotgun, went and found our Barney had been shacked up outside of town with a stripper from Des Moines, blasted her face off when he learned Barney had split, and then went home and killed himself. The money was never recovered.

I could see this was part of the original stash; the mice had discovered a tiny bit and used it for their nests.

"You think there's more money around this house, don't you?" I asked. "Well, they looked, Holly. It was a popular pastime, coming with a crowbar and shovel and hunting the missing ten grand. The whole town's been through this place at one time or another. There's none here."

She drew her chin to her chest. "I thought you wasn't from Dry Falls."

"I'm not. Anymore."

Her teeth edged over her lower lip. "My brothers think I took that Texas slick for at least a couple hundred, but if I tell 'em that I found a piece of old ransom money in the wall, they'll beat me for ten thousand in cash nobody's ever seen. Either way, they want something I ain't got."

"It's only a matter of time before they get here," I said and, before the words were out of my mouth, like I'd tolled my own bell, probability and greed snuck up on me again, and we heard a car approaching down the road.

"Oh hell," she said, rushing to the window; I turned out the lamp but moonlight unfurled through the shattered panes of glass, illuminating the house almost as brightly as if the sun was shining.

A rust-gnawed Plymouth pulled up in front of the house and parked beside the pickup. Three men got out, weaving slightly, tossing beer cans before them. Good, the more drunk they were the better.

Shad Haskell climbed from the passenger seat, as mountainous as Throat, with the same gorilla arms swinging wildly at his sides. He reached into the back seat and removed a shotgun. I remembered Shad used to be the best wrestler in the county, taking pleasure in twisting his opponents' legs up their backs a few too many notches until they snapped. His brother Timber came from the same white trash stock as the rest of his family, except as runt of the litter he'd learned to be twice as sneaky and vicious to make up for the lack of muscle. He favored knives, and now unclipped a Bowie from the sheath on his belt. When I left town twenty years ago, he'd been in jail for raping two fourteen year old girls behind his father's junkyard.

The third member of their little hunting party was the illustrious Fred; holding a rifle, he moved to the front of his pickup and inspected the grille for any damage that may have occurred after I'd absconded with his vehicle. He actually took the time to rub a smear of insect off the windshield.

"Holly!" Shad shouted. "Come on out here right now, you hear me!"

She slid into the crook of my arm and whispered, "That's like calling the catfish out of the lake, ain't it?"

Timber had a weasel's face that hadn't changed much in two decades. He brushed his long, greasy hair aside with the tip of the blade. He spoke in a low, whiny voice that carried further than it should have in the open night. "You're being talked to, girl. We jest wanna know where the rest of the money is, however much, wherever it is you got it from."

Fred moved forward, unsure of where to look as he yelled, "You rotten son'bitch done stole my truck, you I'm comin' after myself!"

"Without your Ma?" I shouted back. I tugged Holly and said, "Let's go," taking her by the hand and leading her upstairs. We stumbled over the rubble of the floor, but once on the stairway we stuck close to the rail and were on the second story the moment the front door burst in. I ran into one of the long since unused bedrooms and pushed her down in the far corner. "Stay here."

"Whatcha gonna do?"

"Have a chat."

"They'll kill you."

The three of them drunkenly clucked and grumbled downstairs, tripping in the twilight and cursing, searching the rooms. I stood at the top of the stairs out of view, shaking my head. I tried to trace my fall from grace and discover when I'd lost the path, but couldn't be certain One step had simply followed another down an ill path. Maybe the fall began the day I joined the force, or when I went undercover for the DEA, or on the night I met Manuel Escobeda's wife, Moira, and decided to take her and a clump of his money. It should have been obvious that a cop ought to know better than to fall in love with a drug czar's wife, but, as they say, at the time it seemed the right thing to do.

In the city, I'd seen men die over a cargo bay full of twenty-five million dollar's worth of heroin, and I'd seen a mugger kill a hot dog vendor over a buck and change. I put this battle for the worthless, shredded hundred dollar bill pretty damn high on the chowderhead scale.

Finally they ascended the stairs, charging up one behind the other like a redneck swat team. Fred came on first. At the top, I spun out fast and took hold of the barrel of his rifle.

He eyed me for an instant. "You phone-grubber! You stole my truck!"

"You were unfriendly," I said, lifting the barrel and shoving him backwards, hard into the others. I had to suppress laughter as they toppled down the flight of steps, spinning and shouting. Shad's shotgun went off and hit nothing but more rotten wall. I heard bone crack on bone, their skulls thick with intent and stupidity. All three struck the bottom with a force that rumbled throughout the foundation of the house. I raced down, picked up the guns and Timber's knife, and threw them aside.

Fred was out cold, and three of his few remaining teeth rested on his collar. Timber moaned and hissed, trying to stand and failing. Shad sat up and touched a nasty gash on his forehead from the splintered railing. He got to his knees and took a swing at me that would have broken my neck if it had connected.

The comforting weight of the .38 in my hand was like the reassuring touch of a guardian angel. It's an old-fashioned gun, unlike a Glock or Desert Eagle, but it fit in my palm perfectly and had a cold, gray steel dignity. I thrust the gun under Shad's chin, the same way I'd done to Throat, except now I hesitated before pulling the trigger. The silky experience of *déjà vu* slipped over me.

"Hi there."

"You," Shad said, gazing at me, blood running down his mouth over his thick, wet lips. "I know you. Don't I know you? Who are you?"

"Been a long time, Shad Haskell."

His eyes cleared in the moonlight, the ignorance bright and alarming, realization dawning. "You're Sheriff Ryan's kid. This used to be your house."

Timber unrolled out of the crumpled ball, his left arm hanging at an awful angle. He was numb with shock, but the weasel remained loose. He'd be whining for the next minute or two, and then he'd start screaming from the pain. "You know where the money is, don't ya?" he said, going for the knife, and, not finding it, going for it again and again as if it might suddenly appear. "Why'd you come back? Where's that ten thousand? You in with Holly? Where is she? Ow, my arm hurts!"

"Listen," I said. "I'm going to say this once and then you stooges are going to get in your trucks and get the hell out of here and go to the nearest doctor before you all drop dead. My father burned the money."

"What?" the Haskells spoke in unison, and then again, synchronized in their belligerence. "What?"

"My father burned the money in the fireplace after he stole it, after my sister was fished out of Sutter's creek. That little burned square of a bill was all that's left, and it belonged to the mice. Don't you understand, boys? He didn't kill and die for the money, it was about vengeance, and the irony of just how deadly greed can be. He was making a point. You ought to learn something from it, but you won't." And then, barely whispering, "I didn't either."

"Huh?" Shad said. "There ain't no cash?"

I called Holly and she came down cautiously, looked at me and said, "Thanks for the help, mister, but it seems you're as much outta luck as the rest of us." I turned away and let her help her brothers. Fred moaned and stumbled to his feet. He took his teeth and tried to reinsert them. By now, Timber was done whining and the shrieks began.

"Get out of my house," I said and watched them go.

I'd meant to spend some time in the cemetery talking to my father, staring down at his headstone and spilling at least a few of my guts now that I knew what it meant to be a cop, to fail in my duty and lose everything that mattered. I thought about how tough it was being an officer of the law, knowing morality from pleasurable evil, to keep your distance without falling too far away from purpose and pride.

I'd have to find another pickup service and lead them back to my car. I still had a little hope for my Mustang. Maybe I'd go back to New York and work the streets a while, finish up with Escobeda, find out if Moira was still alive. Or maybe I'd spend some more time in the badlands that had birthed me, and see if I couldn't track down the shadow that haunted my life all these years: Barney, the man who killed my sister.

I still had a little hope.

VISITING MY BROTHER
EDWARD J. MCFADDEN III

Perhaps there is a story here to tell, perhaps not. Perhaps you won't believe what I say, or doubt the passion with which I tell it. If either be the case, you have never come to see the outlandishly small town of Gree. I chanced upon it while visiting my brother last spring. He being newly retired and me being unemployed, I decided to travel and see the paradise in which my brother had chosen to live the remaining years of his less than fruitful life.

My old car, having barely made the trip, choked and sputtered as it cruised down the long driveway that led to my brother's country estate. I could not help but wonder, as I looked feverishly at the badly groomed landscape, where my brother had come by the money to buy such an extensive, even if it was rundown, estate.

Not being a smart fellow, I assumed that he had somehow conned the money out of an unsuspecting widow or an old codger; yet I still failed to see how he, in his lacking and witless mind, could have accomplished such a deed.

As my car came to an unwilling halt, I craned my tired neck across the massive expanse of my brother's newly, seemingly, found wealth. Images of parties and wine danced in my tired head as I unpacked my meager belongings.

To my surprise I was not greeted by my brother, or some insufferable house servant. Only a solid bell toll rang out, disturbing the crow which sat atop the house's main mast. Clouds hung oppressively low in the heavens and the moon, which had once seemed virile and full of life, sank with a depression that pervaded everything its dreary light fell upon.

With my one small sack hung about my gaunt shoulders, I made my way across the red brick driveway to the oblong door that stood in rancid shadow at the far end of the decrepit porch. The doorbell sounded much like a foghorn and it appeared to alert the entire area to my presence. My brother greeted me at the door.

Had we not lived in the same house, the same room in fact, for over twenty-two years, I would have questioned whether my brother was indeed still my brother. Having never been a man of vitality, I expected his knowing stupendous smile that mocked everything he knew nothing about. What I saw was quite the contrary.

His smile was that of a Cheshire cat and it filled my heart with anguish as I felt his clammy hands removing my coat. His pale dark eyes had taken on a somewhat cheap luster and his pallid skin looked dank and forlorn. He placed my jacket on a tall, newly polished lance, which stood upright in the hands of a statue I did not recognize and looked at me again with his searching eyes.

"How have you been, brother?" He said in a haughty tone as he reached forward to hug my wary frame. My eyes, though I tried to control them, darted about the dimly lit foyer with suspicion.

"Well," I stammered. "It seems you have been better." I finished with a smile that needed work. We stared at one another for a moment until he began fingering the coat tie which hung from his extravagantly embroidered robe.

"Oh, you mean Gree? It is nothing, the smallest of towns, just a mockery of the real civilization in which you live." There was an awkward silence.

"This is Gree, one house?"

His smile turned to a small frown. "This one house, as you refer to it, is Gree, yes. It is a special place," he paused, "as you will see."

I smiled awkwardly.

"Come, Tess has prepared dinner for us." At this my heart skipped a beat.

When I was but a child, my brother chanced to meet a lovely young flower named Tess. She and my brother had loved each other dearly and on a cool day in June, nigh on my sixteenth birthday, they were bound in holy matrimony. This bond came to last but a year, for Tess was killed in what appeared to be an automobile accident. My brother, as you can understand, never really got over the event or over Tess.

Actually, it was not until he announced that he was moving to Gree did we see his lackluster incoherent demeanor fade and his temperament become more bearable. My mother often remarked how a good session with Pastor Hammond would help heal his chronic wound, to which my brother would scowl and mutter unknown words. As for Tess, he spoke of her now as if she had not missed a day.

Thinking my brother had finally lost his mind, I followed him through the desolate landscape of his newly acquired house. Having been there but two months, there was little more than the basic provisions needed to nourish his fundamental needs. While there appeared to be no light fixtures that were visible to the eye, the hall and its adjoining rooms were filled with a pale light that filled every crack with a cold dread. A death light, a light that illuminated nothing and made me fell as if a thousand eyes were watching me.

To my surprise and partial confusion, mixed with euphoria and delight, my eyes beheld Tess as she danced with an almost angel-like grace across the dining hall. My brother's eyes followed her with a fever long smoldering and he could not help but let a thin smile creep across his thin, dull, red lips as he turned to see my reaction.

Tess, upon seeing me, scampered across the room and flung her corpse-like arms about me. She was cold, colder than the hands of my brother as we shook hands and embraced at the door. Once again unable to control my fear, my eyes darted about the dimly lit room, searching for windows or doors, light fixtures or furniture, but only the long dining table with three long backed chairs could be seen.

"Sit, and be refreshed." Tess poured a blood-red wine from an old potter's chalice and waited for me to sit. Her hair had once been the color of the sun, zestful and full of life. Now it hung like ragweed, gray and dirty as if with earth. Her face, while once pretty without the slightest hint of makeup, was white and covered with a concoction that gave her the appearance of a corpse. In fact, as my mind reeled and wondered with what evil magic Tess stood before me, I understood all too clearly that Tess was a corpse!

My brother watched with sick delight as my mind tottered on the brink of insanity and I staggered and almost fell at the realization of Tess' state. "You must forgive my wife," he said with an air of royalty who had been done an injustice, undeserved. "She is a bit under the weather." He paused and helped me forward. "Please sit, eat."

It was then that I mustered the courage that lay hidden deep within my dying soul and asked, "Brother, Tess is dead. How did she come to be here?" He laughed in a low and melodious tone. "And this," I motioned about with my shaking hands. "How did you come by all this? You told us nothing of this when you left. Do you hold some ill will toward the family?"

My words caused his smile to fade and a hard grimace appeared. "Why do you question, young serpent?" asked my brother, and his anger was now clear. "So often you all mocked my very existence, praying and conjuring to make me something I was not. And you, keep your tongue around my dear Tess. She is not used to hearing her master being questioned by an infantile little fool!"

At this the tiny hairs on the back of my neck began to crawl, as if alive with worms. I did not speak, but sat rooted with horror at what once had been a man I knew and loved. It became clear to me that I was present to evoke amusement for him, revenge for injuries that he had concocted in his witless mind. I rose to leave but felt myself yanked back down with a force that shook my insides with a jolt.

He rose and walked toward me, his snarl now replaced with a loving smile. "How did I come by this? Do you mean to say that I attained my newly found wealth in a less than ethical manner?" He snickered. "No, I have paid the price, yet I still owe," he said as he looked at me with a waxen light kindling in his eyes.

The pale light that illuminated the room faded to a dull red glow that hung over all. Tess sat silent, eating, eating. Her plate, which on the surface appeared to be filled with bountiful food, was covered with a brown fowl that seemed to move, almost slither. My stomach wrenched, and I felt my head grow numb.

Abruptly faces appeared within every inch of the room. Dead faces they pressed me, stared at me. I jerked with uncontrollable madness as I tried to free my mind of the staring faces. "They are the faces trapped in Gree, my brother."

The confusion faded, but the faces remained. As I gazed across the wretched collection of pitiful lost souls, I realized the predicament in which my brother had involved himself.

"You sold your soul in return for Gree!" My voice could not hide the utter stupidity I felt my brother had shown.

My brother's eyes had grown hard and lost their gleeful shine. "No, Gree belongs to the master; I live here at his command." My brother paused now and looked hard at me, sizing me up. "And no, not just my soul did I sell. Residing in Gree holds a higher price than one simpleminded fool's soul. No, you shall join me."

I turned, as if chased by hounds, and fled back through Gree like a madman. The once empty walls were now filled with drab ancient tapestries. The faces shown therein mocking me as I ran. My brother waited for me at the door.

"Leaving so soon! And Tess has prepared desert." He mocked me now with self-assured victory. I stopped and backed away like a cornered animal. Lifting the lance from its resting place within the hands of the ancient statue, I drove it forward with a shout of joy.

The lance thrust through my brother with extreme force, pinning him to the wall like a marionette on a string. His legs shuffled, reaching for the ground and his arms flayed wildly.

From Gree I fled aghast, running without heed for my ailing car or my small sack of belongings. Laughter seemed to rise in a giant tumult of confusion from Gree, as light streamed from the house, searching. Hiding within the confines of an old bramble bush, I watched with horror as Gree dissipated like smoke in a strong wind. A hushed silence fell over the dark covered land. I tried to remember my brother, yet his ceaseless laughter in my ears tormented my mind.

After hitchhiking for an hour or so, I was approached by an old man who drove a battered blue pickup truck. "I can take you as far as Gree," said the old man. I didn't wait to hear anymore.

MILKING BELLE
BRIAN PLANTE

After five years, it still wasn't much of a farm, Kara Manson thought. Hell, it wasn't even much of a planet. Pregnant or not, she just *had* to get out there and help Joe in the fields or the work would never get done.

"No, I won't allow it," Joe insisted.

Kara remembered the farm mothers back in her childhood, "On a *real* farm, the women worked right up to the birth, and came right back to the fields afterward. Face it, Joe, you need all the help you can get out there."

It was hard for Joe, managing the stubbornly unproductive land all by himself. For a moment, Kara thought he might give in, but then he refused. "On an *Earth* farm, the gravity's lighter, the air is richer; and there's an ozone layer and Van Allen belts to protect you from the radiation. You're not working on this farm until the baby's safe." Joe stormed out the front door and off into the fields.

It wasn't supposed to have been like this, but with the disastrous crashes of the other two seed ships, Kara and Joe were the only ones left to whip the austere world into some semblance of human acceptability before the big colony ship arrived. Only fifteen Earth years before the hoary horde of humanity arrived to make another new start. It was a laughably short time to make any appreciable improvements in the planet's environment, but with the loss of the other two terraforming teams, the time stretched on endlessly for Kara. Homestead was a lonely place. Thank God she had Joe, she thought.

Joe was out in the soy field, fiddling with the irrigation rigging. He concentrated on the land, and refused to dwell on the disasters that had befallen the others. Like Kara, farming was in Joe's blood. After the high-oxy algae had been dispersed over the oceans, and the nitrogen fixing grasses over the plains, all that was left of terraforming *was* farming, and all the candidates for the seed ships had spent lots of time in the dirt, in addition to the physics, ecology, astrogation, and a hundred other subjects that were required to pilot the seed ships to a likely planet and set up shop. But it was the farm, the spindly slivers of green that would eventually feed them, that would condition the alien air and soil, and one day turn Homestead into the kind of place where humans could live comfortably, that held Joe's attention.

Joe had also planted another type of seed. They had debated whether or not to start a family or wait until the farm was more established. Ultimately they decided that, tenuous as it was, they had enough of a foothold on the planet to take the risk. In four Earth months, the population of Homestead would increase by 50 percent. They would be three.

Kara, in the farmhouse that had once been the seed ship itself, peered through the lenses of a stereo microscope at some native pollen samples to pass the time. The room suddenly brightened, making her look up momentarily from the scope. Before she could turn her attention back to the pollen samples, she heard Joe, calling to her from the fields.

"What is it?" she yelled back, hoping he would hear her through the open hatch that now served as their front door.

"Kara, come look!" was the faint but excited reply from the fields.

Kara switched off the lamp under the microscope and started for the door. It definitely *was* brighter in the room, she thought. She discovered it was not just the interior of the house that was different, but the entire panorama of farmland outside. Where before, the orange light of the K2-type sun, Epsilon Eridani, had always thrown a twilight-like cast over the land, the farm was now bathed in a much more yellow-white Earth-like color. The sun had changed.

Joe stood among his seedlings with his arms upraised, like a conductor leading an orchestra, staring at the suddenly adequate sun. "Isn't this great? How long do you think it'll last?"

From the doorway, Kara looked up at Epsilon Eridani, big and glowing and warm. The kind of light to *really* grow crops by. It must be a solar flare, she speculated, and a wicked one at that.

The light suddenly increased by several orders of magnitude, briefly beyond the warm yellow light she remembered from Earth, into a blue-white fierceness. Her vision was instantly scorched, and her face felt on fire. She stumbled back into the room and looked around, but all she could see was white. A low packing crate as a coffee table tripped her as she staggered blindly about the room. Falling, she heard Joe's cries of delight from the field turn to screams, before she smashed her head on some unseen piece of furniture and lost consciousness.

Kara awoke after a full 39-hour Homestead day, blind and her face still on fire. She rubbed her throbbing forehead and her hand came away wet, as large watery blisters discharged at her touch. Her dry throat and growling stomach told her that she had been unconscious for a substantial period of time.

"Joe," she called, sweeping the room with blind eyes, "are you in here?"

The room remained silent. Kara remembered hearing the screams. Joe had been out in the fields when the flare hit, not protected inside the converted hull of the seed ship as she had been. Joe was still out there. Half the population of Homestead, her husband, gone. Kara protectively felt the reassuring bulge of her belly and hoped all was still well with the baby.

She rose groggily and felt her way to the open doorway and out into the fields. Stumbling sightlessly in vain among the seared crops, she eventually fell to her knees sobbing.

When some measure of reason returned, she realized the gravity of her situation: she was alone, blind, in the middle of a baked soy field, perhaps broiling under the intense radiation from the solar flare. No, she decided, either it was night or the flare had burned itself out, as the skin on her hands felt no heat when she held them out. A cool K2 star like Epsilon Eridani was supposed to have relatively little flare activity, so the danger was probably past. And if it was not, she was surely doomed, so it didn't matter anyway. The most important concerns now were water and food, lest she lose consciousness right there in the fields.

Finding her way back to the farmhouse posed an unexpected challenge. In her blind stumbling, Kara had become totally disoriented, and after feeling her way along the furrowed lines in the soil for an interminable amount of time, Kara reversed direction and retraced her steps, eventually finding her way back to the edge of the plot, and ultimately, the farmhouse.

She nursed herself back to health, although her eyesight was permanently gone. Food and water were not a problem: the seed ship had enough stores to last two people for a decade, and the crops in the silos from the last few growing seasons that had seemed so meager for the coming colonists was more than she alone could eat in another handful of years. The question wasn't whether she could survive the 15 years until the colony ships arrived, but whether she *wanted* to.

Suicide became an increasingly acceptable option in Kara's mind. She was alone and incapacitated. The monumental task of terraforming the planet seemed hopelessly out of reach now. The colonists would arrive to an unexpectedly harsher environment. Not an impossible one, just harsher. There was little Kara could do one way or another to alleviate that, so she was eminently expendable. But there *was* the baby to think about.

Was the baby okay? She wondered. Even protected in the converted hull of the seed ship, she must have received an unhealthy dose of radiation from the solar flare. Having this baby now, without Joe to help with the delivery, with the possibility that the child might be damaged from the radiation, with uncertainty about her ability to care for an infant in her disabled condition posed many risks. Suicide would be an easy way out.

Kara decided the risks were worth taking. If the child was born severely damaged, she would do what she had to, and then end her own life and be done with it. She would not wait the fifteen years, and burden the arriving colonists with an old blind pioneer woman and her crippled offspring. The colonists would find two productive occupants when they arrived—or none.

Kara radioed her situation to the approaching ship. There was no direct conversation possible across the vast distance, but Kara knew the ship would eventually receive the message and be prepared.

That night, as Kara lay in bed, listening to the soft wind blow across the open fields, she thought back to her childhood days on a *real* farm. How she hated the chores—the milking, the mucking, the picking and planting. The work was tedious and back-breaking, as farm work always is, but what she now faced was a farmer's nightmare—alone, disabled, a baby on the way, and with a thousand colonists en route depending on her. How gladly she would have returned, if only she could, to those bad old days on her father's farm to escape the daunting task ahead.

The silence of the place should have made it easier to fall asleep, but instead she found it disturbing. A farm should have animal noises—cows and pigs, chickens, and those damned crows. A creaking windmill and the incessant drone of tractors—these were the sounds of a *real* farm. She even longed for the cricket's gentle chirping in the night—anything to make this world sound more homey. There had been a few orbital sightings made of some curiously amorphous native creatures on Homestead, Kara recalled, but the local fauna as well as the flora was extremely sparse and shy, and nothing as large as a field mouse had been directly observed in the five years she and Joe had been down on the surface. Nothing to worry about.

As she began nodding off, Kara thought there was nothing she wouldn't give for just one dumb old cow to milk in the morning. She remembered pulling the warm teats as the sun came up over the amber expanse of wheat on cold mornings, when the ruddy pre-dawn glow in the sky was nearly the same color as Homestead's normal daylight. Her heart softened as she contemplated the similarity, and she finally began to relax.

As she dropped off to sleep, she could swear she heard a single cow mooing somewhere in the distance.

The next day, she waited until it warmed a bit before going out. She could still hear the haunting cow noises in her mind from the night before, and she wanted to make sure the sun was well up in the sky, even though she couldn't see it, before venturing out into the fields. She tied the end of a spool of fiber optic cable to the front hatch and started walking out into the field, in the approximate direction she remembered, with the cable trailing off behind her. The spool held 100 meters—plenty for the job she had in mind.

When she moved far enough to come to the end of the spool, she began walking perpendicular to her original course, keeping the cable taught and low to the ground. After twenty meters or so, the cable became snagged on some obstacle, and Kara followed it back in toward the house. She came to the point where the cable was hung up, and stopped. Taking a deep breath, she reached down, discovering it was only a protruding rock, and freed the cable.

Kara again paced out to the far end of the line and continued her perpendicular course. The second time the cable got caught, it was on Joe. She tied the cable to his belt and followed the line back to the house to get a shovel. After the burial, she made one more trip to the house, to scratch Joe's name into a metal deck plate, which she laid on top of the mound. When she was finished, many hours later, she deliberately cut the cable ten meters closer to the house than Joe's grave. The 70 or so meters of line would define the limits of her world for now, and there would be no possibility of plowing up Joe's bones, ten meters farther out.

That night, crying in bed, she mentally conjured the image of a great lumbering beast of a cow to divert her attention. She remembered Belle, the milk cow her father had given her as a child, to teach her the meaning of responsibility. "A person don't ever become responsible lessen he has a someone or a something depending on him to get by," he'd told her.

Kara's imaginary beast took on all of Belle's features—the black-on-white mottling that looked like a bell on her flank, the ropy tail swishing back and forth in anticipation of Kara's cool, steady hands, the enormous udder with its long finger-like teats. Belle was more than just a farm animal, she was Kara's pet, and Belle depended on Kara for her daily milking. Like counting sheep, Kara concentrated on the steady *pull, splash, pull, splash* rhythm of the imaginary milking to coax herself to sleep.

The image was helping her relax, and she felt herself dropping off when a familiar sound caused her to rouse with a start. It was a cow sound. "*Aroooaaa.*" A lone cow, Belle, giving her contented "thanks for the milking" bray. It sounded real, not part of her milking fantasy.

Kara got out of bed and felt her way to the front door. She listened by the doorway for a moment, but the only sound was the gentle wind blowing the dust about the fields. Was there something out there or was she just cracking up? She wondered. For the first time since Joe and Kara had arrived on Homestead, Kara fastened the hatch dogs, locking the doorway before returning to bed.

The time passed quickly with so much work to do, and soon the labor pains were upon her. She had prepared a spot on the floor, with everything she anticipated she would need within arm's distance. The floor was safer than the bed, she reasoned, as there was no possibility of the baby falling during the birth. It would also be easier to clean afterwards. When the contractions were close together and lasted longer, she stripped and rolled herself onto the floor, propping herself up with pillows and wadded empty seed sacks.

The pain became much more intense than she had ever imagined. She broke out in a cold sweat and vomited into a bowl that she had placed nearby for washing up in. She tried concentrating on something, anything, to take her mind off the pain. The image of herself as a youngster, milking Belle, came to mind, as it had so often lately, when she was in foul moods and needed something to steady herself. *Pull, splash, pull, splash.*

In a daze, she heard a real splash and felt the warm fluid leaking and pooling under her bottom—her water had broken. The labor seemed to be taking forever, and Kara wondered if everything was as it should be or if there was a problem with the delivery. She dismissed the thought and continued concentrating on the *pull, splash* rhythm for what seemed like hours. Delirious, she reached down and felt the baby's head. She bore down hard, and her sightless eyes nonetheless saw red.

With a wet meaty plop, the baby's head and shoulders cleared her passage. Kara, on the edge of consciousness, weakly reached down for her child. It slid wetly into her waiting hands. She felt it and discovered it was male. It wasn't crying. There was something she was supposed to do, Kara thought, as her mind spiraled down into the haven of unconsciousness.

When awareness returned, the baby was in her arms, suckling her breast. She confirmed that he had all his fingers and toes, and felt his entire body for abnormalities. He was perfect. She cleaned him up with what was left of her drinking water and some towels, and checked his umbilical, which she had somehow managed to cut and tie off in her delirium. A warm, wet lump between her knees told her she had already passed the afterbirth, and she kicked it away temporarily while she cleaned herself up a bit.

There on the floor, she christened him Joe Junior—Joey—the first native-born human on Homestead.

Little Joey gave Kara another lease on life—someone to be responsible for. She had learned responsibility as a child, from caring for Belle, and required it now, to feel useful. Her life fell into a contented routine and her moody periods decreased in number, although she still occasionally used the milking daydream, now and again, to calm herself in frustrating moments. Her greatest pleasure came in the quiet times, when Joey would nurse from her own swollen breasts. Now she understood firsthand the contentedness of the milked cow.

"Aroooaaa," she imitated Belle, crooning into Joey's tiny perfect ears to voice her pleasure. She imagined his cute little face perking up at the strange animal sound. Long before he was old enough to understand her words, Kara whispered wondrous tales of cows and chickens and chirping crickets into the baby's obliging ears.

Outside, for 70 meters in every direction, the field was plowed crookedly and planted in a seemingly hodgepodge manner with a variety of Earth species: soy, bush beans, winter wheat, potatoes, beets. The crops grew smaller and slower than on Earth, but the planet had a reasonably round orbit and no axial tilt, so there was little change of seasons to contend with.

Kara had given up on corn and melons and a dozen other warm weather crops, which never seemed to grow in the dim orange light. Those species, like cows and chickens and chirping crickets, were sorely missed by Kara.

"Mommy, Mommy, it's getting bright outside!" said Joey, all of six years old and the apple of his mother's blind eyes. "It's not red anymore, it's…white! Like Earth, right?"

"Joey, come away from the window, and *don't look at the sun!*" she roared, remembering the solar flare that took the boy's father.

"But, it's beautiful, just like you said! Can I go out?"

"*No!*"

Kara lurched in the direction of the boy's voice, waving her hands in front of her, until she felt the top of his head. She pulled him close to her, enfolding him with her arms, clutching tightly at the one-piece jumpsuit she had sewn by feel from some nylon tent fabric.

"Isn't it like Earth, Mommy?"

"No honey, it could be bad, very bad. You have to stay inside until it's over and don't look out the windows."

"But it looks so nice."

Kara explained the difference between the warm yellow sunlight on Earth and the deadly white solar flares on Homestead. "It's what killed your dad, and I'm not taking any chances on you, little mister."

"Will it hurt the animals?"

Kara was puzzled. "What animals, Joey?"

"You know, like cows and sheeps and horses."

Kara had told Joey about all the different animals she remembered in her childhood. "But those animals are only on Earth. There are no big animals here on Homestead."

"Yes there are! I saw a…a dog in the fields once."

"There are no dogs here, Joey."

Joey bit his tongue at the reference to his mother's blindness. Kara knew Joey always pretended that there was nothing wrong with her so she wouldn't feel bad, and his little slip probably hurt him more than her.

"Don't you worry. When the colonists come, I'm sure they'll have some real farm animals, and maybe even a dog or two. I told you about the frozen embryos, right?"

Kara felt Joey's face wrinkle against her bosom. "Why do we have to have colonists, Mom? What's wrong with just us?"

"I've told you, it's why we're here. We're supposed to prepare the planet for the colonists and build up food stores."

"Well, why can't they find some other planet? You said that with Dad and the other seeders dead, we can't do the terra…terra…"

"Terraforming. Yes, we can't, but we can at least have some decent food ready for them when they arrive. And besides, one day you'll be looking for a nice young girl to settle down with. There ought to be a few colonists your age."

Joey tried to pull away, but Kara held him fast. "I don't want any girls. I just want you, Mommy."

Kara smiled, "Aroooaaa. Thanks, Joey, but you'll see. It'll be good. I promise."

"Aroooaaa," Joey echoed. *Thanks, Mommy.*

He turned out to be a fine farmer by the age of 15. In another year or two, he would be literally and figuratively walking in his father's shoes. The furrows had long been straightened out, and now extended well past Kara's 70-meter limit, except for the grassy mound in the soy field that marked Joe Senior's grave. The silos were filled, and Kara had put away more cans and jars of fruits and vegetables than she could count.

The colony ship was close enough now to hold a real conversation on the radio. She had just transmitted her status report and signed off one day, when Joey came in from the fields.

"Just another 20 days now. It'll be good, I promise."

Joey had grown taciturn and moody as the colony ship approached. As Kara's spirits were lifted by the coming crowd, Joey's sank, and no amount of convincing seemed to help.

"Yeah, Ma. I'll be in the back on the computer if you need me."

She could hear the sneer in his voice. "You're a growing boy. You need to be with people your own age."

"No I don't!" Joey bellowed, slamming the door as he started for the back of the house.

Maybe it was just teenage angst, the "angry young man" syndrome that all kids seemed to go though, but Kara was worried. She wanted him to fit in when the colonists arrived.

"Joey," she called as she shuffled after him, "You know they're going to come whether you like it or not, so why can't you just relax and get used to the idea?"

"I just can't, okay? I don't have to like it, and I'm *not* going to pretend how happy I am to see them."

"But, why do you think we've been farming all this time? It's for *them*!"

He hesitated. "I do the farming because we're farmers. You're a farmer. Dad was a farmer. I do it for you, Mom, not for them."

"Just give them a chance. That's all I ask."

Kara heard him pounding hard on the computer keyboard. He'll change, she thought. It's just a teenage thing.

The colony ship arrived and settled into orbit around Homestead. The first ferry of space-weary travelers screamed across the orange sky late one morning and set down barely a kilometer from the farmhouse. Kara wanted to go out to the landing site and greet the new arrivals, but it was too far from the house for her to venture on her own without getting lost, and Joey was nowhere to be found since she had awoken.

"Joey…Joey!" she called to the silent fields, hoping for a reply. There was none. He was in hiding, so she had little choice but to sit tight and wait for the colonists to come to her.

Come they did, with great ceremony and celebration. It warmed Kara's heart to be with people, lots of people, making people noises, swapping people stories, and bumping into people shoulders in the suddenly cramped farmhouse. It was all very gratifying to be "social" again. But as an undercurrent she wondered when he would make his reappearance.

"I wouldn't worry about it," said Minerva, one of the medical assistants. "He's probably just overwhelmed, like you said, about meeting all of us. He'll come out when he's good and ready."

Kara wondered just how long that might be. He had been steeling himself against this moment for years now. She worried that it might be days before he gave in and returned to the farmhouse and faced the inevitable.

"Would you like us to look for him?" offered Mohammed, one of the ecologists. "We can make an aerial search with one of the flyers."

"Oh, would you, please?" she said. "It can get awfully chilly at night here, and he's never really been away from home. Just be careful not to frighten him."

"We'll be gentle," said an older-sounding woman whose name and function Kara had already forgotten. Could she be the psychologist?

The search went on throughout the long afternoon and Kara grew increasingly worried about Joey, and distressed for having caused so much fuss for her new guests. She spent most of the day serving up freshly made breads with jam, and apologizing profusely to all those within earshot.

Late in the day, the woman with the older-sounding voice that Kara couldn't remember, came to ask a few questions. Yes, Kara decided, she *did* say she was a psychologist or psychiatrist.

"Mrs. Manson…Kara, you've told us all about how your husband, Joe, died. And even though we haven't met Joey yet, I think we've all heard enough to know what a fine young man he is. But…um, you've never mentioned that you had another child. Could you tell us about that?"

Kara hesitated as the words sunk in. "Another child? I don't know what you mean." Kara heard the room, which had been noisy with the chatter of several colonists, grow quiet, with only hushed whispers audible. They were hanging on her words.

"The grave, Mrs. Manson," the woman responded. "The little one, next to your husband's."

"Wh-what are you talking about? I only have one child. Just Joey."

"In the soy field, there's the grassy mound, Joe's grave, with a metal marker, just as you described. Next to it is a smaller mound, with a smaller marker. The marker just says 'baby'."

Kara was silent for a time. "Joey must have done it, Mrs…"

"Kincaid, but please call me Laura."

Yes, of course. Laura Kincaid, the psychiatrist. "Well, Laura, he probably set up the mock grave to send me a message." Kara could feel the tears welling. "Laura, I don't think I like the message. I think we better find my son, and soon."

"I'm sure they'll find him, any minute now," the psychiatrist said. "So then, you wouldn't mind if we examine the little 'grave', would you? We might find some clues."

"No, of course not," Kara said, with a laugh so nervous that even she was surprised at how false it sounded. "Why should I mind?"

"Thank you, Kara," said the psychiatrist, moving off to another corner of the room to exchange muted whispers with the unseen group of colonists.

Toward nightfall, the medical staff returned to Kara with their report. The little grave did indeed contain a body. A human male infant, decayed for many years, consistent with the time of Joey's reported birth. The infant was grossly deformed, they explained, and the autopsy concluded that the child had not lived long after birth.

Laura Kincaid questioned Kara, "Was this child born before Joey, or were they twins?"

"No," Kara replied feebly, "There was only Joey. There was never any other baby."

"It's all right, Kara. The child was really sick. No one can blame you for anything."

"There was *no other child*," Kara insisted more forcefully.

After an uncomfortably long silence, the psychiatrist resumed, "Kara, where are his things?"

"Huh? What do you mean?"

"We've looked around the house for items that might belong to an adolescent boy. Clothing, bedding, toothbrush, that sort of thing."

"His room is down the hall, last door on the right."

"That room is empty, Mrs. Manson."

"What are you talking about? That's his room!"

"There's no sign of a boy living at this house, Mrs. Manson. No footprints in the fields but your own and some animal tracks."

Kara burst into tears. "You keep looking! He's obviously moved his things out, and he's not planning on coming back. *I want him found, do you hear?*"

They wanted to move Kara to the ferry landing site, but she insisted that the farmhouse was where she belonged and would not budge until her son was found. They sedated her and put her to bed. The search was called off for the night, and Kara wondered if it would be resumed at all in the morning. The colonists returned to their landing site, leaving a nurse behind in the farmhouse to keep an eye on Kara.

Kara lay under the open window, listening to the thin wind blowing dust through the fields. The sedative they gave her sent a warm feeling all over her body, though she still remembered something was very wrong. Despite the drug, and try as she might, she could not make herself fall asleep. After a long spell of restlessness, she tried an old trick to calm herself down: she imagined the milking scene, herself and Belle in the old barn. *Pull, splash, pull, splash*, the cadence sounded in her head.

The imagery did not fail her, and Kara felt herself inexorably dropping into a dreamy peace. Unexpectedly, she was roused from her reverie by the sound of something rustling outside.

"Joey, is that you?" Kara called out the window, sitting up. There was no sound from outside, but then she heard the nurse's footsteps approaching from down the hall.

"Joey, they're just people, like you and me. There's nothing to be afraid of. Come on in and let's talk about it. Please?"

The bedroom door opened and the nurse came in and laid a cool hand on Kara's burning forehead. "Please lay down now, Mrs. Manson. Can I get you anything?"

"My son's out there," Kara whispered. "Can't you hear him?"

"Sorry, no, but I don't."

Kara lay back and put her head on the pillow. It seemed to satisfy the nurse, who presently left the room and shut the door behind her. Kara listened to the wind.

"*Aroooaaa*," came the sound from the fields, clear as a summer day in the country. It was not a dream, and it was not Joey, imitating his mother's approximation of a cow. It was an honest to goodness *cow* sound. *Belle.*

"Aroooaaa," the sound repeated.

"Aroooaaa," Kara echoed back softly, before falling off to sleep.

MINES OF MORIA
ANTHONY J. HOWARD

Journal Entry the First/En Route to Ceti Alpha

Art is life
Through it we define who we
are and our place in the universe.
Every sculpture recreates our
physical forms.
Every painter redefines what we
see and how we see it.
Every piece of literature is our
thoughts and every song our
voice and every poem our deepest,
innermost emotions.
Art is our way of becoming our
creator by forming something
from nothing, something beautiful,
something horrible. But something.
Art does not imitate life.
Art is Life.
(All journal entries from the personal
comlogs of Dr. Dawn Bisceglia, PhD,
Art Historian of Excalibur Project,
Jonas Braun, Commanding)

The silver space ship traced its way languidly across the gray sky, back and forth around the great expanse of stone until finally settling in a cloud of fine ash between a pile of jumbled rock and the foot of the mountain. The underside of the saucer opened and a small tracked vehicle scurried forth. Shapes in dark blue jump suits soon followed and began to move busily about, erecting metal posts with lights and small shelters for the stowing of various pieces of equipment.

For one planetary cycle they worked, artificial lights illuminating their labors. At dawn on the second day, they trudged up to the great stone face of the mountain. In a long line they moved up to the plateau, around the mud basin, to the enormous stone doors that stood there. One by one they looked up at the portals that towered over them and then passed through the hole that had been cut neatly through.

One of the last paused a little longer than the rest, her eyes seeing something the others had missed.

"Speak, friend, and enter," she said to herself. And then passed inside.

"I'm sure you've all had time to get acquainted with one another during the long voyage here, and I'd like to thank you for your patience." Dr. Braun, the expedition leader was standing atop a pile of crates and speaking to the assembled members of the team, some thirty in all.

"Introductions would seem superfluous given the inordinate amount of time we've spent in close quarters, but I would like to welcome Dr. Bisceglia to our team." Eyes turned to a dark haired woman near the back of the small room. "As some of you will already know, she is an expert in the area of art history, and given the inordinate amount of carving and artificial coloration associated with this particular site, we thought it worthwhile to include someone of that specialty on this expedition. Please give her every assistance. Now, since most of us will be living and working inside the mine site, a few words of caution are in order."

"Excuse me, Doctor." A hand shot up near the back.

"Please, call me Jonas. When you say 'doctor' in this room, everybody looks." Laughter spread across the room.

"Margaret Grinolds, Geology."

"Yes, Margaret?"

"Has it positively been determined that this is a mining site? I was under the impression that the actual purpose was unknown."

"You are quite correct; no positive determination has been made. That assumption is based on the initial expedition's assessment of the machinery found here. Due to their limited resources, they were unable to stay long enough to provide conclusive evidence for that hypothesis, but for want of a better theory, we are working on the assumption that this is some sort of mine."

Dr. Braun smiled.

"At least until one of you brilliant young minds proves otherwise." Again the polite laughter.

"Now, until the survey team completes their work, I would like everyone to confine themselves to the clearly marked and mapped areas. That includes everything on this level and most of the one below. I'm sure you'll find plenty of material for your various researches until the survey and cartography sections complete their work.

"Dr. Yeh, our resident biologist, can be found on board the ship in the event of a medical emergency or for reference. Our tech support will have databases and containment fields up and running as soon as possible, so bear with them. This room will be the common eating area, and I understand that the crew will be setting up some sort of lounge/entertainment area in our old quarters shipboard. First staff meeting will be tomorrow at 0800 standard, and I hope to see all section heads there. Oh, and remember to keep your transponders with you at all times."

Dr. Braun smiled again.

"Now go forth, and conquer."

"Hi, I'm Mike Bellows. I'm with the survey team."

He was handsome and rugged, with a smile that could have been used to sell toothpaste, and she warmed to him instantly, despite herself.

"You're the art historian, aren't you?"

She didn't answer, waiting to see if any cracks would show in his cool approach.

"I've been on several of these digs before, but I can't remember ever meeting an art historian before."

She stared into his perfect blue eyes and stayed silent.

"Is there something about this one that makes it special?"

She smiled knowingly and said, "It won't work."

"I beg your pardon?" he replied. But she just smiled and walked away, leaving a very handsome and confused young man behind her.

Journal Entry the Second/En Route Day 2
(The following is downloaded directly from Excalibur Mission Briefing, Dr. Jonas Braun, author).

Ceti Alpha 2 is an M type planetary body. It circles a G7 type star at approximately .98 AU with .89 Earth masses and .83 Standard Gravity. It lies at one extreme of what is commonly known as the gray zone, a series of systems in the Gamma Quadrant of the Fourth Sector. The gray zone stretches for well over 700 parsecs in length, three parsecs in depth (Earth relative), and 10 in width at its widest point.

The region is unusual for its abundance of habitable worlds and total lack of indigenous life. Every planet in the zone suffers from a total collapse of the native ecosystem. To term the condition 'catastrophic' is to belittle the extent of the damage to the environments of over 450 worlds. While the affected planetary bodies vary in size density, orbital location, stellar types, etc., they have two factors in common. The first is their suitability to support life, and in many cases evidence that life at one time existed on them. The second is the presence of enormous quantities of fine gray powder that for want of a better term is referred to as ash, although this is a misnomer, as no evidence of combustion exists. Rather, the ash has replaced, either as a result of some catastrophic occurrence or as a cause of it, the entire range of organic and semi-organic matter of the affected planets, thus leaving them, quite literally, as swirling balls of lifeless powder, totally devoid of, and incapable of supporting, life.

(For possible exception, see notes of Galactic Survey Team Maximillian, Encyclopedia Ref. ALC52901-A, "The Suspected Presence of Silicon Based Life Forms in the Crust of Alpha Hydra 3.)

She spent the first few days just wandering. The site was truly awe inspiring in its immensity. Whoever had created the tunnels and chambers had taken great care in creating an environment that was as stimulating as it was functional. Every grand sweep of a chamber was calculated with an artist's eye toward its effect on the viewer. Entire series of rooms were linked by color and effect. If this were truly a mining complex, then its creators had possessed souls of incredible beauty and delicacy. Chasms that dropped off to underground streams were carved and colored on each side as if to lend them beauty that they might otherwise have lacked. In other places, obviously natural caverns had been left in pristine condition, and the whole, when viewed over the period of days, left her breathless. As the survey teams mapped new chambers, new wonders were revealed. In some places ancient machinery was discovered that, like the passages, were things of beauty as well as function. She fell instantly in love with the long lost creators who had worked so hard to leave so much. It was if Michelangelo had been a miner, and the mountain, his canvas.

She had found only one flaw in the otherwise perfect beauty of the entire system. In one chamber, on the deepest level, a shaft had been drilled, or dug, or burned, she supposed, that looked out of place in a room given over to subtle sweeps and gentle angles. The walls were slightly luminescent and hinted of deepest green.

"Some type of natural luminescence." The geologist had assured her. "Low levels of radiation well within normal for such sites," she had said, her eyes never leaving the hand-held instrument. "If we find no other entrances to lower levels, we'll explore that drop in a week or so."

"Doesn't it look unusual to you?" she asked.

"What do you mean?"

"Where it's located. Doesn't it make you feel like it's, well, out of place?"

Margaret had shrugged and put away her instrument.

"A lot of things here seem out of place to me. Look at the statuary in L-9. I mean, what's the point of putting that in what's obviously a cargo loading area?"

The Geologist shrugged again.

"I mean, I like that sort of thing as much as the next person, but what's the point?"

When no answer had been forthcoming, Margaret had shrugged one more time and walked away.

She watched the scientist leave and then frowned and shook her head. "Pearls before swine," she thought, unkindly. "Like pearls before swine." Her only distraction was Michael of the survey crew. He always seemed to end up across from her at mess time, and nearby in her off hours. She had even seen him trying to wade through the dreadful "A Treatise on Art" in the ship's library. She had considered complaining to Dr. Braun, but decided instead to ignore him. If he was that interested, then maybe she'd talk to him after all, and if not, well then he'd just get bored and go away. Besides, she had to admit that he was attractive, in a macho, insensitive sort of way.

Journal entry the Fifth/En Route Day 6
(*Mission Briefing, Cont.*)

A great deal of speculation, nearly bordering on the mythic, has sprung up about the gray zone. Early explorers were dismayed to find even a few planets in close proximity in such a wasted condition. The extent of the zone was not fully known until well over a hundred years after its first discovery, since colonization efforts were quite naturally shifted to other areas. Not until the advent of the Galactic Cartography Corps was a serious effort made to map every star system within Humanity's zone of control.

Early speculation ranged from a purely natural if unknown phenomenon, to the presence of some planet-eating microbe, to an interstellar war that laid waste to the entire region. Several star spanning cultures, or rather the remains of such, have been found, but nothing indicates that these cultures possessed the technology capable of such destruction. In fact, no evidence exists that the various star-faring cultures were even aware of each other, much less involved in conflict.

Some religious scholars have attempted to portray the civilization in the area as some sort of interstellar Tower of Babel or Plain of Armageddon. Of course no evidence exists to support such a hypothesis, but for adherents, none is necessary.

For every interstellar civilization that existed within the zone, evidence of four non-space-faring cultures is present. And, of course, the vast majority of previously habitable worlds contain no traces of civilization at all.

To date, no convincing evidence for any of the multitude of theories has surfaced, although it is hoped that this expedition may bring new material and information to light.

"Well, it's definitely a mining site," interjected Roberts, one of the engineers. "The construction is consistent with an active operation that followed fairly standard mining techniques."

Heads nodded around the table.

"And while I would question some of their choices for supplemental passages, they certainly seemed to be gifted, if somewhat eccentric engineers. Some of the work is almost brilliant, if perhaps a little flamboyant."

"Perhaps they intended to live here once the mining was complete?" interjected an anthropologist.

"That is certainly possible," replied someone from the archeological team, "but we've seen no evidence of living quarters or such amenities as extensive plumbing. And I would add that I've never known of a culture that lived below ground if it could help it."

"I would tend to agree," added one engineer. "With the exception of the inordinate amount of effort put into the beautification of the working areas, it shows no evidence of any purpose besides mineral extraction."

Dr. Braun nodded.

"Well, perhaps out art historian can grant us some enlightenment."

The attention of the staff meeting turned to Dr. Bisceglia. She looked up from her sketches. Everyone waited expectantly.

"No," she said finally, and went back to work.

The room was silent for a moment.

"I'm sorry, what was that?"

"I said no. I don't have any idea."

"You don't even have a theory?" someone asked incredulously.

She looked at the ceiling for a moment.

"They were artists," she said finally. "In every sense of the word." And then she went back to her sketches. Eventually the meeting went on without her.

Journal Entry the Sixth/Ceti Alpha Day 15

Today I viewed the mining equipment of the Ceti Alphans. I use the word 'viewed' just as I would in reference to visiting a gallery or an exhibition of a new artist or the premier of a feature film.

Over a hundred machines filled a large cavern on the second level of the complex; they were parked in neat rows, the orderliness accentuating the individuality of each piece. I wandered among them for hours in quiet contemplation, slowly absorbing the shape and form of each one.

The engineers chatted and buzzed around me, remarking at the lack of uniformity exhibited by the collection. Many of them felt that perhaps this was some museum style display or display of models as in a trade show. But I am convinced that neither theory is correct. Each one will prove to be as functional and efficient as the one we tested, even though each one is as individual as the Ceti Alphan (or Alphans) that operated it.

After a few hours' work, the test machine hummed quietly to life. Silver treads pulled its sleek body forward and back, while a large energy projector glowed to life. It is some type of non-vein burner, I am told, designed to open passages without regard for the presence of valuable ore.

The engineers expressed curiosity at the design of the broadcast unit and shields. It is not that they are inefficiently located, quite the opposite, but they see no need for the extra effort of asymmetrical placement of the projectors, requiring more shielding and a longer carrier. To them, because the design does not add to the efficiency of the machine, it is wasted effort.

The chief engineer seemed surprised when I asked what the machine would look like in operation. After several false starts, he finally described the color and shape of the energy field, and how it would affect the material through which it dug.

I stood back from the machine and closed my eyes, imagining what it would look like burrowing through the virgin rock, hollowing the heart of the mountain. Suddenly I could see. It became a knife, white hot, burning a wound that would never heal. And when I opened my eyes, the machine was gone, replaced by the beautifully crafted knife, a working piece of art, that remained.

The tech crew began to dismantle it for further study. They scurried across it like rats shredding a Monet to pad a nest, or tiny vandals dismembering the colossus.

I stood and stared, tears streaming down my face, until someone, I think it was Dr. Braun, came and lead me away. The stares of the technicians and sound of gnawing followed close behind.

They sat across the makeshift desk amongst scattered crates and boxes in the storeroom that Dr. Braun had claimed for his office. He made a show of reading a hard copy of her latest progress report, his antique spectacles propped on the end of his nose, although she was sure he had already read it at least twice before she had arrived. She realized with a start that she felt like a primary school student that had been called into the Principal's office.

Dr. Braun finished his perusal and leaned back in his chair. He regarded her with a warm smile.

She regarded him with silence.

"Your report is very, um, interesting, dear."

She did not bristle, or reply. He frowned, then continued.

"I must confess to no small amount of surprise at some of your conclusions."

Still she waited.

He leaned forward and flipped through a couple of pages.

"The conclusions concerning the purpose behind the, um, beautification of the mining operation seem fairly straightforward, and while I'm not qualified to remark on the quality of the artwork created, your critical appraisal seems to follow fairly standard criteria with which I am familiar."

He cleared his throat and flipped through to the end of the report.

"The conclusions you draw about the final fate of the original inhabitants, however, well, I must say that I don't follow your line of reasoning."

He took his glasses off and leaned back in his chair.

"Before I enter this into the official record, would you care to expound upon them a little?"

"Am I to understand that if I don't, then my contribution will not be included in the official report?"

Dr. Braun looked pained.

"One of the duties of the Expedition Leader is to see that nothing enters the official record that is, um, ill conceived." He raised his hand quickly to cut off her reply.

"Which is not to say that your conclusions fall into that category. Normally I would simply read the report and either accept or reject it upon its merits, but…"

"But?"

"But your particular, um, specialty lies outside my area of familiarity. And I felt it necessary to ask you to explain some of your theories in a more direct manner."

She let a few heartbeats pass.

"All right, but before we begin there is one thing."

"Yes?"

She leaned forward for emphasis.

"Don't call me 'dear'."

"All right, I can accept the conclusion concerning the sociopolitical system as derived from your interpretation of their art, but doesn't the possibility exist that this site represents an aberration within the greater society as a whole? Some sort of artists' colony perhaps?"

"Of course it's possible, but remember that the incorporation of artistic themes included the design of the mining equipment. And not just in post-production modification as one would expect if the machinery were produced outside the artistic community and later modified, but in the design stage as well. I believe you'll find that the engineering report attached as an appendix will support the hypothesis.

"Besides, historically, pockets of fringe culture tend toward a uniformity of thought, if not style, and the variety of influences shown in the artistic expression of the Ceti Alphans would indicate inclusion in a wider culture."

"You can state that categorically?"

"Of course not. I base it as much on…" She paused to find the right word. "Intuition as on anything else."

"Intuition?"

"Yes. The interpretation of artistic expression is based as much on the response evoked in the viewer as it is on the technical ability of the creator. The cave drawings of a primitive culture can be just as moving, if not more so, as the elaborate painting of a more advanced culture."

"But you assert in your final conclusions that 'the destruction of the Ceti Alphans was sudden, probably violent, and without warning.' And that the culture was probably destroyed from without, most likely by an interplanetary, or at least extraplanetary, agent."

He looked up from her report.

"That's a pretty specific conclusion to be based on intuition."

"That conclusion is not based on intuition, but on an analysis of known data. Look around you. We know that the Alphans incorporate their art into everything that they did. Everything. Yet nowhere do we find any indication of impending disaster in their art. Cultures that fear or even suspect that they are in danger of extinction always reflect this foreboding in their artistic endeavors.

"Take the works of Bosch on Earth. The culture at large was fascinated with the proposed second coming of Christ and the Apocalypse. An expected devastation that didn't occur, but was nonetheless incorporated in a great deal of the art work of that period."

She leaned forward for emphasis.

"We know that the mine seemed to be operational right up until the time that their civilization was destroyed, yet we find no indications of a sense of foreboding in the one medium that would almost certainly contain it.

"It seems reasonable to conclude therefore that since they were obviously advanced enough to recognize the threat of some sort of impending ecological collapse, a threat from within so to speak, yet they obviously did not, that the end came quickly and without warning, and was most likely caused by some outside agent or event.

"The presence of many other inhabitable worlds in the so-called gray zone would indicate that a similar fate befell those worlds as well. And since it seems unlikely that this planet out of so many others would be the source of whatever calamity befell the rest, it seems safe to assume that the cause of the disaster was extraplanetary."

"So something came and just swept them away?"

"It would appear so."

He regarded her in silence for a moment.

"Technologically advanced civilizations just don't disappear."

It was her turn to regard him.

"This one did."

He found her outside. She was sitting on a thermal blanket draped over a chunk of stone that long ago had fallen from the cliff face. She sat facing the enormous stone doors, her back to the mud pond, her head tilted back, staring at the engravings, her voice journal beside her. She didn't seem to notice him.

He crossed to her and sat beside, staring at the doors, but seeing nothing in the seemingly random patterns and shapes. They sat in silence for awhile.

"Is this what art historians do?"

She turned to look at him, but did not reply.

"Stare at things until their eyes blur?"

She looked back at the doors.

"We're much like scientists in that regard."

"How is that?"

"Everyone thinks what we're doing is a waste of time," she turned back toward him. "Until we tell them something they didn't know."

He looked down at his hands.

"I apologize. I didn't mean to offend you. It's just hard for me to see what you're trying to do. I mean, art has its place, I suppose, but, it seems to me that what we're trying to do here is figure out what happened to these people. And I guess I just don't see what good it will do, knowing what they painted on their doors."

He saw her smile in profile, and realized she was more beautiful than he had thought.

"That's because you have no concept of what art is."

"Well, what is it?"

She laughed.

"I've spent my whole life answering that question. And you want it in a hundred words or less."

She laughed again.

"Okay, how can I say this. Art is the expression of what we see and feel. What we think. It's how we pass on our vision. The words become literature. The emotions become poetry. What we see becomes sculpture and painting. What is on that door is something that they thought was important enough to show to all the world. And anything that important to them is something we need to know."

"What if it's just decoration?"

"Then we will at least gain insight to their psychology by knowing what they thought was decorative."

He turned his attention back to the doors.

"So what does it say?"

She sighed.

"I'm not sure, but do you see how bold the patterns are at top? How striking the colors? And then the shapes change, to sunbursts and whorls. And halfway down, the way the interplay of light and darkness gives a sense of, I don't know, of grief?"

He nodded slowly.

"I think it says, 'These are the Mines of Moria that we have carved from the unyielding rock. And these are the stones that we bring forth into the light of day. And these are our numbered dead, who have given their lives that the harvest may continue.'"

He was looking at her, with wonder in his eyes.

"You can see all that?"

"Yes."

She turned to him with a smile.

"Or it might just be decoration."

They found a small storage room and made love on the floor. He held her close and called her Dawn and tears made her cheeks salty. They kicked their clothes and gear into a corner and lay together on the smooth stone and enjoyed the feeling of their heat leaching into the floor. She rolled onto her side and listened to his breathing, slowly running her fingertips across his smooth skin, caressing his chest, gliding her hand down across his stomach, and circling his navel. She marveled at the perfection of it, at how the diversity blended smoothly into the totality of the form.

God is a master sculptor, she thought. She rolled onto her back and stared at the distant, dimly lit ceiling.

They remade themselves in everything they did; even their mines were like them, smooth and clean, blending one form with another. They even drilled like artists, following the veins with an eye to symmetry.

Except for the hole.

They had blended art into their work. Inseparable. Every cut was made with an artist's hand. Everything was a part of the larger vision. Everything.

Except for the hole.

It had dropped from the floor of the chamber without regard for form or beauty or aesthetics. It was strictly functional. It didn't belong. As if it hadn't been made by them at all.

As if it had been made...

...by something else.

She leaped to her feet and grabbed for clothes. He raised onto his elbows, a sleepy look on his face.

"What...."

She jerked on her pants and his shirt.

"The hole, when are they going to explore the hole?"

"What hole?"

"In the green room. When are they going down it?"

"Today. Now. Sometime."

She grabbed his arm and jerked him to his feet.

"That's what killed them. Whatever's in the hole."

Then she turned and sprinted down the corridor, her lover close behind, pulling on his pants as he ran.

She was only heartbeats behind him when he turned and screamed for her to go back. Out of the unnatural hole something boiled. Something dark and terrible that swallowed the light completely and surged forward. It had covered half of the room when it reached him. He had stared without comprehension for an instant, then turned and screamed at her as he took the first panicked step away. The darkness enveloped him and she had one split second's view of the skin and flesh peeling away into ashes, leaving only the rapidly drying bones still trying desperately to save her.

She staggered backwards and sprinted through the passage, slipping and falling as she jerked to a stop, then clawing frantically at the portable force wall. It sprang up as the blackness charged towards her. The wall crackled and flared and the low power warning began to beep. She stared at the charge needle as it dropped quickly to the red. She had time to curse the darkness, and the machine, and then she ran away.

An eternity later, she crawled from her hiding place, waiting until the distant hum of machinery had faded. She had almost died, there in the darkness. She had heard footsteps and eased herself from her hole. As she started to call out, he, she, it, whatever, had turned so that the metal of its face was visible. The body was of Margaret, the geologist, but the face was of some Ellisonian nightmare, all wires and lenses and strange devices.

Only the paralyzation of terror had kept her from betraying herself. Her body locked rigid and her throat tightened, rebelling against a scream too large for it to admit. Soon the thing had turned away, continuing whatever errand its new master had prescribed. For the first time in her life she wished someone was dead.

Finally she groped her way through silent passages, afraid to try to find light, but equally fearful of what darkness she might blunder into without knowing.

That would, perhaps, be best, she thought.

She finally found her way to the small room where they had made love. His face came back to her as she felt along the floor and found their clothes and gear. Tears once again ran down her face and spattered on the floor.

"I am so sorry," she said to the darkness.

With hand torch and laser, she made her way back out, and, risking the light, began to walk toward the exit.

Journal Entry the Last/Ceti Alpha Day 31

I sit atop a pile of rocks near where we touched down. Our silver saucer now juts against the darkened sky, truly phallic in its new dimensions.

The darkness poured out the great stone doors of the mines, slid across the mud flat, and oozed down the mountain nearly two cycles ago. The darkness, like an oily cloud, covered our ship and began to make its changes. A short time later, the surviving members of the expedition marched out the neatly cut hole, down the trail, and into the darkness. For two days they worked, dim shapes moving arrhythmically in the unnatural twilight, doing their master's bidding. Now they move toward my perch, their new machine parts gleaming evilly in the moonlight. I have watched them from my perch for several days, but until now they had ignored me.

I soon realized that it, whatever it is, was not interested in doing to me what it had done to the rest, at least as long as I didn't interfere, and that without access to the ship, escape or communication with the Net was impossible. So I spent these last days in final contemplation of the legacy of the Ceti Alphans. I am still amazed at the simple beauty and quiet elegance of their work. And if anyone had told me that such a highly developed industrial civilization would have been able to remain true to the artist within, I would not have believed it.

I hope that the shades of their dead will forgive me for thinking myself worthy to add to their creation.

I wish that I could have just a fraction of their talent. I wish that I could borrow their soul, if only for a moment, just long enough to prepare a fitting memorial, one that could tell the story of how they died, with the skill that they told the story of how they lived. But how can I do that? How do I write the eulogy of a race of artists that lived here so long ago, loving, creating, until that Thing came down from the stars, fresh from its last kill, and devoured every living thing on this planet? Everything down to the organic molecules in the soil. And how do I explain what I do not know? Why did it choose to wait here, deep in its hole, until we blundered along? Why did it not make the Ceti Alphans into what it has made us? Was it sated from its long conquest of the stars? Did the inhabitants lack some key piece of technology it needed to leave? Something that we unwittingly provided? Or was it simply tired, and wanted to rest, weary from its mission of death among the stars?

I do not know, and the truth be told, I do not care.

Instead, I have spent over half the charge of the laser and what has turned out to be the last hours of my life in an attempt to carve from the mountain my last and only artistic endeavor. It is a figure, burnt black from the heat of the pistol, that looks without hope toward the heavens. I call it "self portrait in stone," and I hope that the dead are pleased since only they will ever see it.

My laser pistol and journal are my only companions.

I do not think that anyone will ever hear this. I seriously doubt that...whatever they are...will bother to download my journal into the Central Net. As a matter of fact, I doubt the Central Net will exist for much longer.

The stars are making a rare appearance. They gaze down upon me, unblinking in the thin atmosphere. I try to look at them with an artist's eyes, but all I can think of is the darkness, and when my eyes fall to the pistol, the burning light.

Soon they will climb to my perch and find nothing except my ashes and this journal, with the spent laser beside.

I wonder how many worlds will join me.

I wonder how long before it once again burns a hole and hides, deep under the ground. I wonder if this time, it ever will.

"To be, or not to be." For me there is no question.

They are coming.

The End is Near.

And there is something that I must do.

THE EXPERIMENTAL THEATER
ARTHUR J. SCOTT

Norman Whitby, walking briskly, turned onto Barrow Street. He was looking for number 217. He crossed the street to the side with the odd numbers. "Let's see, there's 275. It should be near the next corner," he mumbled to himself. And there it was, an old, four-story brownstone in keeping with most of the structures on this historic Greenwich Village block. Up the steps he went—the door was ajar. Norman knocked twice, then stuck his head in. A group of five adults—three women and two men—was seated in an alcove. All turned in his direction. A red door marked *EXPERIMENTAL THEATER* stood just behind them with a sign taped to it:

This Evening's Program
FRAGMENTS FROM HERMETIC LANDSCAPES
(An Exhibition of *Photographic Conjurations*)

Norman stepped inside the alcove and nervously glanced at his watch—it read 6:50 p.m. "Hi. Am I in the right place for the photo exhibition?"

A lady in the group replied with a welcoming smile, "Hi. Yes, you're in the right place. Should begin in a few minutes."

Norman, a friendly, outgoing gentleman of thirty-five, approached the group and sat down. "Great! I'm just dying to see what it's all about. The invitation was so peculiar. Anyone know what *photographic conjurations* are?" (The others shook their heads.) Norman smiled and surveyed the group. "By the way, I'm Norman. Are you folks all together?"

"No, Norman," a distinguished looking middle-aged gentleman replied. "In fact, until you arrived, none of us had spoken a word. Why don't we introduce ourselves? I'm Neil."

"Hello everybody, I'm Cynthia." (Everyone exchanged pleasant *hellos*. Besides Norman, Neil, and Cynthia, there was Erwin, Alice, and Erika.)

Erika, the youngest of the group, said, "Norman, you mentioned a peculiar invitation. Well, that's exactly what it was, peculiar. And can you believe it was mailed from Copenhagen, Denmark? At first I thought it was a friend playing a joke...I was sure it was someone who knew me...but no one I knew was in Copenhagen. Now I'm really in the dark, I just don't know."

"Really. Mine was also sent from Copenhagen and whoever sent it seemed to know quite a bit about me...I mean, things they couldn't possibly know if they weren't watching me," Norman responded excitedly. "I wonder if all our invitations were mailed from Copenhagen?" All present confirmed that they were.

Alice, the eldest of the group contributed with lilt in her voice: "And the title, Fragments From Hermetic Landscapes; in my wildest imagination I've no idea what I'm about to see, but I'm certainly curious!"

Erwin, an intense, nervous gentleman in his forties spoke in a serious, almost somber tone, "Frankly, I'm here because I'm intrigued. Imagine, an invitation stating that I'd been selected from a closely observed group of people—I keep wondering who was *closely observing* me? Now I find myself looking around when I'm on the street. Maybe my telephone is tapped…or who knows what?" Erwin paused for a moment. "They also specified *art oriented people*. Well, I'm a collector and dealer of rare photographs, as well as being a *terrible* photographer personally—there's a great deal more involved in creating a photographic masterpiece than just pushing a button. But I love all of it, so I guess I qualify as *art oriented*!"

Neil said, "How curious that all our invitations were postmarked from Denmark and it was implied that we were being *closely observed* here in New York. As for myself, I'm an art gallery owner, so I suppose I'm an *art oriented* person. Are all of us involved in art?"

"I am. I own a gallery and framing shop in Jersey," Alice confirmed. "And whoever sent my invitation seemed to know a lot of details about my art business."

It soon became apparent that the guests were all art lovers who earned their living in the graphic arts. Cynthia was a commissioned painter of portraits who had established a fine reputation for her skills with a brush. Erika taught European art history at a local university, specializing in Dutch and Flemish painting.

Now the group's attention focused on Norman. "Let's see, I travel a great deal searching for unusual graphics, either paintings, drawings, or photographs. Most of my clients are theater set designers, also a few decorators. I'll tell you, it can be terribly fascinating! You're really working by instinct. Yes, I'm definitely an *art oriented* soul who loves his work. Some of the…"

Norman's ardent account was suddenly interrupted as the door to the exhibition room swung open. It was exactly 7 p.m. An anonymous voice from within spoke slowly and precisely, *"Please enter now. Talking is strictly forbidden in the exhibition room."* The group of six made their way through the entrance into a dark chamber. The lights were very dim, barely sufficient to prevent the guests from bumping into each other. After a moment their eyes began adjusting to the darkness enough to ascertain that they were standing in a room whose widest dimension did not exceed twenty feet. On the walls hung what seemed like framed pictures, but the images were totally imperceptible in the poor lighting.

The voice continued, apparently coming from a speaker somewhere on the ceiling *"Good evening ladies and gentlemen. It is time to begin. As you have gathered from your invitations, the title of this exhibition is* Fragments From Hermetic Landscapes. *These extraordinary photographic images—we used the term* **Photographic Conjurations** *on the invitations— are among the strangest stills ever shot. When the lighting is adjusted you will see twenty-two, 8 x 10 black-and-white photographs hanging in dark wooden framers. The finest white mats have been installed between the prints' edges and the dark frames for contrast."*

"You are about to explore your own inner space. You will examine previously undiscovered movements of your mind. The special lighting will be turned on shortly, at which time you should inspect all the images carefully. Focus your undivided attention on one image, the one that for whatever reason captivates you to a greater extent than the others—you will have fifteen minutes to make that decision. View it as if you were arriving at the summit of a hill and, looking down the other side, the image lay beckoning before you. Consider it as a miniature landscape available for you to enter into."

At this moment the lights came on. (It was effective track lighting with each bulb focusing on a single photograph.) The guests examined the images in awe, moving about the petite gallery trying to select a favorite among the hypnotic collection. The photographs were mysterious landscapes without comparison to anything they had every seen. It was difficult to determine if the images were realistic or illusory, yet something rang of authenticity about them. Most contained a building—or some structure—set in a desolate area, but not a single living creature appeared in any of them. The exhibition room was steeped in silence and only the breathing of the observers was detectable.

After a few minutes, the guests had made their selections. Erika stood motionless before the image of an old abandoned railroad station—it sat alone on a deserted plain. Weeds and grass grew haphazardly about the structure, creating a forlorn atmosphere. To the left stood a disheveled passenger car with broken windows, obviously long out of service. It restsed on two rails—the track ended just a few feet ahead of the coach. Erika's mind was full of questions—her brain entertained obscure thoughts as eerie feelings overtook her. Where is this station? Could it still be there? She wondered how many people once rode in that car and where they were now? Do they still exist? She visualized the station full of life with people coming and going through the doors—now boarded up—some laughing and talking, others somber, alone with their thoughts. Where were they all going on that forgotten railroad car as it raced through the days and nights long past? Erika stepped closer. Strange music seemed to be coming from the station.

Neil concentrated on a tower at the end of a pier. A ladder leaned against the side of the structure. Beyond the tower was what appeared to be a lake. Across the body of water, the vague impression of hills were discernible. The peculiar mixture of light and shadow in the sky was ominous. He was drawn toward the image, compelled to move closer. He could not tear his eyes away.

Alice and Erwin stood spellbound before a small grayish-white house on a dirt road. Uncanny light—perhaps from the moon—accentuated the gloomy hue of the building, outstanding among the shadows. The vague suggestion of a steeple loomed far in the background, adding a further dimension to the composition.

Norman was particularly drawn to the compelling image of a lighthouse on a stormy seacoast, its black door ajar. Cynthia stood next to him, equally enchanted by the mysterious photograph. Eerie fog drifted about the stone structure, its whirling motion arrested in time by the camera's split-second mechanism. His eyes meticulously roamed the unearthly image. Just to the right of the lighthouse, a ghostly figure appeared to be emerging from the vapor; a hollow, shallow apparition with little definition. The mind's eye entered the landscape, proceeding toward the foreboding door. Mysterious music from a harpsichord was audible. The observer reache the threshold of the lighthouse. Music was escaping through the black door's opening, its haunting strain vaguely familiar—perhaps it was *Chopin's Prelude in D Flat*. Dramatic chords heightened the tension. Norman's trembling arm reached forward toward the door. At that exact moment, the music ceased and the lights were extinguished, immediately casting the exhibition into darkness, into silence.

The anonymous voice continued, speaking in non-emotional monotone: *"My dear ladies and gentlemen. You have been invited to this exhibition because you are all artists in one medium or another. Unwittingly, you have become actors and actresses in an experimental theatrical production—this evening's program is a creation of the* **Experimental Theater**—*and your subtle performances have been recorded on film. We are particularly interested in your facial expressions and your postures, of which you were unaware during your concentration.*

"The photographs and music employed were meticulously selected for the sake of this experiment. Now a third impression will be interjected into your experience. You have heard enchanting music, you have viewed graphic images unlike any you have ever seen and, in a moment, a strange piece of poetry will be recited. What you are about to hear is a poem as unusual as the photographs you have been viewing and as eccentric as the music just played. It was discovered by chance, cryptically concealed in a painting that was hung in a European museum for greater than a century. First, you will hear it recited once, without music or photographic images. Then the lights and music will be reinstalled so you may experience all three media

simultaneously. Please close your eyes and listen carefully."

Descend from night tower,
Vision twisted—
The dark vineyard:
"I" fragments languish
In grey obscurity…

The empty road through
Sunflowers bent, dying—
A locked station:
In ghost village silence
One waits moments black…

A rectangle languishes
In Edinbugh—the decaying room
Harbors faint shadows—
The light does not reach
Every corner of the maze…

Beyond the composition
A sitar vibrates in whispers
An ominous warning to artists—
The innocent do not see the coil
Nor hear the hiss…

Insomnia is the loneliest pain—
The rotting poet wanders
A forbidden path—
Twice a female voice alone
Then stillness envelops the road…

A few seconds after the recitation, the lights and music came on and the poem was again recited slowly in monotone. It was repeated over and over as each member of the group intensely focused on his or her chosen image. The harpsichord music was audible, playing softly in the background, but in no way interfered with the comprehension of the poem. After about twenty minutes, the lights were extinguished and the music and poetry ceased. The red door opened and the anonymous voice spoke again: *"Thank you, ladies and gentlemen, for your participation. The program is completed for tonight. There will be another gathering in two weeks, at which time you will receive further information regarding what you have seen and heard this evening. Good night."*

"That's all?" Norman spontaneously quipped, amazed at how quickly the proceedings came to an end.

"Just a minute," Alice yelled angrily into the darkness in the direction of the unknown voice. "I have some questions. Is someone there?"

Erwin raised his voice in frustration. "Yes, many questions. What is this all about? We must have more information to…" Suddenly, the strange music started again, now so loud that words were drowned out by the vibrations of the harpsichord. The guests hurried from the chamber, Erika and Norman with their hands over their ears. The door closed and locked behind them.

Norman was shaking his head. "Some experience! I couldn't describe it in words."

"Exactly. There are no words," an annoyed Cynthia expressed. "We're just guinea pigs."

"I'll bet somebody's having a gigantic laugh!" Alice added.

Neil was quiet, reflecting seriously, then he said, "There's something much more to this than just a big joke. Who would go to so much trouble for something so trivial? The photographs were fantastic—I think that tower on the pier is permanently engraved on my brain. The poetry was extremely unusual—yes, it was somewhat cryptic but, nevertheless, fascinating. And that haunting piece of music—I think it was Chopin—well, the three impressions together placed me in another world for a while! Honestly, I've never experienced anything quite so bizarre—I don't know if that is the proper word for it—but it was not a negative experience. Does anyone else have something to add?"

"The word I would use is *eerie*," Erika said. "But there was definitely something remarkable going on in that room. Those photographs were incredibly powerful. That lonely railroad station; it actually gave me the chills. And the weird music together with that cryptic poem…it really flipped me! It seemed to be coming from the station. I mean, I was there too…Oh, I don't know what I mean, but I'd like to find out more about it…what did they call it, *Experimental Theater*?"

"You know what I think?" Erwin asked, "I think we should take this very seriously. There are so many questions. Why don't we all analyze our experiences for a few days, then get together and try to figure something out. Let's come up with some answers!"

"Well, we could meet at *The Village Lion* some evening for coffee, or even dinner," Norman suggested.

"Sounds great to me," Cynthia said, "but I still can't take this thing too seriously."

"How about *The Village Lion*, 8 o'clock, Thursday?" Neil proposed. All agreed and met on Thursday evening. The six sat in a rear booth at the café. Everyone ordered something to eat.

"So," Neil began lightheartedly, "has anyone come up with anything? Any front row, box seat tickets to the *Experimental Theater?* " Everyone shook their heads.

"I'll tell you one thing about the exhibition," Norman continued, "I can't erase that half-hour, or however long it was, from my mind. I live with that lighthouse. I dream about it. Is there something called permanent hypnosis? And I still hear that music—was it Chopin? In fact, I went looking for the tape this week—couldn't find it, but I will!"

"I think it was Prelude in D Flat—not a very well known piece of his," Erwin said. "You may have problems locating it."

"I can identify with your experience, Norman. I was focusing on that spooky house on the dirt road—you must have seen it. It really grabbed me," Alice anxiously recounted. "Well, I was curious but never anticipated the impact of that exhibition. It's been with me all week and, yes, even when I'm sleeping. That gloomy house; I see myself approaching it but can't find any doors…and the windows are dirty—can't see inside—and then I run away. It's my dream every night. Then there's the poem. Parts of it kind of echo in my mind over and over…*Insomnia is the loneliest pain - /The rotting poet wanders/A forbidden path - /Twice a female voice alone/ Then darkness envelops the road.* And the harpsichord in the background never stops. It's all really too strange. I fear I may be losing my mind. Anyone else feel this way?"

Erwin added to Alice's portrayal of the house. "I share your feelings, Alice. I was also grabbed by the same photograph." (He spoke barely above a whisper, yet with great intensity.) "It was an evening I'll never forget, never. Sleeping has been difficult for me since the exhibition; not only sleeping but being aware—What else is there? My imagination has brought me time and time again to the threshold of that, that…the only word I can choose is *sinister*—that sinister house with the white/grey bricks. How dreary. I also ran…I ran in terror until I was exhausted. And, yes, there's always Chopin's somber strain—such a mysterious Prelude— like from another world, haunting. Words are useless to describe it, but that poem…that poem does something with words. In a strange way it portrays the music…the photographs. I keep hearing it so much I pronounce it to myself; not all of it but certain parts of it…it keeps recurring!"

"The poem did the same to me. It keeps repeating in my mind," Erika added. "It's so hypnotic. Somehow it taps the weirdest part of my brain, sort of makes me think in a different mode. I can't explain it. That part about *the empty road, the dying sunflowers; then, a locked station:/In ghost village silence/One waits moments black.* It creates images, strange ones, but what does it mean? It's like I know I've been inside that station— sometimes I hear a train approaching. Then I get scared and try to run, but my legs…they won't move. The photo, the poem, and the music; they all recur. Well, since that *Experimental Theater* experience…I don't know how to describe it, I think I've undergone some sort of a weird metamorphosis. Actually, it's frightening!"

"I've been sleeping in that lighthouse!" Cynthia exclaimed. "It's everywhere with me. Can you believe I can even visualize the interior. There's a little room up top with a cot, a tiny bath, and one of those small refrigerators, and it's clean! Someone must be living there, but what's funny is that I only saw a photograph of the lighthouse…and only from the outside. How could I know what was inside? Now I feel compelled to go there—wherever it is—just to find out for myself if I've gone mad. When I sleep—of course, that's at home—somehow I'm transported to the lighthouse. Strangest thing ever happened to me!"

"I guess that leaves me," Neil continued, speaking softly in a composed manner. "I think I expressed myself the night of the exhibition. It pretty much reflects the way we all feel. I'll only add that my obsession has grown in a week and that tower—or whatever it is—is with me in my dreams; it's everywhere. I have no idea what has occurred to us—perhaps a kind of hypnotism—but we should continue to probe. Shall we meet again, say in a couple of weeks?"

The group agreed and met again two weeks later at the *Village Lion*.

Neil began, attempting to project optimism. "Well, any news? Any invitations? Anyone contacted?" The member's somber expressions answered Neil's questions.

Neil continued, his tone grave. "Unfortunately, I have a strange feeling we may never again hear from the theater. I've revisited that building where the exhibition was held—not a trace of the *Experimental Theater*. The building's interior is being totally renovated and the room where we viewed the photographs…well it's gone—that whole ground floor has been hollowed out. You might say that the source of our great experience has disappeared without a trace. I inquired with management. No one knows anything about that exhibition, or that there was ever any sort of a theater in the building. Maybe it was there for only one night? So, if we don't hear something through the mail I'm afraid we're left to deal with our fantasies as best we can."

"Ha, ha, ha, what a great big joke," Cynthia said bitterly. "You know, maybe we were never even there. Maybe we're just a bunch of screwballs. I mean, if I ever told some of my friends about my experience at that *Experimental Theater*, they would think I was nuts…I could never prove such a place ever existed. Like Neil said, it's been hollowed out, demolished, ripped apart, destroyed, ravaged, wrecked—whatever you want to call it—without leaving a trace…ha, ha, ha, ha, ha…"

Norman interrupted. "Neil, don't you think it might be best to try to forget about all of this?"

"No, no, let's be patient," Neil answered. "What else can we do?"

This meeting lasted less than a half hour. Reluctantly, the group agreed to meet again in about a month—no date was set. (The group was never to meet again.) Alice dropped out and Erwin moved away from the area. Norman and Erika had become intimate friends—they were living together. Neil and Cynthia occasionally dined together—Cynthia eventually moved back to her hometown in the Midwest. Years passed. Norman and Erika had long since gone their separate ways. There was no longer any contact among the six adventurers who once were so closely united by a mere half-hour experience at the Experimental Theater.

SEASONS & STONE
KATHRYN J. BROWN

Falcon Bertille sat brooding in her courtyard behind the Temple of Justice. Each magistrate maintained a similar garden there, ostensibly as a place to think, but more often used as a meeting place for bribes or threats. Many of her colleagues made elaborate habitats of theirs, filling them with fountains and flowers, but Falcon had little time for such things so she let her guardian, Rotger, do the decorating. He gave it two things: a stone bench and a crab apple tree. And Falcon, who needed neither running water to drown the sound of whispered voices, nor flowers to hide the glint of blood-stained jewels, came to understand the meaning in his choices.

Autumn came early to her corner of the world and the crab apple tree stood like a skeleton, the green flesh of its leaves gone, only its dwarfish fruit remaining like suspended drops of blood. Looking at it, Falcon thought of all the people stripped away from her by the years, old friends lost on fickle currents. "It's been a long time," she murmured.

Rotger sat beside her, his wispy white hair barely stirring in the wind. Beneath it his eyes glowed like embers almost lost in smoke. They and the red underside of his cape were the only traces of color he had. "Since when?"

"Since I last stood in that abandoned storehouse down on Market Street. Falcon Bertille—private advocate, public nuisance—and her menagerie: two prostitutes, a toy maker, and a thief nobody ever saw. The magistrates hated me back then, but they never could ignore me." She sighed, staring up at the autumn sky. "Such a long time ago."

Rotger smiled, just enough to hint at his fangs. He clearly took great pride in his freakish appearance since turning it to his advantage. A red cape assassin could charge high prices for his work, but a red cape assassin who encouraged false rumors about being undead could charge almost anything. "If I may so, I think the forces of law are still every bit as annoyed with you now as when you were a young upstart."

Falcon nodded, reaching into her pouch and pulling out a slice of licorice root. "It's the Crescens case. The courts can't waive a conviction without my vote, and I can't vote without some proof of Damon Nelek Crescens' innocence other than his elevated parentage." She bit off half the stick and chewed slowly, waiting for its cool, dark taste to spread to her stomach.

"I'm sure they've given you other reasons to change your vote."

Falcon laughed harshly, her breath rising in short spurts. "Oh, I've been threatened with bribery and tempted with assassination, if that's what you mean. The usual."

"No."

"I showed that kind of mercy once. Just once. Last month they brought a young man into my court on charges of prostitution. His slim body was like a streak of light on running water and every time his lips moved it was like they were struggling with a kiss. The whole trial he just stood there, staring at me from behind a curl of hair that hung across his face like a jet black talon. He'd obviously been selling his body to anyone for the price of a drink and wasn't about to stop, wasn't even really sorry about it. But at the end of it, I let him go."

A new smell entered the air, a mixture of cinnamon and bitter wine. Falcon recognized the scent as Lady Arcadia's perfume and wondered if Her Ladyship was in the next courtyard, sprinkling it on her drying flowers. For a moment she remembered how each of her old partners smelled, especially Minna's elusive aura of violets. She wondered where they were these days—all of them carried away by the currents of their own lives, except Minna, whose life left her beached on impossible shores. She stayed and Falcon watched her grow sick and thin, until the tailored gown that once emphasized such magnificent curves became a mockery and Minna rattled in it, like fortune telling bones in a silk pouch. When winter came, all Falcon had to bury her with was snow.

She inhaled again and the perfume was gone.

Neither of them spoke for a long time. Then Falcon gestured around the courtyard. "I've come to read my own meanings into this garden, but why did you choose just a tree and a bench?"

Rotger smiled again. "Does it surprise you to find an assassin who is also a philosopher? I assure you philosophy is quite common amongst those of us who aren't insane."

Falcon laughed. His grave manner always amused her, maybe because it was such a careful parody of her own. "But why a bench and a tree?"

"The art of assassination is reduction." He bent over and retrieved one of the fallen crab apples with a black-gloved hand. This he held up before her, like a tiny target. "Every situation is reduced to two opposing principles: blade and shield, pick and lock, sound and silence. Anything beyond the two is clutter. I've seen more than one promising blue cape get killed by clutter."

"So the tree and the bench—" Falcon persisted.

Rotger flicked away the crab apple. "So, the two opposing forces in the world: seasons and stone, mortality and eternity, life and death."

The corner of her mouth curled upward like the slight bend of a flower petal. "I rather thought so."

Again there was silence until he extended a hand to her. "Come, it's getting late and the court sessions are over for today. I imagine you'll be wanting to visit your lover now."

This deduction surprised her more than his elaborate explanation had. "How do you know—?"

"I may not have yet chosen to pardon, but I know why someone would. I'm going to Market Street myself; I'll walk you that far."

Falcon nodded, wordlessly following him out onto the road.

Soon they left the courtyards and law houses far behind and entered the more seasonless section of town. No trees grew there, and even the occasional weed poking up through the dirt looked like it had been dead since the city was built. Rain began falling, filling puddles where birds stood ankle deep, pecking at lice, while random piles of rags melted into the mud that choked out everything. Houses grew smaller and closer together, and finally they arrived at the staircase descent into Medusa's.

The old temple-turned-tavern was busy that night, its patrons seeking shelter from their own leaking roofs. Crowded tables and loud voices drove away the ghosts that haunted Medusa's in its quieter moments, and even the stone serpents that twisted across the ceiling, staring down with their empty, plundered eyes, seemed mundane. On nights like that, only those drunk enough to go treasure hunting in the wine cellar were reminded of what had once been worshiped there. "Would you like to meet him?" Falcon asked, feeling embarrassed.

She watched Rotger's eyes scan the room until they found the young man lying on his stomach by the fireplace. Something about the youth's posture conjured up images of stone snakes warmed to life and made human. "Him?"

"Yes."

"I have other business." But he smiled before slipping back up the stairs, the red lining of his cape briefly tinting her thoughts like a premature sunset. She shook the color loose and made her way over to Alix.

"Hello."

He laughed, rolling over onto his back. For a moment strands of jet black hair ran like cracks across his face, but he quickly tossed them aside. "My Dark Star! You always come to me in the rain. Welcome."

She caught his outstretched hand, pulling him to his feet. The touch of his skin brought a fresh wave of embarrassment. How foolish she must look, a woman of nearly forty consorting with a boy of eighteen—that would make them laugh in their precious gardens. Cold, logical Falcon, taken in by a prostitute. Then she looked at him, the gold chain around his neck and the reckless tilt of his head, all of it like a man about to be hanged, and she knew what anyone thought didn't matter, didn't even exist. Not in his presence. "How are you?" she asked, conscious of the inadequacy of words.

"I have something magnificent to show you." He kept hold of her hand as they left the main room. Medusa's was the one spot of habitation in an old building. Deserted passageways ran like interlocking mazes from its center, but even those foolish enough to descend into the wine cellar never went there. Alix paused to light a candle, then pushed his way into the dust and cobwebs, leaving Falcon to follow as best she could.

Time and space became irrelevant. All that existed was a spot of candlelight on the floor and the shape of her boots as they passed in and out of it. Their footsteps mixed with the sound of falling rain, until one became the echo of the other. Even speaking was an effort, and when Falcon finally managed, it felt like waking from a dream. "I didn't think Idette let anyone go back here."

"She lets me. People let me do what I want, since seeing us together." He laughed. "I don't know who they're more scared of—you or Rotger."

"But you're not?"

"Scared of you? Not at all."

But she knew she should be afraid of him.

They came to a staircase with a banister so rotted the wood felt like velvet when she held onto it. Following Alix's point of light reminded her of following a star, step by step into the night sky, running aft it into deeper and deeper darkness until even the star flickered out. The spot of light on the floor stopped moving and Falcon found herself momentarily outside it as Alix announced, "We're here."

A flash of lightning illuminated the tower room where they stood. Dust lay thick over everything, and bits of the storm swirled in the unshuttered windows like rippling tapestries. Alix stepped inside, and as his candlelight warmed the crumbling walls, Falcon stared past him in astonishment. A woman knelt in the middle of the room, her face bent down, her arms raised toward the windows.

Falcon opened her mouth to speak, but Alix was already crouching down beside the strange figure. "I told you she was magnificent. All the rest have been destroyed, except for bits and pieces, but only Idette knows about this one. And she won't touch it."

"She's stone," Falcon murmured, slowing realizing why the girl had not moved since their arrival. "One of the sacrifices. I had no idea…"

"I found her the other day and just had to sit here and stare. Look at her face. Look how happy it is. I wonder what the last thing she saw was?" He ran a hand lovingly across the statue's stone smile.

"She saw God." The woman unsettled her and she couldn't make herself stop hovering in the doorway, trapped between the darkness behind and the mystery in front. "She saw God and was granted immortality." A clap of thunder answered her like a shout from the divine and Falcon jumped. "I thought Idette got rid of all those things, broke them or threw them in the lake."

"She did, mostly, but not this one. Wouldn't tell me why, either. God, look at her! Aren't you envious?"

Lightning flashed off Alix's features, freezing them in her mind like her last glimpse of Rotger's cape. How long before the faint circles under his eyes grew dark and caved in? How long before the milky whiteness of his skin curdled, turning yellow like old parchment? How long before the slenderness of his body became emaciated and the heat of his touch was no longer passion but perpetual fever? Minna gave away her youth to Falcon, and for what? How long until all she had to offer Alix was a bed of snow? "I don't know."

"I am. I think that's why I keep coming up here." He extended a hand toward her. "Come here, Falcon. Let's kneel and pray for the night to transform us while I'm still young and you're still powerful."

She settled into the dust next to him, touched by a strange yearning, not for perpetual spring, but for some dignity to autumn. As her hands traveled from his throat to the hairless skin revealed by his open tunic, the aching became a sort of tenderness. Across from her, Alix's eyes burned in the candlelight, his face aglow with the love of vanity.

Lightning came again, silhouetting the stone woman beside her, and something in Alix's expression went out. For a moment he looked like he wanted to tell her something real, something that went beyond the sweeping romanticism he wore like a mark of his profession. For a moment he looked like he wanted to tell her what it was like to be gang raped by a group of drunken adventurers, what it was like to give head with a split lip and raging fever. She felt his skin trembling beneath her touch, as if he were about to split open and send everything pouring out—all the things he hid from her, fearing that any trace of grit on her toy would be enough to make her discard it. But all that happened was that his face fell suddenly away from her and his hands came together in an attitude of prayer. "I want to be stone..." he whispered desperately.

Falcon shut her eyes and pulled him close, trying to take reassurance in the warmth of his breath. "I just want to see God."

The next morning she sat in her garden with Rotger, talking of statues and storm clouds, when Lady Arcadia's summons arrived. Falcon rose and started to excuse herself, but Rotger only laughed. "I'll come with you. I know enough of The Lady's secrets to damn her to hell several times over, so I doubt she'll mind if I add this one. Besides, I have an idea what it's about. You may want me."

Falcon nodded, secretly glad of his company. Together they followed the messenger back inside the Temple of Justice, then out through the portal into Lady Arcadia's garden. Like Falcon, Lady Arcadia had a certain aesthetic—her courtyard was dominated by a fountain. It stood nearly as tall as a person, water rattling through its bronze leaves before finally dropping into a pool where the decapitated buds of dried roses bobbed about like shriveled fish. As always, the stale air smelled heavily of perfume. "Lady Arcadia," Falcon murmured, bowing.

The object of her address turned slowly, her silver robe resettling around her body like a freshly torn web. Gray eyes stared at her visitors from some remote place where thoughts hung like icicles and no wind ever stirred the surface of deep snow. "Lady Bertille," she acknowledged, tilting her head in Falcon's direction. Rotger also earned a nod of her head, but to him she gave no name, nor, seemingly, any further thought. "I have called you here because of grave news."

"What is it?"

Lady Arcadia held out a scroll, marked with the familiar half-cat, half-fish of the Crescens' seal. "The Crescens are prepared to bring charges against you that could mean the loss of your seat."

Falcon made a soft noise of contempt. "They can't bribe me and they don't dare kill me, so now they lie. What charges?"

"Patronizing a prostitute."

"What?"

Lady Arcadia nodded, gesturing to the seat around her fountain. For a moment Falcon was too dazed to take in this gesture of sympathy, then hurriedly accepted. Her fingers felt numb as they fumbled with her pouch strings, and the strip of licorice slipped from her, toppling in among the dead rose buds. Lady Arcadia, however, betrayed no notice of this as she sat beside her. "I know. A small enough crime considering what most of us did to acquire our titles, but any violation of law, proven in full court, is enough to cost a seat. You are less than popular, Lady Bertille. All it will take is evidence."

Falcon dipped her fingers into the pool, trying to wash away the memory of Alix's skin. "Can they prove it?"

"That depends. Did you do it?"

There were dark certainties about Lady Arcadia, but Falcon didn't fear her like the others did. Rotger killed for one reason—gold—and The Lady killed only for power. Never in rage, never out of jealously, always for power. That was the one thing Falcon always gave her plenty of. "Yes."

"Then they can prove it."

Falcon saw her world slide away. She couldn't go back to Market Street and start over, not at forty, not without the others. The courts were all she had. "Why are you telling me this?" she whispered hoarsely.

"To warn you. The hearing will not be held until tomorrow. Act."

"How?"

Lady Arcadia's eyes rested briefly on Rotger. "Prostitutes keep no financial records and dead men give no testimony."

Words deserted Falcon in a sudden rush. Her hand jerked from the pool as she leapt to her feet, Lady Arcadia's perfume suddenly burning her tongue and throat. And still she couldn't speak.

Lady Arcadia rose and nodded, turning her back on them. "This talk is at an end," she murmured, fading into the dead plants of her garden.

That night a cold wind spun through the tower room at Medusa's, propelling Falcon from window to window as she scanned the streets for Alix's approach. Rotger stood in the room's center, more like a shadow than a part of the scenery, the rippling of his cape more solid than any of his own movements. In one hand, he held her dagger. "Very nice," he murmured, admiring it in the dim light of his candle. "A bit old-fashioned, of course, but nice. How long since you last used this?"

Falcon stopped pacing long enough to snatch the weapon and tuck it back under her robes. "Not as long as you might think." She started toward the nearest window, but changed her mind, momentarily unable to bear the thought of motion. Instead, she sank to her knees in front of the stone woman, imploring, "What do I do?"

The statue had no reply, but Rotger raised a barely visible eyebrow. "I thought that Lady Arcadia had a perfectly reasonable suggestion."

Falcon shook her head impatiently. "You don't know what it's like— ever since last night, I've had this non-stop background noise in my mind. Do I lust after him? Pity him? Love him?" She tossed her hands into the air sending wind pouring down her loose sleeves like ice water. "I don't know. How can I decide what to do now if I don't even know that."

"Details," Rotger warned softly, "clutter. Focus on the two opposing forces."

"But what are they?"

"That you have to determine for yourself. Choose carefully, Falcon, more than one life hangs on it."

Falcon sighed, feeling hope drain out of her with the last breath. "Thanks. Listen, you better get out of sight. Alix may not be afraid of me, but he might bolt if he sees you, especially under the circumstances."

Rotger nodded, setting the candle beside the stone woman before starting toward one of the windows. He had almost completely settled on the ledge outside before Falcon called out to him. "Rotger, thanks for coming tonight. You're a good friend."

Something flickered across the assassin's face, and he nodded. "I hope so." Then he vanished into the darkness.

Falcon swallowed her licorice when she heard Alix's footsteps coming cautiously up the old staircase. What was he more afraid of—finding her— or not finding her? Then he stood in the room's doorway, warm candle wax dripping on his slender fingers. For an instant they both stood frozen, before Alix's face lit up with joy. "Falcon! My Dark Star, you came!" He blew out his light and let it drop to the floor as he rushed forward, throwing his arms around her. "I was so afraid you wouldn't understand, but you do.

I should have known you would."

Falcon pushed him back, bewildered by the ecstatic expression on his face. Could betrayal be such a joy for him? "Alix? Is it true? Are you really going to testify against me in full court?"

"Of course I am, I have to. But that doesn't matter—"

"Doesn't matter?" Her fingers brushed against the dagger's hidden hilt, aching to draw it. "They'll take away my seat! I'll be finished."

The joy on Alix's face momentarily dimmed from confusion, then reappeared. "Oh, you don't understand. But you still came—how doubly magnificent!" From his sleeve he drew two glass vials, one empty, one still full of a silvery powder. "Falcon," he whispered, touching her arm, "you think I would betray you? The one person I have ever loved like I love the sound of rain and the spaces between the stars at night?"

She stared at him while the wind whipped strands of hair across her face like bars in a clumsy cage. Where was the moment she'd seen last night? Where was the pain that seemed to match and understand her own? "What?"

He drew one of her hands from beneath her billowing robes and pressed a vial into it. "My Dark Star, I haven't turned on you. The Crescens offered me gold, but you give me all the money I need. They didn't dare threaten to harm me. So they asked what I wanted above all else, and when I told them, they gave me this." He held up the empty vial.

A horrible sort of realization began dawning on Falcon, chilling her where the wind had failed. "They didn't. They couldn't."

"Two components, taken in separate doses. Very rare, and very expensive, but what's that to a family like the Crescens? They gave me the first dose today, after we talked. I'll get the second tomorrow after I give my testimony. I made them give me enough for both of us."

Falcon stared at the stone woman and remembered Alix kneeling on the floor, praying to be made stone before he broke open. "They gave you that?"

"They gave us that." He gestured to the powder in her hand. "Take it now, and then tomorrow, after the trial is over, we can both go somewhere—anywhere you want. Some wild hillside or deserted beach, anything. Even that depressing courtyard of yours. And I'll take your hand and look into your eyes, and you'll look into mine, then we'll both take the other component and turn to stone while I'm still young and you're still powerful. While we're still in love."

She reached up and touched his face, able to see what he could no longer hide. She could see that he didn't love her, that he was scared to death that one day he actually might, but he was still willing to give her the only gift he thought he could. Himself. Beautiful. Forever. The voices inside her rose to a deafening buzz, then seemed to reach some sort of conclusion and died. "Alix," she whispered, the one real thing inside her finally breaking loose, "I love you."

His body jerked as if she had hit him, and again she sensed the cracks, threatening to split him open and spill him at her feet. She could see all the hell, all the horror that once revealed can never be rinsed away, pressing at him from the inside. And again he fought it back. "Then this is the only way."

Her hand dropped from his face and she turned away, too broken to think of killing. She would lose her seat, would die old, ugly and alone, begging for coppers on the corner of Market Street, and her lover would turn to stone tomorrow, young and perfect forever. Was there anything more cruel than that? "I won't. I can't."

"Falcon, please—"

"No. Goodbye, Alix."

There was a moment of silence before he spoke again. "I'll do it here, tomorrow after the case is tried. If you won't join me, at least come, so I can carry your image into eternity on stone eyes."

Before Falcon could reply, Alix cried out softly, something about it so different that she spun around. He stood as he had before she looked away, but now his hand was pressed to his neck, and from between his fingers protruded a small, black dart.

"No!" she screamed, leaping forward with the same breath and ripping the dart from his throat. But even as she did it, she knew it was too late. Alix twitched, and the vial fell from his other hand, making a soft clink before it vanished between the boards. A moment later, Alix dropped too, black lines of poison already apparent on his throat. "No!" Falcon repeated, shrieking it into the night where she knew his assailant lurked. Then she sank to her knees beside Alix.

He panted jerkily, each breath forced out of increasingly stiff lungs. As Falcon rolled him over onto his back, she could feel the immobility spreading like some horrible premonition of rigor mortis. "No Alix…I didn't want you dead." As she spoke, she became aware of a figure standing beside her, although she could barely take in its familiarity. "Oh God, Rotger. You've killed him."

"Not exactly. Has it ever occurred to you that statuary is a good deal easier to dispose of than bodies? Of course, the two components are rare and expensive, but what's that to a red cape assassin?"

She looked at Alix. His lips quivered, trying to force out words, but his throat was stiff as marble and refused to allow him sound. Soon even his mouth surrendered its feeble struggle as an icy hardness spread across his face. Her lover wasn't dying. He was turning to stone. "Why?" she whispered.

"Because you spared him. Do you really think the Crescens would trust the life of their son to a prostitute's testimony?"

"They paid you to kill him?"

"They paid me to kill you."

She looked up at him, clutching the frozen body of her lover stubbornly in her arms. "Then do it."

"I would, if you had killed Alix. You credit yourself with mercy because you let one prostitute walk free, and yet it never occurred to you that I murder people for a living. You've made two exceptions, Falcon, and if you had betrayed the one, I would have ceased to trust your commitment to the other."

Her gaze returned to Alix. He was almost completely gone, but faint traces of green still lingered in his eyes. "I love you," she repeated. If he had to carry her image to eternity on his eyes, he should at least carry that on his heart. "I'll come here. I'll remember." Then all color faded, leaving only stone. Falcon pressed her lips against his cold, marble cheek and tried to cry. But despite her burning eyes and tightening chest, no tears would come—not for Alix, young and perfect forever, not for Minna, nothing more than bones buried in snow.

Finally she struggled to her feet and walked to one of the tower's windows. Outside she could see the night sky, and the stars scattered across it like tiny grains of silver powder. They held her motionless until Rotger's gentle voice broke the silence. "What are you doing?"

"Looking for the face of God."

Neither of them spoke again until Rotger placed his hand on her shoulder. "It's late. Let's go home."

SNOW JOB
G. WILLIAM CROMER

I had almost finished shoveling the driveway when the long, black car eased to a stop at the entrance. Two men got out, and I recognized them as cops who'd been here before. Needing a breather, I leaned on the shovel. This had been the fifth heavy snow of the winter and the pile along the side of the driveway was as high as my shoulder, packed solid from the bitter cold.

"You got to be careful doing that," one of the cops said. "Overweight guys like you and me should watch the shoveling." He patted his corpulence with a rueful smile.

I resented his remark because my twenty unnecessary pounds looked nothing like the paunch he lugged around. His round face was heavy-jowled, red-cheeked from the cold. His name was Beader and he was a detective with the local police department.

His partner, shorter and thinner, wore a black topcoat that hung nearly to his ankles. A scarf concealed his neck and mouth, but left exposed a sharp, little nose. His name was Parkinson.

"Any news of my wife?" I asked. Beader stepped over the pile of snow at the end of the driveway.

"We want to talk to you about that. Can we go inside? Unless you want to talk out here in the cold."

Inside the house, I stripped off my parka. They sat gingerly on the edge of a sofa and kept their coats on though the house was warm. They declined my offer of coffee. Beader looked around the room, noting the paneled walls and thick rug.

"Nice place you got here."

"It's OK. Now what about Ellen?"

"If you don't mind, we'd like to hear your story again."

"I do mind. You've heard it three times. Nothing's changed."

"I'm sorry, Mr. Crane, but some of us have to hear things a dozen times before they sink in. Maybe you'll remember something that'll help us find out what happened to your wife."

Parkinson butted in antagonistically. "Are you certain you've told us everything that happened the day she went away?"

I disliked Parkinson and showed it. "What's your problem?"

"Now don't get bent out of joint," Beader said. "It won't hurt to tell us again. Like I said, maybe we missed something."

"You're giving me a snow job to cover your lack of success."

Beader settled back on the sofa and twirled his hat.

"OK, no snow job. There's enough of that outside. We have information that you and your wife had a violent argument the night you say she drove off to visit her sister."

"Who gave you this so-called information?"

"We'd rather not say just now. Is it true?"

"I'll bet it was the old biddy next door, Mrs. Muldoon."

The look on Beader's face told me I was correct. Mrs. Muldoon was an elderly, stout woman who lived in the house behind mine. Although our lots were separated by a dense evergreen hedge, sound carried well, especially in the cold night air. Mrs. Muldoon couldn't see beyond the hedge, but snooped with sharp ears as far as I was concerned.

"Just tell us your story again," said Parkinson.

Obviously they suspected I'd done away with my wife. I threw up my hands in disgust and repeated the details. A few days previously—five now, to be exact—Ellen, weary of the harsh winter, decided to visit her sister who lived three hundred miles south of us. Because the weather was terrible, I begged her to take a plane or train. Ellen liked to drive. Despite my pleas, she loaded a couple of suitcases in her car and drove off, even though it was snowing and the roads icy.

That was the last time I had seen her. The following morning, I called her sister. Ellen hadn't arrived. I phoned some of her friends on the chance she might have spent the night with them. No luck. Fearing she'd been in an accident, I notified the police. They had searched for her since then.

"I hope that's the last time I tell that story," I said.

"I hope so, too," Beader said. "Now what about the argument?"

"We argued, yes, and it might've been loud, but certainly not violent. I didn't think she was skilled enough to drive on bad roads. She didn't agree. That's all there was to it."

Parkinson looked skeptical. "Your neighbor said the argument was violent. She heard screams and thumps. That doesn't sound like a difference of opinion about driving skill."

I shrugged. "If you knew Mrs. Muldoon better, you'd know she's easily excitable and always has her ear cocked for gossip. The TV was turned on at the time to one of those cops and robbers shows that are long on noise and short on plot."

"So why did your wife leave just then? It was getting dark and snowing. Why didn't she wait until the next morning?"

"She thought there'd be less traffic and she didn't want to wait in case the weather got worse. I tried to talk her out of going, but she's stubborn and wouldn't change her mind."

"That was part of your argument?"

They were avoiding the issue and I called them on it.

"Now it's your turn to answer questions. Have you found out *anything* about my wife's disappearance?"

"No," Beader said. "We've checked local hospitals, of course, and alerted highway patrols all along the route you said she'd take. Unless she took another way."

"She wouldn't take another way."

"I'll tell you what I think," Parkinson said. "I think you killed her. Your story is too slick, an answer for everything. You and your wife argued, you killed her, and got rid of the body."

I scowled at them. "What the hell is going on?"

"Take it easy, Andy," Beader said to Parkinson, and turned to me. "Look at it from our point of view. It just seems funny to us, you two having a loud argument which turns out to be a TV show, and your wife leaving in the middle of a snow storm. You can see how it might seem."

"I see you aren't concerned about Ellen. You'd rather invent fantasies than find out what really happened to her."

"Mr. Crane, if your wife had been in an accident, we'd know it by now. That's why we're looking at all the angles. Nobody's accusing you of murder, no matter what my partner thinks."

My voice shook with anger and I began to shout.

"What do you want, a confession? Sure, I killed her. Go ahead, search my house, find the body, look for the bloodstains! You incompetent idiots! Ellen's in trouble somewhere, and you're wasting time chasing shadows."

"Take it easy," Beader said. "We'll find your wife."

"Wherever she is," Parkinson said, grimly uncompromising.

"Be sure to call on Mrs. Muldoon," I said bitterly, "so she can tell you about the violent argument she just heard."

They had nothing else to say except criticism and that wouldn't help. On a tensely polite note they left, jockeying the car around in the narrow street to go back the way they'd come. I finished my shoveling, adding more inches to the hefty pile alongside.

Unable to concentrate on anything because of Ellen's disappearance, I'd taken time off from my insurance business. I puttered around the house or mindlessly watched TV. That didn't help much. Even the local weatherman lost his programmed cheer over continual forecasts for more snow.

I didn't care. My house was the only one on a short street that dead-ended right at my lot line. The city road crews used the dead end as a dump for snow they pushed off the neighborhood streets, creating a mini-mountain of the white stuff that threatened to block my driveway. In my present mood, I welcomed the physical effort of moving additional snowfall.

Early the next morning Beader phoned with the news that Ellen's car had been found. He sounded apologetic. "It was under our noses all the time, parked at the mall parking lot, right out in the open. Some of the stores are open twenty-four hours so cars are parked there all night. On a routine patrol, an officer noticed a car completely covered with snow and checked it out."

He asked me to meet him at the mall. "Bring spare keys if you have them. The car's locked."

I made the mall in less than twenty minutes. Several cars, including a police car with flashing lights, were clustered near the center of the parking lot. Beader and Parkinson were standing near a snow covered mound. I parked and got out and looked at it. It was Ellen's car, cold and lonely.

Inside the car, her purse lay on the front seat. Her wallet and money were intact. Steeling myself, I reluctantly opened the trunk. Her suitcases lay there, undisturbed. I caught my breath, groaning. Someone sighed loudly, either in relief or disappointment that Ellen's body wasn't there. Our collective breaths created a mist that hung in the trunk like a miniature fog bank.

I sagged against the car, my face in my hands. Beader put out an arm to steady me. "Brace up, Mr. Crane. At least we have something to go on. We're checking out the stores right now."

"She's gone," I said. "Someone grabbed her."

"We don't know that. Let's wait till we get some facts before jumping to conclusions."

We waited. Beader's men, armed with Ellen's picture, canvassed the stores, concentrating on the all-nighters, but learned nothing. No one remembered seeing Ellen, which wasn't surprising. The mall was busy at night, even in bad weather.

We sat in the back of a hamburger joint and toyed with coffee while Beader summed up. "We still have to check some of the night crews, but I don't expect much from them. We know she was here. Someone could have picked her up, willing or otherwise."

"What do you mean, willing?"

Parkinson leaned across the table, almost conspiratorially.

"Look, Mr. Crane. Maybe there was someone she liked better than she liked you. She met him here and they ran off together, car, bus, plane, whatever. These things happen."

I glared at him, "Sure they do. And she just happened to forget her clothes and purse. You're snowing me again and I won't accept it. What do you really think?"

Beader sighed. "It's possible that Parkinson is right. But it's more likely she stopped here to buy some last minute thing. Was grabbed by somebody and hustled off. It opens up a new line of investigation and the trail's already days old."

"For god's sake! Ellen is out there somewhere, probably raped and murdered, and you don't even know where to start looking."

Beader clamped a big hand on my arm. "Take it easy. Keep your voice down. Chances are your wife's still in the area. I admit it doesn't look good for her. Your best bet is to go home and try to get some rest."

We jawed back and forth for a few more minutes, but Beader was right. There wasn't anything I could do. He promised to report progress to me daily. I drove home to my empty house.

Unable to sleep, I paced the floor and finally fixed a nightcap. In the mirror hanging over the bar in the family room, I studied my face. It was middle-aged, somber, and drawn. I tried a smile. The smile became wider and turned into a chuckle. Then I laughed out loud and toasted my reflection with my drink.

Things were going just as I anticipated. The only problem had been Parkinson's insistence that I had killed Ellen. I didn't know if he really believed it or was just baiting a police trap.

It didn't matter. They could prove nothing. I'd left no clues. The stick of wood I used to bash her silly head had burned in the fireplace. I had loaded her bags in the car and driven it to the mall, and had returned partly by bus, and by walking the last few blocks on deserted streets to my house.

The story I told the police was essentially true. I had actually made the phone calls to her sister and friends. By improvising an argument with the detectives, I felt I had defused the shaking testimony of Mrs. Muldoon. I hadn't counted on the police taking so long to find Ellen's car but that was a stroke of luck. They were now convinced she'd been abducted.

Why did I do it? Not for any of the usual reasons. I gained nothing financially from Ellen's death, nor did I have a mistress on the side. Call it the accumulated years of her whining and nagging, of her spending money faster than I earned it. Call it impulse when, during the last strident echoes of her voice, I crushed her skull with a cheek of firewood.

The only thing left to do was to get rid of the body. The delay in finding the car had also forced me to delay this final act: transporting the body to some remote stretch of back road and dumping it. Do this at night, I reasoned, and I'd probably never remember where I'd been. Her death would be blamed on the nonexistent abductor. All I needed was another snow night which would surely come in another day or two.

The next dawn brought darkening clouds but just a few flakes fell. In the evening, Beader phoned to report no progress. He didn't sound confident. "We're not giving up. We'll find her."

"I'm praying for your success," I lied.

It was too late for action this night, but I decided to move the body the following night regardless of the weather. I wanted the cover of a snowstorm, but I'd settle for a dark night. As it turned out, I got neither.

Everything went wrong. During the night, the wind changed and by morning the sun shone and the temperature soared well above freezing. The clear, snowless day brought out the busy street cleaning crews with their snow removal equipment. It was the grinding, throbbing noise of machinery that awakened me.

Sluggishly I moved to the window and then, shocked fully awake, started aghast at the sign of the power shovel and trucks. The shovel operator dug a big scoopful from the hug mound of snow at the end of the street and deposited it into a waiting truck. Sunlight sparkled off the gleaming snow and silvered the little streamers of water running along the curbs. It was a sight to warm anybody's heart but mine.

I scrambled out of the house in pajamas and bare feet, and ran to the end of the driveway. "We won't block your driveway for long. Just moving the snow out while we can."

"No, no!" I babbled. "Don't move it. Go away!"

He frowned, but spoke politely, humoring an eccentric. "I know it's noisy. I'm sorry we disturbed you, but we got a job to do. We'll be out of your hair soon, I promise."

The power shovel dug another big pile from the shrinking mountain of snow and dumped it into the truck.

"You don't understand," I groaned. My legs shook and I swayed.

The man caught my arm. "You OK, mister?"

The operator of the shovel shouted loudly and the crew of men surged forward. The last bite of snow had released a miniature slide and with it the frozen, curled figure I had buried there several days ago when even the weather was on my side.

A man yelled, "Somebody call the cops! This is a dead woman here." For a moment, I was forgotten. I staggered back into the house and sat wearily. One day too late. There was no improvisation I could make. Nothing to do but sit and wait for the sound of the sirens.

JUST DESSERTS
PATRICK THOMAS

Things were getting ugly, and it was no slight on the attractiveness of the folks involved. That's the way it is with in-laws sometimes. My wife Elsie died awhile back, but I'd never had this kind of trouble with her parents. Makes me thankful, especially considering the longevity of the feud between Demeter and Pluto. It has run into eons, and shows no sign of being winded enough to slow down to a jog any time soon.

Poor Persephone was caught in the middle. She loved her mother and her husband. Her fondest wish was that the two of them would just get along. That was a wish not even a jinn could make come true.

Usually, the two of them put on a show of civility around Persephone. It doesn't fool her, but it makes her life more pleasant. At the best of times, it was barely enough to camouflage the ever-present storm front between the pair. This was not the best of times.

Today's argument was over the quality of the food Demeter serves here in Bulfinche's Pub. Nobody but Pluto could find fault with Demeter's cooking. In my humble opinion, it is the most wonderful food around.

"Paddy, I can't believe you let your customers eat this rat swill," said Pluto. The boss wisely kept his mouth shut and picked up his broom to go outside to sweep in front of the pub.

"Rat swill?" yelled Demeter.

"You're right. Rat poison is more like it. It does have an up side. At least the kitchen must be vermin-free," said Pluto, laughing at his own joke. I guess when you're a god, you don't have to be funny.

"It will be, as long as you stay out of it," said Demeter.

Persephone shook her head, not bothering to even try to break things up. She had been there too many times before. Instead she walked over to my section of the bar.

"Murphy, I need a drink," Persephone said, rolling her eyes back in her head.

"What'll it be?" I asked.

"Give me a rum and coke," she said, looking over her shoulder. Her mother had just offered to fry up certain of Pluto's body parts. Persephone shook her head sadly as I handed over her drink. "They are so childish. This is no way for them to act. They're gods, for Olympus' sake. Why do we have to do this every spring?"

"We? I'm just serving drinks," I said. Persephone smiled, her first one since she got here.

"You seem to be the only one. Dionysus disappeared down to the wine cellar and Paddy has been sweeping outside for quite a while," she said.

"The boss likes to have a clean sidewalk," I said. Which in New York City requires frequent sweeping. It is one of the few menial jobs the boss doesn't push off on me or Fred.

"It's already spotless. Unless Paddy has hopes of rubbing off the top layer of cement, there is no reason for him to be out there," said Persephone.

Pluto was asking Demeter if she was having Samson pick out her clothes. If he'd been in the bar, Samson would have probably have tripped the Lord of Hades with his cane. Sure Samson's blind, but he feels handicaps are no reason to make fun of anyone. Especially him.

"Oh, I don't know about that," I said with a wink.

"Why are you still here, Murphy? I'm sure you could find somewhere else to be," said Persephone.

"Probably, but I'm enjoying this," I said.

"Wish I could," said Persephone, sipping her drink.

"In a way, you should be flattered. All their bickering is over how much they love you," I said.

"If they loved me, wouldn't they get along? Or at least try?" asked Persephone.

"From what I hear, compared to the old days, this is getting along. Was their bickering really the cause of winter?" I asked.

Persephone smiled and pushed her empty glass across the bar. "How about a refill?"

"I never get straight answers out of you guys about this stuff. You want the drink, you give me an answer," I said with mock severity. Persephone knew the boss would have my hide if I withheld a drink without a good reason. This didn't qualify.

"Murphy, you know winter is caused by the angle of the Earth's axis in relation to the sun. Myths are put into terms the tellers and the listeners can understand. No, what happened was that mother started an ice age. Zeus brokered the deal that I would spend time with her every spring in exchange for her ending it," said Persephone. I handed over her refill.

"So if the groundhog sees his shadow, does your visit get delayed for six weeks?" I asked.

"No," said Persephone, shaking her head and rolling her eyes, this time at me.

Apparently, the sidewalk was entirely spotless because Paddy was on his way back in, and he had a beautiful blond woman with bloodshot eyes in tow. Pluto turned his attention away from Demeter and moved toward Paddy.

"Now, if your husband holds true to form, he's going to hit up Paddy for a job to cater food here at the bar," I whispered.

"Is Pluto that predictable?" Persephone asked.

"Let's watch and see," I said.

"Paddy, how about you let me provide the meals here for a while?" Pluto asked. I looked at Persephone, lifted my eyebrows twice and grinned. Persephone giggled.

"No thanks. I'm more than happy with the cook we have," said Paddy, gesturing the blond woman into a seat by one of the tables.

"How about when Demeter goes on vacation? She could use the time to rest her old, tired bones," said Pluto.

"Who are you calling old and tired, you no—good excuse for a son-in-law? If my daughter had only married Apollo as I suggested..." said Demeter.

"How about dessert then? I have this lovely fudge that people can take home with them," said Pluto. Now that was making more sense. If someone were to eat food from Pluto's realm, they would be forced to go there with him. Problem is, unless they were in his realm, he can't give the food to them directly. Some sort of rule that binds even the gods. Even if Paddy served Pluto's food in the bar, it wouldn't bind someone to Hades. Magic, curses and the like are null and void in Bulfinche's Pub, unless the boss gives dispensation. For a scheme like this, the boss' approval was doubtful. However, if someone were to take the fudge home and eat it outside of the bar, Pluto would have a new denizen for his realm.

Part of what happens to people when they die ties directly into what they believe. The Olympians didn't have a lot of worshippers these days, so business was down for Pluto. He was trying to drum it up any way he could.

"No, thanks," said Paddy.

I whispered to Persephone, "Does he think Paddy will ever change his mind?"

"No, but it gives him something to turn his energies toward," she said.

"I guess even gods need hobbies," I said. Paddy had put his broom away.

"Now if you two can control yourselves, we have a poor lass here who could use our help," said Paddy. Amazingly, the pair shut up. "Can I get ye something to drink?"

"Thank you, but I don't think I should be drinking in my state of mind. How about a cup of coffee?" said the woman.

"Coming up," said Paddy, walking around to the back of the bar, where he poured a mug of java.

Dionysus came out from the kitchen, where the door to the wine cellar was. As he walked out into the bar proper, he looked for Demeter and Pluto. Seeing the pair sitting quietly, he gave a dramatic sigh as he walked behind the bar.

"They shut up. Thank goodness. When the bar went quiet, I thought I had gone deaf," said Dion, grinning.

Paddy delivered the coffee.

"Thank you. What do I owe you?" she asked.

"It's on the house," Paddy said.

"I couldn't take advantage of your generosity. I insist on paying," she said, fumbling in her pants for her wallet. She wasn't carrying a purse.

"You're not. First drink is always free for a guest's maiden visit," said Paddy. The lady looked a little old to still be a maiden, but I was smart enough not to comment. "Now why don't ye tell me why you were walking down the street, crying your eyes out?"

"My name is Helen Donner, but you probably knew that."

Paddy shook his head no.

"The press has been hounding me. You don't recognize me from TV or the papers?" she asked.

"No, not really," said Paddy. He usually went out for a walk and picked up several newspapers. With all the commotion between Pluto and Demeter, he hadn't had a chance to get them yet.

Helen seemed strangely disappointed.

"My husband Jerry and my little girl Tina..." Helen let out a sob. "They were murdered last night. The killer beat me and then he..." Helen stopped and sobbed again. "He raped me."

"You poor dear," said Demeter, torn. She wanted to go and put her arms around the woman, but she knew that many rape victims could not stand being touched. Tears were streaming down Helen's face.

"I'd be dead now too, if the police sirens hadn't scared him off. I might have been better off. I don't know how I'm going to live without my family."

"I'm so sorry," said Paddy. "Do ye need to see a doctor or a psychiatrist? I can recommend someone."

"No, I'm as okay as I can be at this point. I got out of the hospital this morning. They admitted me for shock and drugged me to make sure I got some rest. Being cooped up with strangers was making me crazy, so I left. I started to head home, but the closer I got, the more I knew I couldn't go home. Not after what happened. I don't know if I'll ever be able to go back there again," Helen said. The tears that had been steadily pouring down her cheeks started to flow even more heavily. "My poor Jerry. My little baby."

Demeter hesitantly put a hand on her shoulder. When she didn't pull away, she gathered Helen up into her arms and held her until the sobbing stopped.

"Did they catch the killer?" asked Pluto. He had a special interest in punishing the guilty. Part of his job description.

"No, not yet. The police brought by some books of mug shots to the hospital this morning before I checked myself out, but I didn't see him in there. The detective in charge asked me if I was sure. I was. I'll never forget that face until the day I die," said Helen.

"Who's the detective in charge of the investigation?" asked Paddy.

"Jason Cervantes," said Helen.

"Jason is a good man and a fine detective. If anyone can find him, it's Jason," said Paddy. Jas was a regular.

"I hope so. It was Detective Cervantes who recommended that I come here. He said you people might be able to help me. I'm not sure exactly what he meant, but I took him at his word. Besides, I had nowhere else to go. I have no family nearby," said Helen, staring off into space. When her eyes focused again, she said, "I'm sure Detective Cervantes is a good man, but I know the police have more cases than they can handle, and my family were not important people."

"Everyone is important," said Dion.

"You're right, but I'm afraid that my case will get lost in between the cracks. I mean no offense to your friend. I'm sure he is overworked. I want the man who did this to be caught and punished. When Detective Cervantes said you people could help me, I think he meant in terms of coping, but I need to do something. I'm not going to be able to cope until the killer is caught. I want to hire a private investigator to find the him."

Paddy nodded his head thoughtfully. "I think ye should check with Jason and get his opinion first. Ye don't want someone that's going to get in his way, but if Jason thinks it's a good idea, ye should do it."

"Do you have any idea what that would cost?" asked Helen.

"I'm sure we could find out," said Paddy.

"I'm just worried that I won't have enough money. Jerry and I don't, I mean didn't have much money," said Helen.

"Did you have life insurance?" asked Pluto, who originally had been very amused by the concept, had eventually come to understand the need.

"Yes," said Helen.

"I'm sure the details can be worked out with the PI when and if the time comes," said Dion, trying to change the subject. Pluto was never a big one for tact.

"And I can always lend ye the money in the meantime," said Paddy, overwhelmed by the damsel in distress.

"You would do that for a total stranger?" Paddy nodded. Helping strangers in need is what the boss does. "Thank you," said Helen.

At that moment, John Thanatos walked in the door. His arrival always gives me mixed emotions, which is understandable considering John is actually the Grim Reaper. You wouldn't be able to tell it by looking at him, though. The form he wears when he visits Bulfinche's is my vision of what Death looks like, namely a handsome young man.

(Why do I picture Death that way? I can't explain my subconscious. Well, maybe I can, but usually it's easier not to try. After the death of Elsie, the love of my life, I subconsciously envisioned Death as the man who had stolen my wife away from me.

John and I had a confrontation after I had traveled through several afterlives looking for Elsie. John gave me a chance to see Elsie again, something I'll always be grateful for. Maybe even grateful enough to one day forget that he took her away from me in the first place. Not that it's his fault. Even Death has rules he has to follow.)

It seems Death is a lonely guy at heart. He and Paddy have a deal, allowing him to come around as John Thanatos. The sole stipulation is that only Paddy and I know who he really is. I think Hermes suspects, but Pluto, who owes his divine livelihood to John, has never recognized him. Neither have any of the other death deities who have shared bar space with him.

John looked troubled and stared at Helen. He came over to my station at the bar.

"John, is everything okay?" I asked, worried at the way he was looking at Helen. Poor lady had been through enough already, without joining her family in the afterlife. "You're not here on business, are you?"

John took his eyes off Helen and looked at me. John's eyes looked normal enough, but I swear when I look in them I see things that mortal, living men were not meant to gaze on. It sends chills up, down, and across my spine.

"Not exactly. Murph. Can I talk to you in private?" asked John.

"How private?" I asked, thinking we could just move down to the end of the bar.

"Extremely," said John.

"John, you don't have an appointment with me that I would want to know about, do you?" I asked.

"No, Murph, it's nothing like that. Please," said John. I stepped out from behind the bar and waved at John to follow me. I pushed open the men's room door.

"Step into my office," I said.

John went in first and I followed. The bathroom was empty. I saw John staring at the urinal. It was set up like a drinking trough, so that more than one guy could use it at once. Instead of flushing, a stream of water ran along the sides, cleaning it.

"Guess indoor plumbing is something you're not used to, huh?" I said, making conversation.

"Murph, when I'm in mortal form, I have mortal needs. Besides, many people die in bathrooms," said John.

"Lots of people fall getting out of the shower?" I asked.

"Some, but far more die on the toilet. They bear down and push during a bowel movement. It increases the pressure in their thoracic cavity, which can give them a heart attack or stroke."

That was more than I really needed to know.

"I was looking at the urinal. I haven't seen this type in years," said John.

"You know the boss. He's had the bar over a hundred years and he won't get rid of anything just because it's old, so long as it still works. He did update it slightly," I said, pointing to some devices mounted on the wall. "Motion sensors control the water stream now." Which made it kind of like a flush. The only reason the boss did it was to save water, which in turn saved him money. "But I'm sure you didn't ask me in here to discuss the evolution of urinals."

"No, I didn't," said John. "This is very hard for me. Although it's not technically not against the rules, I tend not to get involved with the who and how of people's deaths. By coming to you, I am violating the traditions of ages."

"What are you trying to say, John?"

"That woman out there is lying. She murdered her husband and daughter," said John.

"How do you know?" I asked. John gave me a look.

"Her daughter Tina told me," he said.

"But her daughter is dead," I said.

"Your point?" he asked.

"Sorry, I forgot who I was talking to for a second. Tell me the whole story."

"When I went to take them, Jerry came quietly. Being murdered by a loved one tends to have that effect. But Tina wouldn't leave," said John.

"Does that happen a lot?" I asked.

"It's common enough, spirits staying behind to take care of unfinished business. Usually, I let them be. It's best for people to resolve these things first, before moving on," said John.

"So what was different this time?"

"Tina was crying and I..."

"Were a sucker for a little girl's tears," I finished.

"Yes," said John. "It's been so long since I was affected so deeply. The influence of spending time here among the living is reawakening parts of me," said John. I smiled. John smiled back. He didn't notice me shiver. "I actually stopped and asked her what was wrong. Tina told me what happened. Her own mother had slit her throat with a switchblade, but she didn't die right away. Jerry walked in and tried to stop Helen from killing their daughter. He was stronger, but she was faster. She hit him in the head with an iron, and then strangled him while he was unconscious. Tina watched as her mother slew her father, then died herself. Tina wants her mother to pay for her crimes," said John.

"Are you going to... take her too?" I asked.

"No, that would be against the rules. Tradition I can break, but the rules are not to be toyed with lightly. I thought that if I told you and Paddy, together we could come up with a solution," said John, knowing full well that Paddy's solution would be non-lethal. That's just how the boss is.

"Can't you bring the little girl here and have her confront her mother?" I asked. Being confronted by the ghost of her murder victim might be enough to unhinge Helen, maybe even get a confession.

"Spirits can't come inside Bulfinche's," replied John.

"All right. Wait here and I'll send Paddy in," I said, exiting the men's room. Paddy was still doing his best to comfort Helen, who was speculating on where she was going to live now.

"Well, I can understand ye not wanting to go back to your apartment, after all that happened there. I may have a solution," Paddy said. Helen's act was so good that it even fooled Paddy and his normally excellent judgment. I knew what came next. He'd done it for me and dozens, maybe hundreds, of others. He was about to open his home and offer her a room upstairs, until she could get her life back on track. I had to stop him before he made that mistake.

"Boss, there's a problem in the bathroom," I said.

"So take care of it, Murphy," said Paddy.

"It's something that needs your personal attention," I said.

"I'm a bit busy here. It'll keep," said Paddy.

"No, it won't," I said. "You need to get in there now, before anything else happens."

"Murphy, I said I'd get to it later," said Paddy.

"It really can't wait," I said.

"John Murphy, ye of all people should have your priorities straighter than this. It wasn't so terribly long ago that ye came here needing help. We gave ye our full attention. Ye can at least do the same for poor Helen, here," said Paddy. Helen looked a bit confused, as did everyone else. I may wise-crack, but I rarely ever directly contradict or try to overrule the boss. Normally, it would be a losing battle. This time I had to make sure it wasn't.

"Paddy, trust me. If you don't come right now, there will be a much bigger mess to clean up later," I said. Paddy looked at me, wondering why I was being so persistent. "It'll cost you more than you should have to pay. Padriac, please." I had never called Paddy by his proper name before, at least not when I was addressing him directly. It got his attention.

"Helen, please excuse me. I need to take care of this. Dion, do ye think ye can get your bloated carcass out here and freshen Helen's coffee?" asked Paddy.

"I think I might be able to squeeze out," said Dion, coming around the bar with the coffee pot. Paddy followed me away from the table.

"Murphy, what's going on?" whispered Paddy.

"I really don't think you want to help Helen," I said.

"Why not?" he asked.

"Because she killed her husband and daughter." Paddy looked shocked. "I got it straight from the ultimate death authority." Paddy raised an eyebrow. "John's in the bathroom. He'll fill you in on everything. Meanwhile, I'm going to call Jas and see what he knows."

I snuck into the kitchen with the cordless phone. I got through to Jason on his cell phone. He bent a few rules by telling me everything he had on the case. Helen had supposedly been hiding and gotten a call off to 911, while the "killer" was in the other room, attacking her family. By the time the police arrived, Jerry and Tina were dead. Helen was badly beaten and claimed that the intruder had run off when he heard sirens. There was evidence to support rape. There were traces of semen found on Helen and her clothes, and odds were the lab would prove that it didn't match her husband's. Helen claimed her daughter had answered the door and let the stranger in, before she could stop her. He was supposedly wearing gloves, so no fingerprints were found.

"So do you believe her story?" I asked.

"Everything's checked out so far. She seems on the level. Why?" Jason asked.

"Because she killed them," I said.

"How do you know?" Jason asked.

"I can't give the source." Part of my deal with Death was not to let anyone know who or what he really was. I couldn't tell Jason. "Let's just say it's a Bulfinche's thing," I said. Jason didn't question me. He had been coming here long enough to understand what I meant.

"Is there any way your information could be wrong?"

"No," I said.

"Will your information hold up in court?" asked Jason.

I could see it now. *'The D.A. calls the Grim Reaper to the stand.'*

"Not a chance. Is there enough evidence to point a finger at Helen?" I asked.

"Nope," he said.

"Didn't she have her daughter's blood on her?" I said.

Jas paused several moments. I could imagine him going over the details of the case in his mind. "A good defense attorney will argue what I believed up until this conversation. The killer got the blood on her during the alleged rape. Hell, she was so thorough, they found the daughter's blood during the rape physical. This lady is one sick puppy, but she seems to have thought of everything. I've been a detective a long time. This frame job of an unknown intruder was done expertly. As a matter of procedure, we'd investigate her, but without physical evidence, she'd never be suspected, much less charged. So, unless we find the knife with her prints on it, she's in the clear. Judging by the way she planned everything else, I doubt that will happen. Murph, I don't want her to get away with this. What can I do to help?" asked Jason.

"Right now, nothing. If we come up with anything, I'll let you know," I said. A plan was forming in my mind.

"I can be at the bar in ten minutes. One of the benefits of having a car with a siren," said Jason.

"Actually, I think I have a plan and if you were to suddenly show up, it might not work," I said.

"You'll keep me informed?" Jason asked.

"You know it," I answered. We said our goodbyes and hung up. As I came out of the kitchen, Paddy and John were exiting the men's room. Paddy did not look happy. I told them what Jason had said.

"So there's no way to have the cops handle this?" said Paddy.

"Not really. But I have a plan," I said, and explained it to them. Paddy and John both smiled. Paddy had a great smile, but John's still made me nervous. Here Death was being a stand-up guy, and I couldn't shake my paranoia of him.

"I like it. Ye have my dispensation to do it," said Paddy. The three of us returned to where the others were. Helen's cup of coffee was almost empty again. I walked over and picked it up.

"Let me refill this for you," I said, bringing it behind the bar and pouring more coffee in. I picked up a piece of the fudge Pluto had left on the bar and put it on the saucer, then brought it back to her.

"Here you go," I said, handing her the coffee.

"Thanks," she said.

"My pleasure," I said.

"Fudge?" she said, picking it up. I nodded.

"Since you're not drinking, I figured I'd give you the next best thing to booze for easing your troubles: Chocolate," I said.

"That was very thoughtful of you," Helen said, taking a bite. It wasn't a big piece and she had it finished in two more nibbles.

"That's just the kind of guy I am, but what I'm really interested in is what kind of woman could kill her husband and child," I said. Helen's head shot up so fast I'm surprised she didn't get whiplash.

"What?" she said.

"Murphy, what are you..." said Demeter, but stopped when she saw Paddy shaking his head.

"I mean it's one thing to kill them during a fight, but to have planned the whole thing in advance? That kind of twisted mind frightens me. So tell me, what makes a homicidal maniac like you tick?" I asked.

"Are you trying to say I killed Jerry and Tina?" she asked, hurt and indignant. Pretty convincing too.

"I'm sorry. Did I stutter? Of course that's what I'm saying, you murderous twit," I replied.

"That's slander. I'll sue," Helen threatened.

"Go ahead. I'm a bartender. I don't have any money," I said. It's not exactly true. Paddy pays well and I still live upstairs in one of those rent-free rooms Paddy is so generous with.

"How can you say these horrible things?" Helen whined.

"Maybe because they're true. First, you slice your daughter's throat with a switchblade. Your husband walks in and tries to stop you, so you smash his head in with an iron. Then you strangle him with the cord. But the thing that really gets me is, in order to make the rape seem real, you had to go out and find some poor sucker to have sex with you right before you did the dark and dirty deeds. I bet your description of the intruder matches that sucker to a T. Probably told him you were into S&M, and liked it rough. Rough enough to give you some fresh bruises for the cops and doctors to see. Plus, if you need to produce the killer, the DNA evidence will nail that poor guy, letting you off scot-free," I said.

Helen looked at Paddy. "Are you going to let him talk to me like that?"

"The gig's up, Helen. We know ye did it," said Paddy.

"I don't have to stay here and take this," said Helen, storming toward the front door. Paddy nodded and Dion beat her there, then blocked her way.

"Actually, you do. Sit back down," said Dion. Helen grabbed his arm and tried to move him. Dion didn't budge. Hercules may be a better bouncer, but Dion's no slouch. He led conquering armies in his younger days. A single mortal woman was not going to tax him in the slightest. She tried to slap Dion's face, but he caught her hand without blinking, mostly by reflex. Dionysus has been slapped by women more than once over the centuries. Helen brought her knee up in an attempt to crush his groin, but the god of wine and orgies is just a bit protective of that region. Dion turned his hip, bringing his own leg up and sweeping Helen's feet out from under her. She landed on her butt. Dion shook his head and said, "Murderer."

"I didn't kill anyone. You people are all insane," she said.

"Kind of you to notice. You are amazingly observant for a cold-hearted bitch," I said.

"Help!" she screamed and kept screaming. Paddy put a quarter in the jukebox and turned the volume up high, drowning out her cries.

"You can't prove any of this," said Helen, but the look in her eyes was that of a frightened and cornered animal. We were getting to her.

"We don't have to," said Paddy, turning down the jukebox volume. "We're not the cops."

"Yeah, we're just interested parties. Tell us how you did it," I said.

"Let me go," Helen demanded. Paddy and Dion shook their heads no. "This is kidnapping."

"Let's see. It's your word, against that of seven of us. Kidnapping? Prove it," shot back Paddy. "Ye are not leaving here until you tell us the truth."

"This is coercion. It'll never hold up in court," said Helen.

"I told ye, we're not cops. We have no plans to do anything that would bring ye to court. We want to hear the truth," said Paddy. Not that he didn't believe John, but he had to be entirely certain she was guilty.

"You'll really let me go if I tell you? And you won't tell the cops?" asked Helen, wavering. Her options were limited at this point.

"I give ye my word that when ye leave here, I will do nothing to hold ye back. I also will not do anything that would get ye arrested for these heinous crimes," said Paddy.

"Then why find out at all?" asked Helen, confused.

"Because I have to know," said Paddy.

Helen started pacing back and forth nervously. John walked directly in her path. He said nothing, but looked her directly in the eyes. She stopped short, and stared at him like a deer caught in headlights. When he frowned, she stepped back, suddenly afraid for a reason her conscious mind could not fathom.

"You aren't taping this?" she asked. John's stare had broken her resolve.

"Turn the jukebox back up. That would mess up any recording," I said. Helen walked over and did just that.

"Fine. I did it. I killed my husband and daughter. Happy?" barked Helen.

"Far from it," said Paddy, his voice twinged with sorrow.

"Well, that's it. I'm not giving you a blow by blow. I won't tell you where the murder weapon is. This one seems to have more information than he should have as it is," said Helen, looking at me.

Persephone looked stricken, as did Demeter.

"How could you kill the man you love? Did you fall in love with someone else and want to be with him instead?" asked Persephone. Helen laughed. It was a light, happy laugh, with not a hint of evil in the tone. It made it that much more disturbing.

"No, there was no one else. As for love, don't make me laugh. I never loved Jerry. I planned this before I even met him. I wanted to be rich, but I knew the odds of winning the lottery were low, so I made my own. It had a guaranteed pay off, as long as I was willing to wait a few years and put up with a few minor inconveniences. The only reason I married Jerry is that he fit my criteria. Right age, right job and income range: high enough to buy me a comfortable life up until he was horribly murdered, and high enough that a million-dollar policy would not seem unusual. I had him insured up the yin-yang," said Helen.

"But why your daughter? Certainly you loved her," said Demeter.

"That brat? Tina was nothing but an albatross around my neck from the day I found out I was pregnant. I was sick for nine months and I didn't feel much better once I got the brat out of my womb. She was the reason I moved up my schedule. I had originally wanted to have three kids, and insure each one at a million apiece. I just couldn't last that long or survive another one like her. Two million, plus the rest of what Jerry left me, is enough if I invest it right. Plus we own the apartment. We inherited it right after his poor mother died. It was so sudden that no one expected it. Well, almost no one," said Helen, smiling at her implied confession to yet a third murder.

"You are an evil and despicable creature," said Demeter.

"Maybe, but no one outside of this room would believe that I am anything other than a grieving widow. I'll never be convicted," said Helen.

"Ye're probably right. Okay, Dion, there's no need to block the door anymore," said Paddy. Dion gave him a questioning look, but stepped aside.

"So that's it? I can go?" said Helen.

"I won't do anything to stop ye," Paddy said.

"Then I'm out of here," said Helen, walking toward the front door. She paused at the door and turned back. "Just a friendly warning: I don't get mad, I get even. I'd watch my back if I were you. The bunch of you are probably going to have some real bad accidents."

"Did you just threaten to kill us?" asked Demeter.

Helen shrugged her shoulders and smiled innocently. "I never said that."

"I don't think we really have anything to worry about from ye," said Paddy.

"Really? Why's that?" asked Helen. Paddy ignored her and turned to Pluto.

"By the way, Pluto, did ye happen to notice that Helen ate a piece of your fudge earlier?" asked Paddy.

"Yeah, so? She ate it in your bar," said Pluto.

"True, but I gave that one piece of fudge dispensation," said Paddy.

Pluto practically jumped to his feet. "You mean...?"

"She's all yours," said Paddy. Pluto walked over to Paddy and shook his hand vigorously.

"Moran, thank you," said Pluto.

"It was Murphy's idea," said Paddy. Pluto turned to me.

"Murphy, I owe you. Any boon you want that I can grant is yours," said Pluto.

"Thanks, Pluto," I said. He gave me a look. As a god, he feels mortals such as I should address him as Lord Pluto and not dare familiarity. I meant the thanks. A while back, I was in Hades and, at Demeter's request, fed halves of her foods to several of its inhabitants. The end result is that Demeter can take all those that ate her food away from Hades and Pluto for half the year, if she so chooses. Pluto doesn't know about it yet. Demeter is saving it for a special occasion, and when she tells him, I could be in some serious trouble. I think I'll save this boon until then.

"You people belong in a freak show," said Helen, who had delayed her exit because she was shocked and a bit disappointed at our lack of reaction to her.

"Pluto, you have dispensation to use your influence over her until both of you leave the bar," said Paddy. Pluto winked at Paddy. Helen gave up on getting any attention and went to push the door open.

That's when Pluto spoke up. "Not so fast, Helen Donner. Freeze where you are."

Helen found herself immobilized and unable to speak, and her expression became one of sheer terror as she realized she was no longer in control. John smiled, then nodded at Paddy and me before quietly sneaking out the other door.

Pluto said goodbye to his wife. He had to leave soon anyhow. Over the years, Demeter had softened enough to allow him to visit his wife, but never during her first week on Earth. He was like a kid with a new toy, as he ordered Helen to follow him out the door to the parking garage. It led to a nexus with a path to Hades, among other otherworldly places. He was so excited he didn't even insult Demeter as he left.

"Wait a second," I said. I tossed a couple of dollar coins at him. "Charon's ride is on me. Tell him I said hi."

The boatman and I had shared a ride a while back, although my ticket was had been for a round trip. Helen wasn't going to be so lucky.

"And to think you said you'd never give Pluto's food dispensation," I said to Paddy.

"Well, sometimes ye have to fudge the rules a wee bit," said Paddy, with a wink as he followed Pluto and Helen out.

The boss had to reign Cerberus in. Paddy had won the three-headed watch dog from Pluto in a poker game some time back, so the dog worked for Paddy now. Pluto had never fed or otherwise taken care of Cerberus, leaving him to fend for himself while chained to a rock. While Paddy still keeps him on a chain, it's a long one. Plus, the boss not only feeds the Hades-hound, but plays with him. Needless to say, Cerberus has a major grudge against his former owner, and Paddy had to go to make sure Pluto didn't get hurt.

John told me what happened later. When he stepped outside, he reverted to his Grim Reaper persona, since a big scary monster is how little Tina's mind perceived Death. He went to get Tina and was waiting when Charon's boat pulled up on the near side of the banks of the river Styx. Charon was in a robe similar to that of the Grim Reaper's, pushing his boat with a long pole. (The ferryman's boat actually sported a high-tech motor which he kept hidden. Pluto and some of the other deities Charon ferried for were suckers for tradition, not wanting anything to change. I guess they found it comforting in a world that had all but forgotten most of them. If Charon were left to his own devices, he'd be sporting a captain's hat and fishing all day.)

"GREETINGS, LORD PLUTO," said Death. When John is outside of Bulfinche's, his voice is majorly different, hence the capital letters. It had taken him ages of practice to be able to sound like a human inside the bar.

"Lord Thanatos, a pleasure to see you," said Pluto, still not making the connection with John. Of course, John's face had flesh instead of the skull he sported in Grim Reaper mode. "I have a new subject. Quite an evil one too. I'm going to have to get my creative juices flowing to come up with suitable punishment."

"THAT IS THE REASON I AM HERE," said Death.

"She ate of my food. She is mine, fair and square," said Pluto nervously. Even gods fear Death.

"I AM NOT HERE TO CONTEST YOUR CLAIM. I HAVE A SOUL THAT NEEDS TO GAIN CLOSURE BY SEEING THAT HER MURDERER WILL BE PUNISHED," said Death. He stepped aside to reveal the spirit of Tina. The four-year-old looked much as she had in life. She was still wearing the pink feetie pajamas she died in, and her hair was pulled to the sides in pig-tails. She hid shyly behind Death's robes.

"This is the daughter?" asked Pluto.

"YES."

"Stay," Pluto said to Helen, then he bent down on one knee to talk to the girl. "Hello, Tina. My name is Pluto."

"Like Mickey's dog?" asked Tina. Pluto cringed. He predated the cartoon mutt by thousands of years. Sadly, the dog had a better publicist and hung out in a theme park.

"Yes," said Pluto. He was amazingly good with kids. He and Persephone had been trying to have children of their own for almost forever, but had come up empty so far. It was something Demeter reminded him of constantly. "You realize that sometimes people do bad things to good people, even good little girls like you."

"Why?" asked Tina.

"I wish I could answer that, but even a god doesn't have all the answers. Your Mommy was very bad, and I will make sure she gets punished," said Pluto.

"Promise?" asked Tina.

"I swear it on the River Styx," said Pluto. Tina didn't realize it, but she couldn't get a better promise. That was an oath that no Olympian could break.

"Mommy always made me say I was sorry when I was bad. Mommy

should say she's sorry to me," said Tina.

"Excellent idea. Ms. Donner, why don't you apologize to your daughter?" asked Pluto, freeing her vocal chords.

"I'll see you in Hell first," said Helen.

"You seemed so bright topside. It's Hades, not Hell. Not that you'll be able to tell the difference. I command you to apologize, and sound sincere about it," ordered Pluto.

Helen struggled and lost. She was Pluto's, body and soul. She had to jump through his hoops. "Mommy is so sorry that she killed you, Tina. It wasn't your fault. I was very, very bad. Do you forgive Mommy?"

"No," said Tina. "You always hated me. Daddy was the only one who loved me and you killed him too. He was going to sing me to sleep and you killed him," said Tina, with the logic of a four year old. "I hate you."

"You have a good head on your shoulders, girl. I will take your mother away now," said Pluto.

"You seem nice. Can't I go with you, Puto?" asked Tina, mispronouncing Pluto's name. Pluto looked at Death. He knew that the girl was too young to have a developed belief system. In a sense, her soul was up for grabs, and she had just offered it to Pluto on a silver platter.

"Tina, you will always be welcome in my realm. For now, I think it will be the best thing for you to go with Thanatos. He will bring you to meet a guide, who will show you your options. If you still want to come with me then, I will be happy to have you," said Pluto, showing real class. His realm had fallen a bit on the dreary side of late. Not the best place for a child, even a dead one.

"Okay. Bye bye, Puto," said Tina.

"Bye bye, little one," said Pluto, bending down to kiss her on the forehead.

She waved to Pluto as he stepped away into Charon's boat with Helen Donner in tow.

"Is it time to go now?" asked Tina.

"YES."

As they walked across the field, a mist appeared and surrounded them.

"Will I be able to see Daddy?"

"THAT WILL BE UP TO YOU AND YOUR GUIDE."

"Would you sing to me, until I can see my Daddy and have him sing to me?" asked Tina.

If a skull face could show conflicting emotions, the Grim Reaper's would have.

"UM... I SUPPOSE SO. WHAT SONG DID YOUR FATHER SING TO YOU?"

Tina told him, then reached up to hold Death's bony hand. As she did, his aspect softened and became less fearsome. Flesh began to cover the bones, and his hood disappeared and was replaced by a baseball hat, as Tina's idea of what Death was changed.

As they vanished, hand in hand into the mist, the sounds of the Grim Crooner could be heard.

"HUSH, LITTLE BABY, DON'T SAY A WORD. PAPA'S GONNA BUY YOU A MOCKINGBIRD..."

MIND WORKS

No neon signs
    to advertise feelings,
No spell checks
    to correct ideas,
No road maps
    to unfold,
No one-way traffic
    to worry about,
No vacancies
    To be filled,
Just
    rainbowed, star-filled wishes
    gently swirled into delicious dreams
    dancing with whipcream ponies
    creating and recreating
    an unruly universe.

-Linda D. Addison

THE SILENCE
STEVE HAMILTON

Do you really want me to tell you what happened? You want the real story? All right, then. This is how it's going to work. I'm going to tell you this story once, and then I'm never going to tell it again. You got that? I'm going to tell it to you straight through. I don't want you to interrupt me. Even when I get to the part where you might not believe what I'm saying, I just want you to sit there and listen. I want to tell it to you and get it off my chest once and for all, and then I never want to hear about it again. We got a deal?

It all starts three years ago. I'd been off the force a couple years, after I took that bullet in my hip. I was doing some security work, collecting the disability, you know, just sitting around on my butt most of the time. I really hated it. And I was driving my wife crazy. I get a call from my buddy Sal. We were in the service together. Turns out he's gotten into local politics since then, and he had just gotten himself elected mayor of this little town called High Falls. It's a couple hours north of here, way up in the woods, middle of nowhere. You probably never even heard of it.

Anyway, he's the mayor, and he wants me to move up there and be the constable. That's how small the place is. They don't even have a police chief. The mayor just appoints the constable.

So the wife and I go up there to look around. She loves the place, and I'm getting sick of being a security guard, so we say, what the heck. We made the move. They had about eight or nine policemen full time, most of them good guys. A couple I wouldn't have hired if it were up to me, but not so bad they were going to be a problem.

I'm on the job about a year. It was pretty quiet most of the time. A couple break-ins, a marijuana bust, nothing much else. Sal's kid Tony would tear around in his truck sometimes, thinking he could do anything he wanted to do because his father was the mayor, but aside from him I really didn't have anyone making my life miserable. Not like when I was down here in the City. High Falls was a really nice little town. That's a quaint name for a town, isn't it? That's just the kind of place it was. Real quaint.

Most days, I'd have breakfast at the diner. Not that I didn't want to eat at home. It's just a good idea to get out and see the townspeople every day, and everyone seemed to stop in at the diner on the way to work. So I'd just sit there for a while with my paper, say hello to everyone. You know, keep in touch.

It was a hot July, I remember that. I was in the diner one morning, and I noticed a man sitting at one of the tables. He was maybe 35 or so, tall, kind of thin. I was pretty sure he didn't live in town. I had certainly never seen him before. He caught my eye because he was taking up a whole table to himself. The diner was always packed in the morning, and people who were there by themselves were naturally expected to sit on one of the stools at the counter. But he was just sitting there by himself, taking up a whole table. So right away I knew he didn't have any manners. He was still sitting there when I left.

I went into the station and did my usual routine. Read the mail, checked the messages. I was usually there by myself most of the day. I had a phone, of course, and a radio there on my desk so I could keep in touch with the officers on duty. When I had first started on the job, they'd always be calling me every hour just to check in until I finally said to them, "Hey, you don't have to keep calling in if nothing is happening. Just go on about your business and let me know if you need anything." So they finally got used to that, and I'm sure they appreciated it that I trusted them enough that they didn't have to call me on the radio every time they used the bath-room.

I sat there finishing the newspaper and doing whatever odds and ends I had to do. When I looked up, it was lunchtime. I hadn't gotten any calls on the radio, and I don't think the phone even rang once the whole morning. But like I said, it was a quiet town. Some days were like that.

I went back to the diner for lunch. The stranger was still there, sitting at the table. Jenny, one of the regular waitresses, seemed a little on edge when she served me, so I asked her what was up.

"It's that guy at the table over there," she said. "He's been here since this morning."

"Yeah?"

"I don't know. He just keeps looking at me. He's giving me the creeps."

"Probably just lonely," I said. "But give me a call if he does anything else."

"I'm sure he's harmless," she said. "Like you say, he's probably just lonely."

I went back to the station for the rest of the afternoon. I found myself getting sort of bored and restless until I finally realized that I still hadn't gotten any calls on the radio. I wondered if maybe the radio was broken, so I tested it. "Dave, are you out there?"

"Right here, Chief," he said. He always called me Chief, because it just didn't sound right to call me Constable.

"Everything okay? I haven't heard from you today."

"I'm out by the highway, Chief. Nothing happening."

"Okay, just checking."

I went home that night. I swear there wasn't one call all day long. But heck, I figured it was just a fluke. Next day, I was back at the diner in the morning, and there was the stranger, sitting at the same table.

"I see your friend is back," I said to Jenny.

"He was here when I got here at 6:00 a.m.," she said. "He's been watching me all morning. It's really starting to get to me."

"Maybe I'll have a word with him," I said. I went over to his table and asked him if I could have the seat across from him. As soon as he looked at me, an alarm went off in the back of my head. It was the same alarm that would go off three or four times a day when I was in the City.

"Sorry to bother you, Sir," I said to him, "but Jenny here tells me that you've been staring at her all morning."

"I'm sorry, Officer," he said. His eyes seemed to look right through me. "I didn't mean to make her uncomfortable. She's a striking woman, that's all. Very striking, don't you agree? Please tell her I'm sorry. I won't do it, again. I'm very sorry, Officer."

It didn't sound like he was being insincere with his apologies, but there was still something not quite right about the way he was talking to me. It sounded like he was reading me a line off a cue card.

"All right, then," I said. I didn't know what else to say to him. I just got up and left.

I sat in the station all morning again, and I'll be damned if I didn't get one single call. "Are you out there, Dave?" I said into the microphone.

"Right here, Chief. Something wrong?"

"No, just checking in. I hadn't heard from you yet today."

"I'm over by the highway again, checking speed."

"Gotcha. Jim, you out there?"

"Right here, Chief. Just cruising Main."

"Fine, fine. Just checking."

When I went to the diner for lunch, the stranger was gone. "Look what he left for a tip," Jenny said. She showed me a fifty-dollar bill.

"Not bad," I said. "Kind of makes me feel bad, though. I only leave you a dollar."

"For fifty bucks he can stare at me all he wants," she said.

I didn't sleep very well that night. My hip was hurting me, which usually happened when it was going to rain. But the skies were clear. I got up and went outside and looked at all the stars.

When I went back to the diner again the next morning, the stranger was back at his table. He gave me a little wave when I came in.

"He's back, I see," I said to Jenny.

"Yeah, he apologized for yesterday," she said. "He said he couldn't help but stare at me, because I reminded him of a girl he used to be in love with. That's why he left me the fifty, said he was sorry he made me feel uncomfortable."

"Well, just be careful," I said.

"Ah, he's all right," she said. "Just a little weird."

"I don't know," I said. Whenever I looked at him, that little alarm kept going off. "Just be careful."

Dave was waiting at the station when I got there. He had his radar gun in his hand. "I think it's broken," he said. "All day yesterday, it seemed to be stuck."

"What do you mean?" I said. I took it from him and examined it.

"Every car I shot, it kept saying 54 or 55."

"Well, did the cars seem to be going any faster than that?"

"Actually, no," he said. "Far as I can tell, everyone was going exactly the speed limit."

"Were you over by that billboard? Your usual spot?"

"The Dunkin' Donuts billboard, yeah."

"Well, there you go. People must know about that spot now. That's why they're all going 55. Find a new spot."

"Good idea," he said. "I guess that's why you're the Chief. Or the Constable, whatever."

A couple officers would usually man the station in the evening and log any activity. The page from the previous evening was blank. Not even a noise complaint. I sat there next to the radio all morning, waiting to hear something. Nothing. I finally called Dave just before lunchtime. "Any luck?"

"No, Chief. This thing must be broken. I keep getting 54 or 55."

"Does it look like they're going faster than that? I mean, has anyone come tearing past you? Obviously over the limit?"

"No, not really," he said. "But still, this can't be right."

"Well, don't worry about it. We'll look at the gun when you come back in."

I picked up the phone and listened to the dial tone. Seems to be working just fine, I thought.

When I walked over to the diner for lunch, my hip started hurting again.

"What's the matter with you?" Jenny asked when I limped into the diner.

"Ah, it's just my hip," I said. "It flares up once in a while. Must be fixing to rain soon." I looked over. The stranger was sitting at his table, staring out the window.

"It's not going to rain," she said. "There's not a cloud in the sky."

"I tell you it's going to rain," I said. "This hip is never wrong."

But it never did rain that day. And I didn't get any calls on the radio. When Dave brought the radar gun in, I ran all the diagnostics on it, but could find no problem whatsoever.

The radio was silent all the next day, and then again the day after that. There was only one plausible explanation. My officers had to be goofing off. Either they were sleeping in their patrol cars, or else they were all together having a party somewhere. I pictured them drinking beer, keeping an ear on their radios in case I called them.

I took my car out and drove around the town, hoping to catch them. I found Jim driving through the neighborhoods. Roy was on foot on Main Street. I found Larry driving through the park. They were all doing their jobs just fine. I swung over to the highway and found Dave sitting in his car under a big oak tree, just over a big hill, his radar gun pointed out the window.

"What's up, Chief?" he said when I pulled up next to him.

"Just felt like getting out of the station," I said. "Is that gun working now?"

"Nah, stupid thing still says 54 or 55 every time," he said. "I tell you, it must be broken."

"Here, let me see it," I said. He handed it to me through the window. I aimed it at the highway as a few cars came over the hill and passed us. 54, 55, 54, 54, 55. "For God's sake," I said. "These things cost, what, two thousand dollars. You'd think--"

I was interrupted by a loud roar. I knew who it was as soon as I heard it. It had to be Tony, the mayor's son, in his big truck. I pointed the gun at the highway, waiting for him to come barreling over the hill.

It was Tony, all right. The gun read 54 when he passed us. And I knew just watching him that the gun was right. I turned on my flashers and chased him. I swear to God, I pulled that kid over and got out of the car and went right up to the driver's side window and stuck my face right in his. "What's the big idea, Tony?"

"Excuse me?"

"You want to tell me why you were only going 54 miles per hour?"

"I don't know," he said. "I wasn't even thinking about it. Was I going 54?"

"Yes, Tony. You were doing 54, right on the button. I have it right here on the radar. You want to see it?"

"I don't get it," he said. "You pulled me over because I *wasn't* speeding?"

"I just want to know why," I said. "Why are you all of a sudden driving under the speed limit?"

He was at a loss for words. "I don't know," he finally said. "I just didn't feel like going any faster."

Dave pulled up behind us and got out of his car. "What's the deal, Chief?"

I realized then just how ridiculous I must have looked, pulling this kid over because he wasn't speeding for the first time in his life. "Nothing, Dave," I said. "I'm sorry, Tony. I was just curious. Go on, get going." Tony shook his head and pulled out onto the highway, leaving me there with Dave. He looked at me with obvious concern.

"Are you okay, Chief?" he said.

"I'm fine, Dave. It's just that... have you noticed anything... peculiar lately?"

"How do you mean?"

"I don't know. Maybe I'm just imagining it. It just seems like, well, nothing has happened the last couple days."

"So what's wrong with that?"

"No, I mean *nothing*. Not one single thing. Nobody doing anything wrong. No calls, no complaints. Nothing."

"Sounds pretty good to me," he said. "Sounds like we're doing our job."

"What about the radar gun?" I said. "Why isn't anybody speeding? Doesn't that seem strange to you? *Nobody speeding?*"

"Hey, don't fight it," he said. He put on a fake cowboy accent for me. "Varmints 'round here know there's a new sheriff in town, figure it's high time they stopped rustlin' them cattle."

"You're a funny guy, Dave," I said. I rubbed my sore hip. "Did you hear anything in the forecast about rain?"

I went back to the station and sat next to the silent radio for the rest of the day. My friend Sal the mayor called me that night. I had to explain to him why I pulled over his son for not speeding. "It has just been a weird week," I said. "Ever since, what, Monday morning I guess it was, there's been absolutely no calls. Not one."

"That's why people love this place," Sal said. "That's why they move here from the City!"

"Yeah, I guess so," I said.

"Would you rather we have *more* crime? Are you not feeling useful enough? Come on!"

"Yeah, yeah, point taken," I said. "It's just a fluke. I'm sure I'll get a call tomorrow."

But I didn't. The log from the evening shift was blank again the next morning. And the radio was silent again, all day long. When I went into the diner at lunch, the stranger sat at his table in front of three empty plates.

"He won't let me take the plates away," Jenny said to me. "He says he wants to keep all the plates he's eaten off today right there on the table."

"Are you kidding me?"

"He gave me another fifty dollar tip, too."

I sat there and looked at him for a while. He was just sitting there at this table, staring at the three plates. Monday morning, I thought. Monday morning. That's the first time I saw that guy in here. That's when our little dry spell started. That's when we stopped getting calls.

Oh for crying out loud, I said to myself. Listen to you. You are really losing it. This thing has really gotten to you. What next?

But the silence continued. I couldn't sleep at night. My wife started to worry. I paced back and forth, trying to figure it out. When the reporter from the local paper came by to collect the weekly log sheet, he looked at the blank sheet and laughed. "Okay, very funny," he said. "Where's the real log?"

"That's it," I said.

"There's nothing on it," he said.

"You're very perceptive," I said. "I can't imagine why you're still stuck on a small town newspaper."

He ran a single line reading "No activity to report this week" under the Police Beat. People asked me about it at the diner. Sal called me, wanted to know why people were asking him why the police weren't doing anything.

"It's like you said, Sal. Remember? This is paradise. There's no crime here."

My officers were getting nervous. They kept driving around, looking for something to happen, anything. Nothing did. We called the company that made our radar gun, asked them to send us another one. Dave took the new gun out on the highway. 54, 55, 54. I sat by the radio, rubbing my hip. Nothing. Silence.

After ten days of this, I was ready to explode. People started to avoid me. I sat at the counter in the diner and no one would say a word to me the whole time. On the eleventh day, I was sitting there in the diner, watching the stranger at his table. This time he had empty coffee cups on the table. He must have had thirty of them there. I went to his table and sat down across from him.

"Officer," he said.

"What's your story?" I said. I couldn't even put my arms on the table, with all those empty coffee cups in the way.

"Excuse me, Officer?"

"Why are you here? Why do you keep sitting here in this diner, day after day?"

"I like it here," he said. "Is there something wrong with that?"

"What's your name?"

"My name is John."

"John what?"

"John Smith."

"May I see your driver's license?"

"I don't have a driver's license," he said. His face was calm. He looked at me like he was looking at a goldfish in a bowl.

"How did you get here if you don't have a driver's license?"

"I rode the bus."

"John Smith," I said. "That's a pretty common name."

"If there were no John Smith's in the world, it wouldn't be a very common name, would it," he said. "I happen to be one of them."

"Where are you staying?"

"Excuse me, Officer. May I ask why you need to know all of this? Have I done something illegal?"

I looked at him for a long moment. "No," I said. "You've done nothing illegal." I got up from the table. "But maybe we'll talk again later."

I went outside and sat in my car. I turned the air conditioner on. I didn't know what to do. I didn't want to go into the station and sit there next to that silent radio. So I just sat there in the car. My hip was throbbing. Even though it still hadn't rained yet.

I don't know how long I sat there. At least an hour. The stranger finally came out of the diner and started walking down the street. I didn't think he saw me sitting there in my car. I got out of the car and followed him on foot, hiding as well as I could behind the parked cars in front of the businesses on the street. I didn't have to follow him too far, because he went right into the Lucky Day Motel on the corner.

I went into the office and asked Gene the manager to show me the register. John Smith, Room 6. Paid in cash, every morning, every day for the last eleven days. As I stood there in the lobby of the motel, I saw John Smith walk right past the front window, back towards the diner. He was wearing a baseball hat now. He had it on backwards like a catcher. In his hand was one of the coffee cups.

I sat on the edge of my bed that night, looking out the window at the heat lightning. It still hadn't rained yet. My wife slept soundly on the other side of the bed. I couldn't remember the last time she had spoken to me.

The next day I walked up and down Main Street, looking at all the people. What is wrong with you people? I wanted to say out loud. Why are you doing this to me?

John Smith was at his table. I knew that wasn't his real name. I hadn't even bothered to run it through the computer. John Smith, my ass. He was reading the back of a sugar packet.

"What happened to you?" Jenny said when she served me. "You look like hell."

"Has our friend Mr. Smith over there left you any more big tips?"

"Yeah, a couple days ago," she said. "It was just a twenty this time. I think he's getting cheap."

"Has he been bothering you? Do you want to fill out a complaint?"

"A complaint?" she said. "Why would I want to do that? He just sits there. I don't even notice him anymore."

"If he does anything suspicious, Jenny, if he bothers you in the slightest way, I want you to call me and I'll come down here and arrest him. Okay?"

"What's gotten into you, Chief?"

I shook my head. "I'm sorry, Jenny. I'm just... I'm sorry." I got up and left. On my way out, I stood over his table and just looked at him. He kept reading the back of his sugar packet for a long while, and then finally looked up at me. He smiled.

There was no evening log, of course. There were no calls. The silence continued. My hip kept hurting. I didn't think I could last much longer without going crazy. I called Dave on the radio. He had been sitting there day after day with his radar gun. "All I want is one 56," he said. "One lousy 56, that's all I ask. Some bastard comes by here going 56, he's gonna get a speeding ticket, I swear to God."

I sat in the station all day, my face pressed into a towel. The man from the paper came by again. He took one look at me and walked back out the door.

I went home. I didn't eat dinner. I got back in my car, drove all around the town. Main Street was quiet. The neighborhoods were quiet. The park was quiet. There were no teenagers out playing their radios too loud. No one drag racing on the straightaway by the lake. Nothing.

The call came that night. I was in bed, only half asleep.

"Chief," the voice said. It was Marty, one of the night officers.

"What is it, Marty?"

"Chief," he said.

"What, Marty? What it is?"

"The motel."

"What about it?"

"I'm at the motel. I'm at the Lucky Day."

"I'm on my way," I said. I raced across town to the motel. Marty was standing outside Room 6.

"What happened?" I asked him.

He just looked at me.

I grabbed him by the shoulders. "Marty, what's wrong?"

He didn't say anything. He just looked at the ground.

I opened up the door to the room. It was Jenny. What he did to her. Holy Mother of God, what that man did to her.

I was up the rest of that night. Calling in the description and the alias, getting the coroner up there. I interviewed the other guests in the motel and the other waitresses at the diner. I was just going through the motions, doing the routine.

The whole town had to deal with it. Everyone was in shock for a while. But slowly, things got back to normal. It finally rained. My hip stopped hurting.

And a couple days after the murder, someone called in a noise complaint. And then there was an accident. Nothing major, just a fender bender. Dave started clocking cars over 70 on the highway, wrote a dozen tickets. By the time the summer was over, all of my officers seemed to have forgotten about the silence.

But I didn't forget. I couldn't. I was the one who had to sit there next to the radio, all day long, waiting for the calls to come in. Sometimes it would be silent for a few minutes. Ten minutes of silence, that's all it would take. I'd start sweating. Twenty minutes of silence, my hip would start hurting again. Thirty minutes of silence, and I'd be climbing the walls, wondering if he had come back.

CALL FORTH THE DEAD
J.L. HANNA

The hunters found Chrys Madreen in the Eshai Woods before dawn, after his car broke down.

The engine died in silence, as though the battery's contacts had rotted through. A possibility; it wasn't his car. He coasted to the side of the road out of habit, not expecting other traffic on *this* highway.

He pulled up the parking brake, took the flasher from the dashboard socket, and slid his door open. A rabbit or some other skulker darted across the highway ahead of him, startled by the light or his presence. He was about to flip the motor compartment open when headlights flashed over the hill behind him.

Hunters.

That was his first thought. Perhaps it was paranoia. Then the idea firmed; no one else took the ancient road from Mahoneel to Bethrem—not with their lights, openly, as if they had a right.

He reached into the driver's compartment and pulled his keys and the heavy leather backpack with his notes and finds out. Nothing else in the car to link it to him, not until they checked with the University motor pool and beat up the right people.

He looked up at the stars, finding the Fisherman and north. The inner moon was a red dot in the Starship and the thin wire of the space elevator was washed out of vision this time of year by Sister Sun's light—five hours to sunup.

Madreen sprinted across the highway and down the embankment on a course that might take him back to the city if he survived. Around him the plant life glowed faintly in the light of the stars and the Sister Sun. This was Parklands. Crai preserves, a plant kingdom as alien to Argos-natives as to the near pure terran transplants of Analayne continent.

Madreen made it half way up the side of the hill before he turned back. If the other car sped past he could return and work on his engine, if not…

The car slowed police wise and stopped behind his. The doors slid open.

Hunters.

He was dead. His luck had run out.

Quickly he pulled his binoculars from his backpack and focused on the enemy. A light came on when the door opened revealing two of them. An older man, hard-bitten, his age, with a look on his face that said he would kill his mother for the line of Zherar Heunis, and…there was a chance he wouldn't be dying after all. The other man was Phar Rowlwen, who'd taken his night course two semesters past. If he could be reasoned with, shown the *m'shee* in his backpack…

He'd have to get Rowlwen alone, even to speak to him.

He watched the policemen examine his car. They spoke a minute. Perhaps they might think it had been there for hours…

Obviously, they didn't. The older man clapped his hands and an enormous hound—one of the hunting breed the Crai had developed—leaped out of the police car and began to sniff around.

He didn't see what happened next because he was running as fast as he could through the shimmering forest. From the back of his mind he called up mental images of Parkland memorized from a stolen map, recalling all he could about his people's past masters, their technology and their world. The High Lords of Kentaret had an estate nearby, and there were roads of a sort once you got over the hill. As his run slowed to a trot to conserve energy ideas began to form.

"Bruno, here Bruno." Stanen Lane clapped twice and his Hound leaped from behind the back seat to join them. The animal immediately found where their quarry had broken through the bushes lining the road.

"Stay, Bruno, stay." Lane went back to the police van and Phar Rowlwen, who was on the radio.

Lane's ears pricked up when he heard the voice through the static from the other end.

"…wish to have to deal with Scholar Madreen. That would be unfortunate. Is that clear?" The question was totally unnecessary.

"Yes, Citizen General," Rowlwen said. The younger man looked up at Lane, shrugging. Lane's Hound would probably do the killing; Rowlwen thought that was a pity.

"Anything Scholar Madreen has with him is to be brought to me immediately, unopened. I am especially interested in his notes." No doubt orders had sent other Hunters to Madreen's lab and house, but he would have been a fool or mad to have left anything there.

They signed off. Lane got out a map of the area and looked it over. "Couldn't you have gotten one with details of the Preserve?" he snapped at Rowlwen.

"No. General Gelter said only the First Citizen had them, and he wasn't giving any away."

His flasher showered the area with a blank oval, surrounded by mixed terrene and argolid forest.

"At least we know the boundaries," Rowlwen quipped.

Behind Lane, Bruno had trotted up to them, then sat to heel, and slowly wrapped his long tail three times around his handler's legs. Lane idly leaned down and stroked the feathery head.

The hound's shoulders came up to Lane's waist; its hairless body was a mottled brown in color. The outline of the head was generally canine, but the genengineers had imported the fangs from one of the Old Terran big cats, Lane wasn't certain which one. Because of his need to bond with the animal, Lane had raised Bruno from a puppy, which had tended to restrict the people he could invite to his home to close relatives and fellow cops, though Bruno was always gentle until given his orders. While Morneen had been sick Bruno had snuggled up to her in the bed, and after the funeral the animal had been disconsolate for months.

Thinking of Morneen's death made Stanen Lane want to kill—who really didn't matter. A Crai would have been ideal; before the Conquest most cancers had been curable. That much even Lane remembered from school.

"It's up to you, boy," Lane told the hound as he wrapped the map back up. "You have to find the Enemy of Humanity, Scholar Chrys Madreen." He suddenly looked at Rowlwen. "What would Madreen know about the Preserve?"

Rowlwen had pulled out backpacks and semi-automatics. He thought a moment before answering. "His profession is learning. And he remembers everything. I got to observe him working for Intelligence. I know he can read Crai symbols—I saw a few Crai books, ones he could have legally— in his library. I'd say he could know more about the Crai and the Preserve than we do."

"He's a bookish type then? Slow…" That would make it easy and quick.

"No," Rowlwen said. "His legal work is on Analayne, in the First Settlement ruins at a thousand meters' elevation. Heavy machinery's expensive, shovels aren't. He spends three months a year playing ditch digger, and he isn't carrying much extra weight." Rowlwen snapped a round of explosive cartridges into his rifle.

Lane brought the hound over to the University car and let Bruno sniff the seat and steering wheel until he was satisfied the hound really had the scent. He spoke softly into the rear set of ears. "Enemy, Bruno, enemy. Kill enemy, Bruno, kill." Then he pulled off the collar and the hound bounded off across the old Crai highway. Shouldering their rifles, Lane and Rowlwen followed.

"First Citizen." The servant's murmur came over his shoulder. Jonas Coraish, heir to the Heunis lineage, half-turned angrily, then made himself listen. After all, he had given orders not to be disturbed.

"Pardon me." The First Citizen of the Republic of Argos got up from his gaming table. His guests smiled back at him, grateful that he was caring for their welfare.

"Security reports a break into the Crai Reserve." The servant spoke more audibly once they were away from the public.

"Have they identified the trespass?"

"A University Scholar. Madreen. Works in early and mid-post-settlement archaeology. He's been trouble before. General Halding has ordered termination."

"Halding's an idiot. Call him back and cancel it. We want him alive for questioning so we can identify his nest."

"The policemen have already crossed the boundary." The servant left the pertinent fact unspoken: they can't be called back.

"Get me a flyer and two Loyal guards, and tell the General I'll be on my way to the Reserve myself. I'll be a minute telling my guests they will have to entertain themselves for a while."

Humans had been on Argos for three thousand years, Madreen thought, and still the terrene ecology often came out second best to the argolid. Yet in the three hundred years since the Crai Conquest and the seventy-five years since the Expulsion nothing had troubled the pristine *Crainess* of the Preserve. No imported terran birds sang from the trees, no moles or voles burrowed in the soil beneath the phosphorescent plants; the native argolid worms and soil bacteria came up against a barrier and stopped.

The moss of the Crai highway grew perfectly, as though it were still gardened by patient fourfingered hands.

There were still signs in Crai characters, as there had been on the day they'd left. So this was the *Glory of the Hunt Joypath*. He knew all about it, if only by reputation.

He wasn't the first human to run it, nor the first to be chased by a mutated Hunter dog. The human tribute of old had a 3% chance of survival and had been rewarded with breeding rights and a chance to serve the masters that, the official histories told, only one man had rejected. That one man led the revolt, which culminated in the Expulsion and human freedom.

The official histories lied.

The *m'shee* was proof—could be proof if it could be shown.

A gate stood down the end of a short alley off the Joypath; he went up to it and looked over the symbols. Beyond was a breeding unit compound— the human cultural anthropologists, who studied the Crai during the Conquest, before they were extirpated, called the breeding units septs—space enough for a group of sisters and their current inamorata and the young. No symbols indicated residence; it must have been abandoned prior to the Evacuation.

He turned and went back to Joypath. A wind stirred the trees and flowers; the trees chimed, the flowers were aromatic, and made his nose itch.

This was still the Border, close enough to the Wild that a compound had been abandoned. Further on in a man could drown in the perfume.

He turned down the Joypath and ran, feeling for his pulse and trying to keep his lungs active. Soon he'd be sneezing.

The Joypath widened into a circle surrounding a monument. He stopped.

It was a giant *m'shee*, dedicated to the first Crai to find Argos, the female who commanded the troops who rode the elevator anchor on the inner moon, turned off the planet's power, and took control of the world. Her holo stood pedestaled. As he came near she spoke, became alive. He understood the words.

"I am Ganerath Ahdissa of Lysaagh of the Mehedern sept which has served the race for ten thousand years, as my sept will always serve the race with wisdom and success. I thirsted for glory and led my sisters to this world, and made its race an appendage of our own. We control their economy, determine their breeding. To all who come after me I say Thou shalt keep faith with our Glory..."

Madreen turned away; he'd heard it all before.

A few minutes later he came to another side-path and another gate. Here the symbols were up; the Dalashg sept declared that those who trespassed herein would feed their young.

He went back to the road to where he'd seen a pedestrian bench; a metal grating two meters long held up by concrete pedestals at either end. The metal was simply slotted into the stone. He lifted it up; it was fairly light, probably aluminum.

He brought the bench seat back down the path; from two meters away he threw it as hard as he could into the gate. Then he fell on his face and covered his head.

The gate wasn't locked, naturally. The Crai never locked anything. The gate flew open, and the metal bench seat exploded when it struck the disrupter field. A moment later the path ahead glowed white hot where pieces of metal had activated anti-personnel mines.

That seemed to be standard with Crai household defenses, more pro forma disinvitation than anything really deadly. After all, the Crai were occupiers on a hostile world, so they limited their aggressiveness toward each other, for as much as they found it disagreeable. He'd learned a lot about Crai household armament in the past few years.

He got up and advanced toward the gate, picking up loose pieces of the bench that had splintered and almost impaled him. He threw a few shards down ahead of him onto the path, but nothing happened. Then he was through the gate, and within the Outer Defensive Ring.

Now the only traps would be natural, if just as deadly. After all, this was the children's playground.

"Stinkin' Crai...this place should have been cleared out years ago." Lane looked warily at the old monument. "Stay, Bruno!" Stay meant for Bruno to run no more than ten feet ahead of his man.

"Then we'd have nothing to remind us of the Tyranny," Rowlwen said. "Of the need to keep vigilant against Enemies of Man." He had the political litany memorized. "I'd say he went this way." He pointed to torn moss on the Joypath. "And Bruno thinks so too. Want to let him have a go?"

"No," Lane refused. He was senior, after all. "I remember too many stories."

Rowlwen laughed. "With luck the old Crai traps will leave enough of him to identify so we can get our bounty."

"Heel, Bruno." Lane caught the dog and attached the leash. "Bruno cost the State more to train than you did, Phar."

"The way you treat him you'd think he was a lap dog," Rowlwen said. The younger policeman went into his backpack and pulled out a series of twister trap sets; he keyed them to the control on his rifle butt. They were transparent and the size and thickness of a large sheet of writing paper. "We might want to leave a few of these around in convenient locales. He might actually outwit us."

Lane grunted and took several.

Bruno led them down the right path; the gate had yet to grow back.

"Why would he head in here?"

"He's spent a lifetime studying the traps," Rowlwen said. "He thinks he's going to use them against us." The younger man bent and picked up some metal debris and stones. He tossed them onto the path ahead to see what would happen.

"He might have doubled back," Lane suggested. Bruno pushed forward.

"Only if he went off into the trees." Rowlwen pointed to the groves on either side. "You remember what an *iashlag* is?"

"Yes." That let out doubling back using the trees.

"So he went right ahead into the nest."

"And the worms."

"Better a worm than an *iashlag*."

The Crai had never liked roofs; if humans in their architecture had recapitulated the cave, the Crai continued to live in giant nests. The roofless walls might tower and peak fancifully, projections of concrete and metal drapery, but what they surrounded were still nests for birds that had been barred from the skies for most of their evolution.

And nests could also be traps.

Madreen had managed to spend half an hour prowling the nest and the verge of the surrounding trees. He was fairly certain he had spotted most of the threats, but something could come shooting out of the underbrush before he had a chance to move aside. His hunters had been wise in not rushing in after him. There were *iashlag* in the trees, bladebirds, and any number of toxic thorns and bushes.

Madreen spent some time watching the worm hole at the base of the inside wall near a line of ancestor statues. For the moment the worm was the least of his worries, and he had plans for it.

As if sensing him the creature stuck one horn out of its hole; the horn was a pheromone detector as well as a weapon. It could smell you, gut you and drink your blood. But only if he was unable to control the stink of fear.

There wasn't much of a breeze, and he had done his best to stay downwind of most of the threats. Of course experienced hunters could find him that way too. He hoped they thought that's what they were doing.

He'd taken off his backpack but it really hadn't contained much more beyond his finds, note pads, and a half-eaten sandwich. The sandwich had proven the most useful. It was sitting out in the open; several bladebirds had descended upon it and were gorging on the peanut butter and jelly. Already one or two of them were beginning to show signs of drunkenness. They were clearly ignoring the worm's horn.

The 'nest' proper was some thirteen meters in diameter, a raised marble bowl intricately carved with the creatures of human fantasies and nightmares. In the years since the Crai evacuation nothing had taken up residence in the bowl itself; nothing would. The moss surrounding was flat and trim, free of fallen leaves and branches as the day the Crai had left.

Hopefully the hunters would not know why.

He heard them before they came into view. Anything could have heard them. Everything did. In a terrene or argolid environment noise was a safety factor; most animals tried to get out of the way of human beings. But not here.

Madreen caught sight of the dog first; it advanced warily towards the nest, sniffing the air, clawing the ground with front and back paws. The dog was enormous; the short saber fangs were a recent addition to the canine lineage. The fur was black, and the scientists had clearly modeled much of their work on illustrations of Indian tigers rather than wolves.

But I'm not afraid of you, Madreen thought. The dog could only tear him to pieces.

The drunken bladebirds screamed and dove. Drunk, they were little danger to the hunters, but looked frightening. Rowlwen went flat; the other man batted at one of the birds with his rifle. The dog caught two bladebirds with its paws, then wiped smears of blood on the moss.

That brought out the worm. It reared out of its hole at least three meters high, its horn twisting, mouth pulsing as it sought the scent of blood.

The dog surged forward, protecting the older man; it knew what to do, certainly. It pushed him behind it, growled and brushed the lunging horn out of the way.

In an instant Chrys Madreen was behind Phar Rowlwen, a blade at the man's throat.

"Don't move," Madreen whispered. "If you want to live look at this." With his free hand Madreen placed the *m'shee* on the rim of the nest beside them. He had already activated it.

"Take a look at it; don't turn around." Madreen blacked away into the bushes; a bladebird slashed at him.

Bruno leapt into the air and caught the worm with all four claws, ripping open the torn mouth. After a moment the worm collapsed on the ground.

Lane got to his feet slowly, then shot a pair of drunken bladebirds out of the air.

"Rowlwen." Lane looked around. His partner was out of sight, behind the curve of the nest. In a moment he found the man looking at a smaller version of the Crai *m'shee* that stood in the middle of the Joypath.

"Over here," Rowlwen called. "Come here and look at this." Rowlwen shot at a bladebird. "Have you ever seen one of these?"

"Sure. It's Crai…" It took Lane a few seconds to realize the figure was human and the language comprehensible.

"Know that I am Zherar Heunis the Loyal, Defender Unto Death and After of my mistress Elosang Ahdissa of Argos of the Mehedern sept that has served the Race for ten thousand years and will always serve the Race in wisdom and success. I have drunk the blood of the Race's enemies and befuddled their minds so they yet serve while thinking they are Wild…"

Rowlwen fingered the twister trap control. The traps hanging from Lane's belt exploded around him. The older policeman sprawled on the ground, squirming in the sticky twists. Lane managed to hold onto his rifle, but it was wrapped around his chest pointed at his face.

Bruno ran over to his master, then looked at Rowlwen and back to Lane. The beast tried to get a grip on the twists with his jaws but they were too tight.

"I thought that might have some affect on you," Madreen said from behind a bush.

The dog howled, then barked in Phar Rowlwen's direction. Rowlwen went over to the *m'shee* and picked it up.

The image of Zherar Heunis, Liberator and first First Citizen of Argos, continued to proclaim his undying loyalty to the Crai race and his mistress' lineage. The rebels on Verren had been routed and emasculated because of his betrayal. Tedryng Faber, the politician who had nearly united the Revanchists and Union Party had not died of a heart attack before victory, but from poison administered by one of the Loyal; the jump gate to human space had been disabled through *his* doing.

"And Heunis's heirs are still traitors to the human race," Madreen said, walking into the open. "Coraish and his clique are just waiting for the Crai Empire to expand again and overwhelm Argos."

Then Madreen heard Heunis' declaration of Loyalty switch off; through the leaves he saw Rowlwen's hand move casually across the base of the *m'shee*. And Madreen stopped moving.

He's one of them.

"I'll drink your blood, traitor!" Rowlwen put the *m'shee* down on the ground and hefted his rifle again. "Then I'll feed your body to the worm." Rowlwen stepped over to Lane and made certain the man was still incapacitated. "Don't waste your time, Bruno. He's worm-meat."

Madreen sank deeper into the underbrush. *Stupid, stupid I should have killed him.* Rowlwen fired into the underbrush. It was the safest approach.

Madreen looked around. He stood five meters from the Wood. There was another worm hole ahead of him, but no way to attract bladebirds. There were a number of gorgeous flowers with toxic pollen, but he doubted he could wait the six or seven days before Rowlwen died. A blast of metal pellets shattered a gold blossom; the wind carried it away from Madreen.

Madreen had a fairly good map of the area in his mind. He needed to be about fifteen meters north, at the edge of the Wood.

The dog howled again. He ignored it.

And while I am moving from one square to the other to outwit my opponent, where is he moving himself?

Finally, the scholar positioned himself.

Rowlwen came closer; Madreen could hear the footsteps on the moss. The man walked much more carefully than earlier. Not silent enough for the Crai Preserves, but he knew what he was supposed to do. Every so often he fired into the underbrush. Eventually he'd find his target. In the distance the dog was still howling.

Madreen dared not move. He had to be completely still, completely silent. He couldn't look to see if Rowlwen was where he had to be.

Now!

Madreen cast his mind down into terror. His memory sorted out everything and isolated the one memory he knew would produce the desired result. Once while he was a student they had been been testing one of the big cats from Analayne in the lab on a caged treadmill. It was a mass of muscle and white and black stripes and its limbs were a blur at 40 miles an hour. Then, without thinking, Madreen had walked directly in front of it.

The big cat had looked at him; the digital counter on the treadmill climbed to sixty.

Madreen had known fear.

The fear was in his mind; he let it overpower him until he stank of terror, and the wind carried his stench downwind.

The worm erupted from its hole. Rowlwen saw it and fired; he missed and had to dart backwards to avoid the horn.

Then he was in the trees.

The *iashlag* struck, wrapping its tentacles around the policeman; Rowlwen was snapped backwards and lifted into the brush. The *ialshag's* tentacles were toxic to human beings. The man had gone into shock, and his heart had stopped beating before he had a chance to make a sound.

Madreen found Rowlwen's gun; it had fallen from his dead hands and hit the ground almost directly below the *iashlag*. That was probably the safest spot in the entire Wood, underneath a feeding *iashlag*. Madreen recovered the gun and checked it; several hundred minibullets left.

He walked back to the nest. The dog crouched over its fallen tangled master, head darting right and left, striking out with forelegs and hind claws; a pair of worms approached it from both sides.

Madreen shot the worms. The dog looked at him quizzically, sniffing, remembering his scent.

Madreen went over to the *m'shee*. Lane lay a few meters away, looking in his direction. The dog moved between them, ready to die or kill if its master gave the word. The cop was silent.

"Hello boy," Madreen said to the dog. "I'm a friend of sorts, I guess."

Madreen pressed the control stud on the stock of the gun. The twister net began to flex.

"I take it you watched this." He picked up the *m'shee* and placed it back in his pack. "Our glorious First Citizen is a traitor. They betrayed us seventy years ago. We're just sitting out the recession in the Crai Domain, waiting for them to expand and rule us again. They cut us off from the rest of the human race…."

The policeman tried to stand, but the twister net was still too tight.

Can I trust him? Rowlwen didn't, but he might very well want to move into the ranks of the Loyal, and my head will do it for him. I can't take the chance.

"I took Phar Rowlwen's car keys. I can make it back to the road before you get free. Don't follow me."

Away from the nest Madreen went into an easy lope, the gun in his hands, the pack swinging gently on his back. After working at two kilometers for most of the past season he expected to be able to keep this up all the way back to the road. He'd avoid the trees and be moving too fast for whatever worms were in the area to respond to him. He was feeling overconfident and didn't see the flitter until it was almost on top of him.

A four-man government job with Protectorate markings, and someone was aiming a weapon at him out the side window.

The only cover nearby was a grove of trees; a good way to get killed by a *iashlag*. He headed for it anyway, but the ground ahead spouted gouts of dirt and flame.

Pebbles and mud whipped his face, Madreen half-turned away and raised his own weapon, firing blindly in the direction of the flitter. Another explosion caught him from behind and threw him to the ground.

When he awoke they were breaking his legs. He fought not to scream and failed.

"...thought that might bring you around. It's remarkable what a little pain will do." He'd have recognized Jonas Coraish's voice anywhere.

Two beefy men in security uniforms stood over him. One had a foot on his chest.

"That was your right tibia," Coraish said. "Your left femur will be next."

One of the Security goons had a metal bar. While the first held him down, the second raised Madreen's left leg and struck it deftly with the bar. Agony swept over Madreen and he shrieked.

"That's better. Breaking your left tibia and your right femur will be even more interesting..."

There was a shrill sound. Through a haze of pain Madreen vaguely recognized it as a com beeper. It came from five meters away, where they had landed the flitter.

"I'll have to get that," Coraish said. "Your shots took out our pilot." He told his men, "Don't do anything fun until I come back."

Coraish walked to the flitter and climbed inside. It would be some official or semi-official call in his capacity of First Citizen, to some Argolid Citizens who didn't know he was First Traitor. The two goons just stood around Madreen, waiting for orders.

Stupid of me. I should have known they'd send someone after the cops... Three people had died to steal the *m'shee* from the graveyard where the Loyal interred their dead, all students of his, and he had failed them....

The police dog made no sound until it was on top of the Security men. Madreen first saw it as a black blur flowing over him, reaching out with claws to push one disemboweled man down while it drove its saber fangs into the other one's throat...

When he heard the explosions in the distance, Lane broke into a run again; a couple of his ribs were broken and it hurt like hell whenever his feet touched the ground. He had barely gotten out of the underbrush and seen the landed flitter and the three men before Bruno leapt from him.

"Bruno!" Lane shouted; before he could act the dog was on the Security guards, its massive temporal muscles crunching the skull between maxilla and mandible.

A moment later the civilian had jumped down from the flitter; his machine gun cut through his own dying guards and Lane's animal. Bruno flew backwards in a spray of red and lay twisting on the ground.

Madreen tried to get to his feet but both his legs were broken; he floundered and bit back screams. The civilian was walking toward Madreen— Lane recognized the First Citizen Coraish immediately.

"Don't move," Coraish was saying to Madreen. "I need you alive for a little while longer...." Coraish ignored Lane; he was just another policeman who would take whatever orders he was given. As Lane limped toward him

Coraish seemed to notice him for the first time.

"You, Sergeant Lane is it? Go to the flitter and bring me the first aid kit…"

As the First Citizen spoke the policeman found himself standing over his dead dog. Bruno lay eviscerated on the gray moss.

"Sergeant, I am the First Citizen, your commander…." The voice was strident and insistent, ready to break into a declaration of loyalty to the Crai on his *m'shee*….

Lane raised his weapon. It was the last thing the First Citizen ever saw.

Chrys Madreen wiped blood from his shirt and pushed the body that had fallen on him to one side. The First Citizen had a look of total bewilderment frozen onto what was left of his face. The police special Lane had used caused an enormous stink.

Lane sat on the ground with the head of his dead animal in his lap, rocking back and forth. Of all the mistakes Madreen had made in the last two days, this was the one he would regret the most.

And my legs are still broken.

Coraish had said the first-aid kit was in the flitter, hadn't he? Five meters away. There was no way he could crawl that far.

Madreen turned back to the dead First Citizen. He slid through the mess Lane had made of his master. Madreen found a private pocket phone in Coraish's vest pocket. A few centimeters lower and Lane's gun would have taken it out as well.

Anyone he called would have their phones tapped, but he could think of things to say that would only be understood by friends. They'd get help out here before sunrise. He punched out the numbers.

IN THE GARDEN ON THE FAR SHORE OF THE STYX

CHRISTOPHER STIRES

A half-day's ride from the city of Daarmoor, as we traveled east along the old spice merchant trail, Kree and I first smelled the stench of the funeral pyres on the wind. With each passing mile, we saw gray-and-silent farmhouse after farmhouse with P carved on the doors. Plague. Still we continued toward the city. We had ridden for three months to find a mage called Yulin and I would not relent. I could not.

Kree twisted in the saddle of her claybank mare as she scanned both sides of the road. "This isn't good, Novarro. It's been the same since daybreak. No birds in the trees. No cattle or sheep in the fields. Not even a dog anywhere to be seen."

"Go back," I said. "You're not known in that border town we passed."

"I've thought about it. More than once. But no, I'd just end up in jail again."

"A thief and gambler of your caliber? You'd have the entire town fortune in your pocket within a week and the people electing you magistrate."

Kree brushed the dust from her thick arms and smiled. "I know," she replied. "It's just, well ... I figure, with you, I might accomplish some task that will make my parents proud of me for once."

"Feeling sentimental?"

"It's a failing I've worked hard to overcome but, occasionally, childhood teachings rear their ugly head. Usually when you least need them, too."

"Whatever you're going to do, Kree, do it quick." I motioned toward the horizon and the quintet of smoke columns rising into the black sky above Daarmoor. "Because if you stay with me, I hope you're not planning on living forever."

"Well, yeah, I was. Live forever, be very rich, and much loved. That's my basic strategy."

I shook my head.

The frontier city before us had emerged around the sweet-water wells of Daarmoor. Since before my great-grandfather's time, spice merchants and silk traders had crossed this trail between the western European provinces and the territories in the Far East. The city of Daarmoor had blossomed and prospered. The other route was around the Cape by ship. That took a full year. Last summer, however, King Harold's son finished building his railroad through the northern mountains. The merchants switched their caravans to the new transportation and the old trail was abandoned to smugglers and bandits.

While crossing the border, Kree and I had heard curious stories about Daarmoor. The citizens had remained within their city. Not one family or individual had left to join the new towns springing up near the railroad. The king's soldiers sent to investigate did not return. No smugglers or bandits had been seen.

The reason was now more curious. With plague claiming the borderlands, there should have been a mass exodus.

As we entered the city, we saw an ox-drawn death wagon parked in the shade of a crumbling arched arcade. Hooded soldiers, exhausted, lay among the weeds. The driver dropped a water bucket beside the thin oxen. None looked at us. Corpses, tiny and large, filled the black wagon bed.

"What's that lettering say?" Kree asked, pointing at four symbols scrawled on a shattered wall.

"Those aren't letters. It's hieroglyphics. Pre-Thurian. It means Protect Us from Evil."

"Didn't work."

I reined my Appaloosa to a slow walk. The narrow street before us was deserted and still. Ash floated in the breeze. All the stone buildings had their windows shuttered and doors barred. In front of the tavern were three bodies tied and wrapped in burlap shrouds. The burlap twitched and bulged. Two more corpses were outside the cobbler's shop. Their shrouds were ripped wide and fat gray-brown rats, dozens, crisscrossed the bodies. One rat, amber rimming its muzzle, sat up on its hind legs and hissed at us.

Kree sighted her crossbow.

I tapped her shoulder. "Save your arrows."

"Yeah, you're right, there's too many," she replied, then she fired. The rat dodged sideways and the arrow ricocheted off the shop wall.

I spurred my Appaloosa forward.

Following, Kree reloaded her bow. "I'm going to be nicer to cats. Do you think this Yulin can do half of what they say?"

"What is happening here is not happening by natural means and Yulin is not a student of white magic."

It was said that Yulin had been an apprentice of the necromancer of Camd'n Rin. He'd learned to navigate the tides of the River Styx and had mapped the Nine Rings of Hell. His coffers were brimming, the rumors claimed, with treasure looted from the Damned. I did not know whether the stories were true or not except one part. There had been a necromancer in Camd'n Rin. I knew this because I had killed him. Now, I had come to Daarmoor to seek the assistance of his apprentice.

I glanced down at a child's ball, forgotten, in the muddy gutter. Two young rats were batting it back and forth between them. A third, older rodent watched me. Behind us, on the second floor of the baker's shop, a window shutter creaked open.

Kree nestled her bow in the crook of her arm.

"It's him," a faint voice echoed along the empty street. "He's come."

"O' merciful gods, please, let it be him," another wept.

The door of the tinker's shop flung open. A gaunt, sallow-eyed woman stepped from the shadows. She clutched the doorframe and stared us down as we breasted the shop. Kree scowled back at her.

"Is it him, Idanna?" a man's weak voice called.

"Don't know. Looks like two damn fools to me." Idanna pointed a skeletal finger at me. "Are you him?"

"I'm no one," I answered.

"Does he carry a weapon?" the man asked.

"Yes," Idanna replied. "But I've never seen the likes of it before."

The man, blood-scarred cankers etching his face, lurched into the doorway. He smiled and inhaled deeply. "That, dear daughter, is a revolver pistol. It was designed by the great gunsmith of Shankur and there is none like it on the frontier. The smith gave it to the man who rescued his children from the Griffin Vampire."

"Novarro the Crusader," Idanna spat.

Doors opened wide and people—nearly two score—staggered into the dim sunlight from the shops and houses. They surrounded us, touching and clapping our mounts, as we moved down the street. Most were weak and pale with seeping lesions branding their faces and bared arms. Several clung to one another to keep upright. A hunchbacked man, his left eye and ear devoured to nub, handed me a tankard. I took it, nodding thanks, and sipped the cool water.

"Save us, Crusader."

"Thank the gods you've come at last."

Now I understood what was happening here.

Kree yanked away from the caressing, grasping hands. "I'm not with him. Keep back. Don't touch me."

"Destroy the curse that keeps us here, Crusader."

"Save us from Prince Yulin," the hunchbacked man said.

"I'll do all that I can," I answered.

"Damn you!" snapped Idanna, grabbing my saddle and pounding my thigh with her frail fist. "You should have been here long ago!"

The tinker's daughter collapsed, sobbing, against my Appaloosa. I brushed the tears from her cheek. She bolted back from me.

"No!" Kree cried as a young man, his nose split from crown to tip, hugged her leg and kissed her knee. "You don't need to touch me."

I reined the Appaloosa to stop. Kree twisted toward me. Her expression pleaded for us to get away. Fast. The crowd grew silent. I rose in my stirrups, listening. On the breeze, not too far from us, I heard a lute. And laughter.

"Where?" I asked.

"In the plaza," replied Idanna. "Those who are allowed to remain inside the plaza are safe from the plague."

Kree trotted her mare ahead of the crowd. "What's in the plaza?"

"Yulin," I said.

"Let's go introduce ourselves. He's gone to such lengths to lure us here."

I spurred the Appaloosa forward and rode toward the plaza. Kree slipped beside me as the townspeople, Idanna in the lead, followed. We rounded a bend in the street and the music and laughter grew louder. Banners of rich orange and blue stretched between the buildings.

Kree double-checked her crossbow and loosened the wheel-lock pistol in her belt scabbard. "I know that you can't kill him," she whispered tightly. "I'll do it."

I motioned upward to her. Positioned, along the rooftops, were archers and musketeers.

"Anything else I should know?" asked Kree.

"This is more than a trap for me. Yulin enjoys this. Follow my lead. Don't get impulsive."

"Impulsive? Not me."

We rode into the plaza.

The circular courtyard was jammed with over one hundred people dressed in bright colored silks. Kree grunted in surprise. Tense laughter vibrated from the surrounding walls. Long tables, scattered everywhere, were over-flowing with meats, vegetables, cakes, and pitchers of wine. Jugglers and fire-eaters snaked through the crowd. A jester performed sleight-of-hand with scarves and flowers on a raised platform to our far right. On the left, a whimpering nobleman his face painted as a grinning clown knelt before a masked executioner. In the center, musicians played the lute and dulcimer and twelve naked dancers twirled in perfect rhythm to one another.

"Quiet!" a harsh voice ordered.

Instantly, without comment, all voices and movement ceased.

Straight in front of us, on the opposite side of the plaza, a man bounded onto the main table. He was short and round-bellied and dressed in a purple tunic and breeches. The right side of his broad face was fair and unblem-ished. The left, however, was dark and tattooed with a swirling, twisted cross.

"Welcome, Crusader, to the Feast of Nod," he called. "I am your host. I am Yulin. You could not have arrived at a more opportune time. I was becoming bored. These people die so slowly."

He hopped down from the table and the crowd parted between us.

I dismounted as Kree glanced from Yulin to the townspeople blocking the street behind us.

Yulin smiled broadly. "I knew you would be unable to resist stories about a mage who could descend into Hell. The mere appearance of a chance to rescue the Lady Lenore would bring you running."

"That's why you've done this?" I said. "You cannot defeat me."

"Perhaps not. Let us say that the bounty Lord Satan has placed on your blood has made it well worth the challenge."

I stared evenly at the prince.

Yulin walked closer. "Gentle people of the realm," he announced, "our honored guest today is the hero of Shankur and Herron. He is the warrior who destroyed the necromancer of Camd'n Rin. May I present to the court, Patrick Novarro of Valon, the Crusader."

Several nobles near me edged away.

A lady, dressed in ivory-yellow, stretched her hand toward me and mouthed, "Save us, m'lord."

"He has not always been a warrior," Yulin continued. "Once the Crusader was a scholar of books and letters. A blade, let alone a pistol, had never crossed his delicate hands. He was married to the loving and beloved Lenore. His life, and the world about him, were to him perfect." He pivoted toward me. "Am I correct so far?"

I remained silent.

"I am." He dunked his fingers into a noble's goblet then sucked the wine from his flesh. "Then late one winter night, a highwayman attempted to steal his meager purse and, during the robbery, the Crusader's heart was pierced by the outlaw's blade. As he lay dying, no doctor or shaman able to save him, Lenore bartered a covenant with Satan. Her immortal soul for her husband's life and for him to live the remainder of his years without harm from Satan or his servants. No demon or angel could have imagined the warrior he would become. Except, I presume, his beloved bride. And thus was born the warrior for Heaven who is shielded by Satan's own oath."

I rested my hand on my pistol. "What's to prevent me from ending your reign over this city?"

Yulin signaled to an archer on the rooftop. The archer fired. The arrow thudded deep into Yulin's chest. He rotated for all to see. Then the prince wrenched the arrow from his flesh. No blood spilled across his tunic.

Several nobles weakly applauded.

"This isn't good," Kree said.

Yulin gestured to a musketeer. The man sighted and fired. The bullet slammed into Yulin's forehead and the prince reeled backwards. He smashed into a table, sending platters and bowls spiraling to the ground, and started to his knees. Then, he leapt back upright and bowed to the crowd. No blood appeared from his head. He pressed his forefingers into the wound and, a minute later, tugged the round-shot from his skull. The wound seared together as if it had never been.

"We are both blessed," Yulin told me, tossing the shot onto the cobblestones. "I tricked the Archangel Zebadiah almost as cleverly as Lenore did Satan. I shall not be harmed by mortal hand or by Heaven's lackeys."

"Then we have a stalemate," I said.

"Not quite," Yulin responded. "There is a way for us to duel."

"How?"

Yulin waved to the crowd and they began to chant as one. "Tanith ...Tanith ...Tanith..."

I first heard the myth of Tanith when I was a boy in Valon. At six years of age, Tanith had perished in a blizzard. The child followed the Damned who departed the Boatman's ferry at the gates of Hell. She went into the Great Hall and knelt trembling with the others before Satan's throne to receive their punishment. Satan gazed down at the child. She was pure and innocent. No traces of sin marred her white-gold aura.

"Why have you come before me, little one?" Satan asked.

"I was bad," she said.

"How were you bad?"

"Mother and Father told me not to go outside," she answered. "A storm was coming and I knew my pony would be cold. Father said she would be all right but I was worried. After Mother and Father went to sleep, I took my blanket and sneaked outside. The snow was blowing fierce. I couldn't find the stable. Then I couldn't find my way back to the house. I lay down and went to sleep. When I woke, I was on the ferry. I disobeyed. I know where bad people go when they die. Mother and Father told me."

Satan smiled and the fallen rebel angels within the Hall cowered behind pillars. "Go back to the ferry, little one. The Boatman will take you where you belong."

"I must stay here, sire."

Satan signaled a demon king to escort Tanith to the river but the child was pure and the demon unable to touch her. Other demons attempted to trick her into returning to the ferry. They failed. Angels beckoned to Tanith from Heaven's shore and tried to coax her to the ferry. They failed also. "I was bad," she answered to all who spoke to her. "Bad people go to the Bad Place. Mother and Father told me this is so."

Finally, Satan called upon the Archangel Magdalene. "Come and get the child. If I could throw her across the river I would but, just as no demon or damned can enter Heaven, nothing touched by the hand of Hell can enter Heaven either. You have my oath that you may enter my realm, gather her, and leave unmolested."

Magdalene, weeping, shook her head. "It is written and so it is that no one can be forced to accept Heaven's embrace. All have a choice. Tanith truly believes she has not earned Heaven and I cannot command her to cross to us."

Satan roared and demons, high and low, hid from his sight. He walked his realm and all those he encountered felt his angry wrath. As he stood on the far shore of the Styx, where the river emptied into the abyss, he glared across the waters at Heaven. The Archangel Magdalene knelt upon Heaven's shore praying.

"I should throw her into the abyss," Satan said, "and be finished with her."

"You could have done that without calling for my assistance," replied Magdalene. "You seek another solution."

The Boatman called to Satan and Magdalene. He pointed to a tiny island, in the center of the river, near the falls of the abyss.

"Neither Heaven nor Hell," Magdalene said, nodding. "But how shall we lead the child here when none can compel her to leave your palace?"

Satan waved his hand and a bridge of bones rose between his shore and the island. He snapped his fingers and Hell echoed with the sobbing of a pony.

Tanith came, as swiftly as her small legs would carry her, to the far shore of the Styx. She crossed the bridge to the island. On the island, Tanith found a satin-lined bed growing from the rocks and perched on the pillow was a cloth, button-eyed pony. As she gathered the pony into her hands, a deep trance engulfed her, and she lay down to sleep. Angels seeded the barren ground around her with flowers and plants. High demons placed gifts around her.

"Here," Satan said, sweeping away the bridge, "the child shall sleep until one who is not yet demon or angel comes to escort her to her rightful reward."

Magdalene agreed.

"But it must be one who is worthy," added Satan. "All pretenders will go alive into the abyss."

Magdalene trembled. "Why? Why these conditions?"

"Because, my sister, I am who I am."

And, since that time, long ago, Tanith has slept peacefully in the garden on the far shore of the River Styx.

"I can induce the Boatman to take us to the garden where Tanith sleeps," Yulin said. "You and I will go there, Crusader."

"To what end?"

Yulin brushed the cheek of a young dancer. The man shivered and retreated into the crowd. "Where Tanith sleeps is neither Hell nor Heaven and, by our own hand, by our own actions, the oaths that shield us cannot protect us."

"By our own hand," I repeated.

"There is one true treasure on the island. All else is false. Choose the one and I will be sent into the abyss to plummet through the darkness forever. Choose wrong and you shall meet the same fate."

"Who has told you this?"

"My Lord Satan."

"Satan is a liar by word, deed, and omission."

"Of course," Yulin responded, confused. "I don't understand your meaning."

I mounted my Appaloosa.

Yulin bounded forward. "If I'm destroyed, my curse will be lifted from this realm and the people freed. The plague shall end. The tortures shall end. If I remain, all shall be dead within a fortnight and I'll move on to new lands. I've heard much about Valon."

"What do you gain if Novarro's destroyed?" Kree asked.

Yulin glanced at the thief. "The reward Satan has placed on the Crusader's blood is more power than can be envisioned. I can envision a great deal." He turned to me. "Satan will observe the contest. Lenore will accompany him."

A fiery chill settled around me.

"Wasn't a good idea to come here," muttered Kree.

"When shall we depart, Crusader?" Yulin asked.

"We don't," I replied.

"Coward!" Idanna yelled at me. "Damn coward!"

The lady in ivory-yellow dropped to her knees and raised her clasped hands toward me.

The hunchbacked man, tears filling his good eye, touched my leg. "Please, sire."

"You do not fear Hell," said Yulin. "Or the abyss. That I know. Save these simple people. Come with me."

"No."

Yulin pivoted toward the crowd. "I will open the invitation to any who are bold enough to journey with me."

I reined the Appaloosa around. Idanna spit. The townspeople and nobles moved away from me.

"I'll go," Kree said.

I twisted toward her.

"And I," called Idanna.

"Good," Yulin shouted. "Will you reconsider now, Crusader?"

I spurred the Appaloosa to a walk.

"We don't need that coward," said Idanna.

"Quiet," Kree growled. "Leave him alone."

I stopped the Appaloosa. Satan was a liar by omission. When he told me of his covenant with Lenore, he explained his oath of protection over me. What he didn't tell, what I didn't discover until I'd killed seven of his soldiers, was that Lenore would be impaled with burning spikes upon each death. The first impaling only lasted for a mortal day but the torture would be doubled for each succeeding death. When I decapitated the seventh, the necromancer of Camd'n Rin, she was impaled for sixty-four days. When I learned of this, it was almost more than I could bear.

I looked from the townspeople to the nobles. I had no doubt that they all would be dead within a fortnight. But the price was too high. For the next death, Lenore's torture would last one-hundred-and-twenty-eight days. I could not cause that suffering. She was so gentle and frail in life. An unkind word would pierce her heart. This was too much to ask of me.

"Ride on," Kree shouted as if reading my mind. "No one will fault you. Ride on, Novarro."

I gripped the reins. Lenore would. If I allowed a single person to perish, she would blame me. She would hold me accountable despite the consequences to herself. I touched her cameo that I wore around my neck. I feared one thing above all else in this world and the next—Lenore ashamed of me. I turned the Appaloosa and trotted back into the plaza. I stopped beside Yulin.

The prince smiled.

I kicked him in the face.

Kree stared at the swift, churning water as the Boatman steered us south along the coastline of Hell. "This is not one of my better plans."

Idanna tugged her cloak tighter around her bony shoulders and sat facing Heaven's green shore. Angels danced and played among the lush meadows. A herd of unicorns wandered among the woods. Doves and sparrows etched the clouds.

From the bow, Yulin watched us as he sipped from a wine tankard.

I scanned Hell's shoreline. Fire and ice merged among the hills. The veiled sky buckled. The wailing of the Damned echoed toward us. We had sailed past the palace city with its flaming walls. Giant dragon-hounds guarded the gates. Fallen rebel angels, who had forsaken Heaven with their master, enthralled at seeing four live mortals with the Boatman, called for us to join them from the ramparts. We saw the lustful, their flesh torn to ragged strips, as they were savaged by horned demons and the gluttons, their mouths staked open, drowning in pools of rotting garbage and urine. Shrieking murderers dangled by their necks from barbed ropes as spiders nested in their eviscerated bowels. Suicides, bound hand and foot, writhed among flames and jagged blades.

Kree shuddered. "Don't think I want to see thieves' fate."

From under the water, a man clawed desperately to the surface near the boat. He stretched his hand toward us. Pleading. Begging.

Idanna leaned forward.

"Don't," I said. "He'll pull you in with him."

She sat back, silent and hating.

The man disappeared under the tides.

Yulin smiled. "Non-believer. If one truly believes in no Hell and no Heaven, then that is what one receives. The abyss. Forever falling through the darkness. All of you will soon know first-hand of the abyss."

Kree shifted toward me. "Remember my basic strategy. I've changed it. I don't have to be much loved and moderately rich will be just fine. To live forever, though, is non-negotiable."

Up ahead, I heard the thunder-roar of a mammoth waterfall. We were quickly approaching the garden. "I shouldn't have let you ride with me."

"My choice," Kree responded. "You told me that life is not predetermined. That all of us have choice. We have free will. I believe it."

"I'm not so sure any longer."

Idanna pointed at the island.

"Novarro, I know how devoted you are to Lenore," whispered Kree. "I know I'm not pretty and delicate and refined like she is. But I wish that just once you'd made a pass at me. I wouldn't have been offended."

I shook my head, dumbfounded.

Yulin rose to his feet.

The Boatman steered the ferry onto the beach. Huge rainbow-colored flowers and emerald-green plants bloomed across the island. A cool breeze caressed my face. To the east, the Archangel Magdalene and others prayed on Heaven's shore.

Yulin tossed his tankard into the water and jumped from the boat. The dark tattoo on his cheek glowed as he motioned for us to follow.

"Stay here," I said to Kree and Idanna. "This is for me to do."

Idanna climbed from the boat onto the beach.

I stepped ashore. Not too far from us, the river emptied into the abyss. The man we had seen earlier rose from the water screaming madly. A moment later, he plunged over the falls into the pit.

Kree sighed and hopped from the boat to my side.

To the west, along Hell's shoreline, loomed towering cliffs. Flames curled from the arctic crevices. Demons scampered along the upper rim. Suddenly, they dropped to the ground and bowed their heads.

Satan stepped to the edge.

He was beautiful. No sculptor or artist could capture the seductive allure of the banished angel. Rich blond hair feathered around his chiseled-perfect face and down to his massive shoulders. His eyes were deep indigo-blue and his mouth firm and inviting. A gossamer, fire-yellow tunic was molded over his lean, muscled torso and arms and ice-black breeches cloaked his long legs. Formless and enticing creatures lingered in his mammoth shadow. Fear and Madness. Horror and Sin.

As he stood on the cliff rim, he peered, damning and unforgiving, down at the garden.

Beside him, chained to him, was Lenore. My voice failed as I attempted to call to her. She was dressed in a flowing, pale-white gown. Her long dark hair cascaded along her slender spine. An angel trapped in Hell. A cyclops demon crept behind her and stroked her hip with its hoof. Lenore swiveled and slugged the beast in the eye. It screeched and scurried away as the other demons cheered.

Lenore looked toward the garden. "Patrick!"

I rushed forward, into the river, the tides grasping at my boots and legs.

Satan waved his hand. Flames erupted from the water and I reeled backward.

Kree grabbed my arm. "Not today," she whispered harshly. "Someday you'll find a way to rescue her, but not today. There's too many and they're ready for you."

I nodded, tears stinging my eyes.

Demons pranced along the rim and mocked me.

As I continued gazing upward at Lenore, and she down at me, Kree and I walked from the beach and into the garden. My heart felt as if it would implode. My hands and legs trembled. Kree gripped me upright.

Idanna and Yulin waited beside a tiny bed rooted to the clover-seeded ground. A child, innocent and sinless, sleeping peacefully, lay on rose-colored satin sheets. On the pillow near her head was a cloth toy pony. Scattered along her side were four idols that the high demons had left: a small crown, designed to fit a child, bejeweled with shining rubies and bright sapphires; a crimson-flamed diamond the size of a titan's double-fist; a golden angel with ebony wings and lyre; and a silver chalice filled with amber liquid.

Yulin tapped the headboard with his fist. "There is one true treasure before us. If you choose wrong, the river will claim you. You shall go over the falls and into the abyss *alive*. No judgment day. No balancing of the scales to determine if you have earned Hell or Heaven. Only falling through the darkness of the pit forever. If you choose correctly, I shall suffer the same fate."

"You don't pick?" Idanna asked.

The prince shook his head. "I lose only if you win. Who shall be the first to choose and perish?"

"I am," I replied tightly.

Yulin smiled. "No, Crusader. You will be last. My master wishes it so."

Vines exploded from the rocks ensnaring my legs. I grabbed at the thick boughs as they tightened, burrowing, into my flesh. I slumped to my knees.

"Why?" I yelled.

"You will watch the others perish," Yulin replied. "And the odds will be in your favor when it is your turn. But it won't make any difference."

I twisted toward Kree and Idanna. "Don't choose. Go back to the ferry."

Idanna walked, without a single word, around the bed. She snatched the jeweled crown from the linens and raised it in her fist above her head. Her eyes blazed as she stared at Yulin.

"A popular choice," said the prince.

The crown sailed from Idanna's hand back to its place on the bed.

"But wrong," he added.

A savage, hot wind slammed into Idanna. She fell, wind-milling her thin arms, into the river. Black whirlpools surrounded her.

I struggled against the vines. They burned deeper into my muscles.

Kree jumped forward, to the shore's edge, and thrust her hand toward the tinker's daughter. "Take it!"

Idanna glared at her as the current sucked her from Kree's reach. A moment later, she careened over the falls.

Angels wept. Demons danced.

I lowered my head. Idanna did not deserve this fate. Nor Kree. I did, but no other. I should have forced Yulin to leave them behind. This was for me to do.

"Patrick," Kree said, using my given name for the first time.

I looked up at her.

"May the gods guide us," she said.

I held out my hand.

Kree shook her head, smiled, then marched beside the bed. She straightened her shoulders and traced the back of her hand across Tanith's tangled hair. "Diamond, angel, or chalice?"

I rose slowly to my feet.

Kree nodded to herself and, with both hands, picked up the cloth pony.

On the cliffs, the demons applauded.

Kree glanced at me. "Not good."

The pony glided back to Tanith's pillow.

The ground under Kree buckled and collapsed. She tumbled into the river. The whirlpools engulfed her and pulled her away from the island. She fought violently against the current as she neared the falls.

"Patrick!" she cried.

No! She was going into the abyss *alive*. Alive!

I drew my pistol and fired twice. The bullets ripped into Kree's breast shredding her heart. She toppled facedown in the water. The limp body swept over the falls.

"You can't." Yulin pivoted toward the cliffs. "That's not damn you!"

Satan stood motionless on the cliff rim. Demons scurried, cowering, away from him. Lenore smiled and clapped.

The vines uncurled from my legs and retreated into the rocks.

"Put the pistol here," Yulin ordered, pointing at the corner of the bed. "You will not use it on yourself. You won't cheat the abyss."

I holstered the revolver and limped toward the bed. "Take it from me."

Yulin looked upward. Satan motioned to continue.

I studied the sleeping child and the idols beside her. Not the crown, not the pony. Diamond, angel, or chalice? Choose the one and only treasure. Or walk away. I could still do that. I glanced toward the Boatman. He nodded his gray head and grinned.

"The moment of truth, Crusader," Yulin announced. "You will have forever to ponder your decision."

I looked again to the cliffs. Lenore smiled and folded her arms across her chest. Then she rocked her elbows from side-to-side.

"Choose," demanded Yulin. "The citizens of Daarmoor await my return."

I brushed my fingers along the angel. High demons had placed the gifts beside Tanith. There was only one true treasure. One. Of course, Lenore, I understand. Yes. I swept all the idols from the bed and gathered the child into my arms.

Tanith murmured and her tiny arms encircled my neck.

"No!" Yulin cried. The wounds on his chest and forehead burst wide. Then other wounds erupted. Dark blood spilled from him. He screamed as vines from under the water speared forward wrapping themselves around his legs. The tattoo on his face peeled and bubbled. He grabbed the bed's headboard. Bones cracked and shattered as the vines pulled viciously on his legs. He held tighter, his fingers locked on the headboard.

"Not by mortal hand shall you be harmed," I said. "Like hell."

I spun and quick-smashed his hands with my boot heel.

Shrieking, Yulin released the headboard and plunged into the river. The black whirlpools churned and swirled about him. A vine arrowed around his throat. The tides claimed him.

I faced the cliffs. All were gone. The demons, Satan ... and Lenore were gone. The island garden vanished as if it had never been and never would be again. I hugged Tanith against me.

Yulin, screaming, hurtled over the falls. Into the abyss.

I walked to the shore and stepped into the ferry. "Shall we take the child to the angels?"

The Boatman nodded yes.

I motioned toward the falls. "Kree?"

The aged ferryman shook his head—No.

"Where then?"

He pointed toward Heaven's shore.

Brushing a curl from Tanith's face, I said, "At your convenience, sire."

The Boatman looked behind me.

I turned.

Satan waded into the river. The waters parted from his path. "I knew you would succeed where no other had. Now the little one will be where she belongs."

"Lenore," I whispered.

"Lenore will not be harmed. This time you have done *my* bidding. Besides, she welcomes the torture. She laughs at me. The torture means you have won again. I have to create something new for her punishment. Until we meet again, Crusader. I believe that will be sooner than we both envision."

The Boatman steered away from the island and, as Tanith began to wake, we sailed upriver to where the Archangel Magdalene and the other angels waited.

HEART'S DESIRE
JEFFREY VALKA

A woman named Helena contracts a fatal virus and falls into a burning fever. She alternates between fits of helpless delirium and thrashing, violent outbursts. One moment she will tear at her sweat-drenched bed sheets and scream as if in the throes of a particularly long and painful childbirth, but then suddenly she stops and grows very still, murmuring incoherently. Day and night her family watches over her and cares for her, but they can do little more than try to alleviate her suffering and make her comfortable. It's only a matter of time before she can fight no longer and succumbs to the illness, they say to each other.

A single white dove sits perched on the windowsill of the sick room and watches in silence. The family mostly ignores the bird except for a few attempts to shoo it away, but their attention remains focused on Helena and her immediate care.

Days wear on and the sickness worsens, becoming more difficult for Helena to fight. She grits her teeth against the pain raging through her body as the sweat running down her face and neck begins to take on a milky coloration and thicker consistency, a symptom no one has seen until now. Many of the family members fall to their knees and wring their hands in prayer, certain that the end has finally come. The milky white sweat runs more and more slowly down Helena's anguished face until it comes to a stop at her bare collarbone and appears to solidify, ripening like an apple into a small, round bead. She screams as if being touched with sizzling hot brands along her skin, as if this tiny bead were tearing the very life out of her.

The bead falls from her body and clatters onto the floor where it rolls around like a marble. Helena faints with exhaustion, and her breathing becomes shallow and ragged. Her family stands there for a moment, stunned by this new development. Helena's brother John drops to the floor and crawls around until he recovers the white bead. He holds it up to the light and exams it with a cold, scientific look. He rolls it between his thumb and forefinger, studies the bead up close and from far away. "It looks like a pearl," he says and passes it around to the other relatives for their own inspection. Eyes light up as the bead passes from hand to hand, each person rolling it in their palm and glancing over at Helena who is now deeply asleep, and then back to the white bead. Nervous glances fly between them as they pass it along, fingers hesitant to let go of the potential treasure. Nobody speaks a word to anyone else as they pass it around.

Later that day John takes the bead to a jeweler for an appraisal. He confirms their suspicions: the milky white bead is in fact a genuine pearl,

and quite valuable. Upon this realization, the family members all take a re-
newed interest in Helena's care. Before they used to take turns at her side
reading poetry and favorite stories to her and wiping her brow with a damp
cloth; now they steadfastly refuse to leave any one person alone with her
for fear that Helena will produce another pearl and the one watching her
will quietly pocket it and turn a small profit. Deep within each relative's
own thoughts, however, they guiltily imagine what could be had if they
themselves were able to sell one of the pearls. Unspoken distrust crackles
between them like an electric charge. They stare edgily at one another and
walk around the room like jungle carts on the prowl, one eye on Helena and
the other looking over their shoulder.

Two days later another violent fit racks Helena, only this one is much
worse than the first. She shrieks and flails about mindlessly like a frantic,
overturned turtle, desperately crying out for someone to bring an end to
this. Her fever burns so hot that those standing next to her can feel the heat
and break out into a sweat themselves. They move her from the bedroom
to the adjacent bathroom where they submerge her in a tub filled with the
coldest water they can muster. They ladle water over Helena's head and
dump buckets of fresh ice into the water to bring the fever down. With
sobs of pain and tears streaming down her cheeks, Helena produces another pearl which plunks into the water and rolls around on the bottom of
the tub. Someone thrusts an arm into the water and quickly retrieves the
pearl, and takes it back into the bedroom for inspection. This one is slightly
larger and a purer white than the first pearl, obviously more precious and
more valuable. Two of her aunts who remained behind lift Helena from the
tub and towel her off while the rest of the family marvels at the new wonder. The white dove continues to observe in silence, by now completely
forgotten.

A vigorous discussion breaks out between the relatives as to what they
should now do with Helena. Her condition has obviously become more
serious, and several argue that she should be taken to a hospital. Others say
no, that if she is to die, then she should die in her own home surrounded by
her family. Finally, after a great deal of talk, John says, "I will sell the pearls
so we can bring a doctor here to take care of her. She will receive the best
possible care and still remain at home."

The family agrees, and they bring in a doctor to watch over her during
the day. A few try to hide their disappointment at the sale of the pearls, but
they grudgingly tell themselves that it is all for the best. The doctor brings
with him the finest machines that money can buy, and suddenly Helena is
surrounded by tubes and wires that run in and out of her nose and arms,
and blinking monitors that measure all of her vital signs. Under the doctor's
care her condition stabilizes, but he tells them that there is little hope of her
ever recovering from this illness. "All I can do at this point is prolong her

life and provide her with a small amount of relief from her pain," the doctor says.

Every two to three days she produces another pearl, which is immediately sold in order to pay for the doctor's services. Eaten up by their own unrequited greed and avarice and unable to stand it any longer, a few complain about this. "Why should the doctor get rich at her expense?" they say. "She never knew him, and to him she is nobody, just another sick person. Wouldn't she want her own blood to profit from this, and not some stranger?" Many of the relatives nod their heads in agreement, relieved that someone has finally given voice to the thoughts that they themselves had been harboring like a shameful secret. A few try to argue on Helena's behalf, but they are outnumbered and quickly intimidated into silence. The family decides to cut back on the doctor's services, and have him visit just once a week instead of every day. They disconnect the machines deemed superfluous and send them along with the doctor.

Like witches around a bubbling cauldron they sit at her bedside, waiting for Helena to produce another pearl. She looks back at them all, knowing what they all want, but she says nothing. Eventually another violent, agonized seizure takes hold of her just as before, and someone scoops up the latest treasure. All but one of her family members goes off to sell the pearl and to celebrate their newly found fortune. One of her aunts, Aunt Nora, who helped Helena from the tub, remains behind to watch over her. Nora takes a seat by the bedside and reads a book while Helena sleeps, but eventually she too nods off into sleep.

The white dove flies from its perch on the window sill and alights upon Helena's chest which rises and falls in ragged, fitful breaths. Her eyelids flutter open and she sees the bird for the first time, uncertain of whether she is awake or dreaming. In a voice like sandpaper she whispers, "What do you want, bird? Are you hoping to get rich like my worthless family? I'm afraid I have no pearl to give you right now."

The bird cocks its head to one side and stares back at her, as if sizing her up. After a moment the bird says, "I'm not here to profit from your misery, but rather to grant you a favor."

Convinced now that she is either dreaming or in the midst of a fever-induced hallucination, Helena says, "What kind of favor can you do for me? You're not even real."

"I can bring an end to your suffering and carry your soul into paradise. But to do that, you must first give me the pearl of your soul, the very essence of your being. Until then, you will remain trapped here in this body."

Helena is silent for a moment, then says, "I'm not going to give that to you...you can't have it. You're just like the others. Even my dreams are hoping to make an easy fortune off of me!" Weakly she raises her arm and tries to wave the dove away. "Go away and never bother me again."

Without a word the dove flies from Helena's chest and back to its window sill perch. It sits behind her just out of sight, and waits.

The next morning Helena's family returns after having spent the night on the town with the money made from the sale of the pearl. Nora frowns as they enter and gives each one a lacerating stare, but says nothing. They are loud and boisterous despite having been out for the entire night. Already they begin making plans for how the money from the next pearl should be spent.

From the next room Helena hears everything that they say, feigning sleep but feeling disgusted beyond measure with her family's behavior. How could they have sunk so low, so quickly? She thinks. I will die before I give them anything more.

Late at night when everyone is asleep, the dove visits Helena once more. She awakens feeling lucid and clear for the first time in several days. "Have you changed your mind?" the bird asks without a trace of irony.

"Yes…yes I have. Take me away from this place," she says, bitterly at first, but then simply tired, resigned. "How do I give up the pearl of my soul?"

"You must go deep within yourself and bring together everything that you are. Your loves, your fears and all of your desires. Focus it all on a single point, then push it away and let it go. I will do the rest."

Helena closes her eyes and does as the bird asks, concentrating intently upon her life from her earliest memories to the present moment. She imagines herself wandering through a vast mansion with each room holding a different memory. She opens the doors, walks into each room and carefully examines what she finds there. Gradually her mind begins to bustle with the thoughts of all the places she's been and all the people she's known. Helena smiles as she remembers childhood friends and old loves who all parade before her. She works at this mental inventory methodically, considering every memory and feeling one at a time, examining every facet. This will take months, she thinks, despairing.

Suddenly the memories rush out like a tidal wave, as if a cork has been pulled out by the act of unearthing these forgotten things and triggered an overwhelming avalanche. I'm drowning! I'm drowning! she thinks, unable to process the thoughts quickly enough or to stem the tide. She thrashes weakly in her bed and knocks the IV out of her arm.

"Push it away," the disembodied voice of the bird tells her. "Push it away and let it go."

"I can't…" Helena says, sobbing. "I can't do it…"

In a blinding flash the lights come on in the room, and John stumbles in. "What's wrong?" he asks, confused and still half asleep. The flash of light and sudden intrusion of her brother shocks Helena back into the present. All of the feelings and memories dredged up suddenly vaporize, blown away like a deep, heavy sigh. A stunningly gorgeous pearl, the largest and most beautiful one yet, rolls from her chest into Helena's lap where it lays nestled in the sheets like a newborn baby.

John's eyes grow large and hungry as he spies the pearl which glints in the moonlight spilling into the room. Sleepily he reaches for it, unaware that Helena has stopped breathing. The dove swoops down from above and takes the pearl into its talons before he can reach it, however, and soars through the open window into the enfolding arms of the night.

LIFE GETS BENT
BRETT HUDGINS

"Astounding Andy! Yoo-hoo! Astounding Andy!"

Andy froze, alarmed by the call. A woman's voice, excited, verging on desperate and thoroughly out of place in the grungy backstage alley. Hardly one of the vagrants he often encountered when leaving work, fellow natives of a cruel world.

"I see you, Astounding Andy!"

Having completed his second show of the night to drunken heckling and blind indifference, Andy wanted only to go home. He was parked at a meter that took slugs and Canadian coins, the Holy Grail of city life, but that was over a block away from the run-down Grand Imperial Theater. Saving a fortune suddenly paled against saving his life. Such as it was.

"Astounding Andy! Yoo-hoo! I have something for you!"

Andy didn't doubt it. With his luck, the business end of a really big knife. A little knife he could handle, but not one of those suckers that could cut through a mattress as if it were a sandwich.

Gauging his distance from the approaching woman, he started briskly in the opposite direction. Behind him his pursuer increased her pace to an unsteady jog, or so the clatter of her high heels indicated.

Andy followed suit. Minus the high heels.

"Why are you running, Astounding Andy?"

Andy smiled grimly as he heard the woman crash into a cluster of overflowing garbage cans. She went down hard, crying out, and Andy thought he heard a bone snap.

It wasn't one of his, though, so he kept moving.

The next evening Andy visited the Grand Imperial's owner in his office, as requested. It was the first time Andy had seen the wizened little man since auditioning and being told, "Good enough." He didn't even know the owner's name; he got paid in cash once a week by a hulking usher named Turk and advised not to loiter. The owner's expression, what wasn't obscured by a huge cigar, didn't bode well.

"Look, if this is about the trouble last night—"

"What trouble?"

"In the alley...er, never mind." He sat in a chair facing his employer's desk, eyes watering in the acrid cigar smoke as he waited to hear the real reason for this meeting.

"I like you, kid..."

Wonderful. False praise, probably softening him up for a pay cut. And what could he do but nod and say, "Thank you, Mister..." Uh-oh. What *would* he call the guy? Mulva?

"...But you draw more flies than paying customers."

Stinky, Andy decided. From this moment on, he'd call his employer "Stinky."

"You're too weird, too cerebral. It'd be different if you had boobs. I gotta let you go."

Oh crap. "Pardon me, Stinky?"

"Huh? What'd you just call me?"

"Stinky."

"Oh." He frowned. "Hey!"

Andy interrupted. "I show up sober, do my best, and don't hit on the ticket girl. You can't fire me."

"Wrong. I gave you a shot but you're too boring."

Andy snorted. "How boring *should* I be?"

"Real funny. This ain't a charity, kid. I gotta draw the line."

"In blood across my throat?"

"Heh. Yeah, I guess you could say that."

Andy slumped in his chair, not feeling particularly astounding. "Man, you stink."

"Bite me," Stinky growled.

"Seriously." He straightened, with indignation if not pride. "I'm pretty good. I have a hook, a sense of humor, and I demonstrate during the act that I'm no fake."

"People just don't care."

Andy imagined Stinky falling backwards out of his chair into the hottest fires of Hell, his screams continuing to echo as slavering demons danced through his ashes.

"What're you smiling about, kid?"

"Nothing." Too true. A sheen of fantasy couldn't stand against acid reality, or the realization that he was now one step removed from a freak show or a government lab.

"Buck up, then. Ask around, put some irons in the fire. Word of mouth keeps a lot of losers in work. Just look at pro athletes. Hell, if you don't find another gig within two weeks, I'll eat my shorts. Speaking of which..." He spat his cigar onto his desk and rummaged in the wide, flat middle drawer.

Andy stood to leave. Anything for which Stinky's ginch could serve as a reminder held little appeal.

"Hah." The little man triumphantly raised a scrunched-up ball of fabric. He lobbed it to Andy.

Curious despite himself, Andy unrolled the ball and found he was holding a pair of slinky yellow silk panties. Printed on the crotch in red lipstick were the words: COME UP AND SEE ME SOMETIME. "What the hell is this?" he asked, aware that he was sweating.

"I don't know. Well, I *know*, but I don't *know know*. You know?"

"No."

"A woman dropped 'em off during your first performance tonight, then paid to see the late show. Said she's a big fan of yours, whatever *that* means. You mighta just missed her leaving when you came in here. Or maybe not, people weren't exactly bottlenecked at the exit. She's a real looker too, even with a broken wing."

"Oh." Uneasy on a number of fronts, Andy occupied his hands with neatly folding the underwear. "Well...I guess I'll be going now. I wish I had a locker or a dressing room to clean out."

"No you don't."

"You're right." Turning for the open office door, he said over his shoulder, "These panties had better not be yours, dickhead."

Holed up that night in his one-room apartment, where the grime ate wallpaper and shat roaches, Andy drank. Cheap rotgut fit only for lubricating his temporary escape from despair, hopelessness, and the dread certainty that he'd never amount to anything.

He was roadkill.

And he dreamed. Trapped in the Grand Imperial, chasing a stinky little gnome through one wrong door after another while a woman with a broken wing hovered in the shadows, chirping her mocking call: *Yoo-hoo, yoo-hoo...*

He awoke clenching the panties so tightly his palm sweated through the silk. He unfolded and stared at them. The lipstick invitation was smeared and illegible and about as enticing as the rest of his prospects.

Andy skipped breakfast. No way he'd be able to keep anything down. Instead, he went outside to his ancient brown Honda Civic, intending to leave the city for a few hours. To collect himself in a more pleasant environment.

His hubcaps hadn't survived the night. Big surprise.

Once in the car he rooted through the glove compartment, hoping he'd left some money. No such luck. Muttering, he gunned the Civic's weak engine and, without checking over his shoulder, spun away from the curb into an illegal U-turn.

And a head-on collision.

A red Buick Skyhawk, swerving to avoid his reckless move, met him in a crushing auto French kiss.

Actually, Andy noticed this with the same dazed, absent awareness with which he knew his legs were working and his nose was bleeding, the two hoods did sort of look like tongues. And there was plenty of mingling fluid.

Andy staggered from his car, ignoring ominous creaks from his aching back. The two cars, hissing and gushing and groaning, were more compact than ever; they wouldn't be pried apart any time soon. Damningly, no one had emerged from the apartment buildings lining the streets to investigate the commotion. Probably too busy gloating over their new hubcaps.

To hell with them, Andy thought. He limped to the Skyhawk. The unconscious driver was roughly his age, early thirties, with wavy blonde hair now matted with blood from a wound to her temple. A thick cast sheathed her right forearm.

The broken wing.

Oh geez. What she did to herself was one thing but this was his fault. *His*. And it wasn't a mess he could abandon or deny, as he'd done for so much of his life.

Andy looked around frantically and stifled a scream. No aid was forthcoming. God knows he'd wanted to move from this neighborhood due to the living conditions and atmosphere, but now he was doubly intent on leaving, and it was a matter of principle: his neighbors were all selfish, apathetic bastards. And only five minutes ago he'd been one of them...

He wrenched furiously at the Skyhawk's driver-side door in conjunction with using his "weird, cerebral" talent, managing to snap one of the hinges and bend the door aside. He eased the woman from behind her wheel and gently stretched her out on the pavement, using his foot to clear a patch of broken glass and twisted metal. Though her bleeding had almost stopped, she was too pale for comfort.

Andy tried to think back to all those first aid courses he'd taken as a teenager. What was the correct procedure in such an instance?

That's right, it was his best friend who'd taken all those courses. Damn.

Around him, neighborhood residents carried on their lives behind shuttered blinds.

Andy swore. The woman's breathing was shallow but regular, and none of her limbs seemed twisted wildly out of position, to quote Stinky, "good enough." He gathered her limp form into his arms and carried her awkwardly to his building, weaving badly on the climb to his third floor apartment. He cleared his bed of bottles and laid the woman down. She hadn't stirred during the trip.

Wondering if he should call an ambulance, Andy retrieved a wet cloth from his kitchen alcove and set about cleaning the woman's head wound. Her eyelids fluttered open at the cloth's first cool touch.

Andy jerked back from his bed. "You're awake."

The woman's eyes found him, wobbling slightly in their sockets. "Astounding Andy."

He shrugged and nodded.

"Yoo-hooo..." She collapsed back into unconsciousness.

Outside, traffic swerved, not stopping, to avoid the wreckage.

Several hours later Andy and the mystery woman were seated at his tiny folding dinner table, gazing into each other's eyes and flushed with excitement.

"You were magnificent, no, *astounding*," she told him in an awestruck tone that went straight to his head.

"Um, thanks."

"The way you bent and straightened it without using your hands. Woowww..."

Oh man. This was too good to be true. "You really find that attractive?"

"More than anything." Confidentially, she added, "When you tied it into a knot, I thought I'd *explode*."

Andy was enchanted.

"I've had the most gigantic crush on you since I first saw your performance. Pure schoolgirl flutters."

Beyond enchanted, in fact. And why not? His life had just taken a more dramatic U-turn than his car. More to the point, he'd finally met someone who thought his odd talent was impressive. A woman, no less, who found him, Astounding Andy, the man who could bend spoons and other small metal objects with the raw power of his mind, irresistible.

His eyes wandered from the crumpled, knotted spoons on the table to the cast on his admirer's arm and he grew sheepish. "Sorry I didn't stop to help."

"I don't blame you. I went a bit overboard and you have to look out for yourself, right?"

"So what you said you had for me was actually your underwear?"

"Uh-huh."

"And the invitation over the, er, crotch, that was, um, serious?"

"Deadly."

"And we totaled each other's cars while you were on your way over here to, well, follow through on that invitation?"

"Exactly." She spoke without self-consciousness, hesitation, or regret.

"Wow." Andy rubbed his forehead.

"My name's Nina, if you're interested."

"Nina." Andy closed his eyes and let the name roll around on his tongue. "Nina, pretty ballerina."

"Pardon?"

"Just the title of an old song."

Nina blinked. "You think I'm pretty?"

"You're gorgeous," Andy affirmed, his eyes still closed.

"Thank you."

Andy's eyes popped open. "Would you move in with me, Nina?"

For the first time her forthright confidence faltered, but only briefly. "Shack up? Just like that?"

"Yeah. Another thirteen days to ourselves in this dump. Then we'll have to get out of town."

Nina's eyes sparkled and she didn't question the deadline. "Just the two of us?"

"Yeah."

"Like Bonnie and Clyde?"

"The law might become involved."

"I like the way you think, Andy."

"And I like you, Nina."

"Think the city'll get around to cleaning up our accident?"

"Naw. No one cares."

Nina rolled over onto Andy in their bed, pressing her breasts into his face. The morning sun bathed the couple through the recently washed apartment window. "Guess what, lover?"

"Mmmph!"

"Oh, sorry." She rolled off again.

"Thanks." He licked his lips. "Both times."

She grinned at him. "Today's our one-week anniversary."

Andy kissed her. "Not regretting it, are you?"

Nina kissed him back. "You kidding?"

"I'm glad."

"I quit my job to be with you. You'll never be rid of me."

"Gee, poor me..."

She studied his face for a moment. "Well, wanna do it?"

"You bet." Andy moved to kiss her.

"Not *that*, silly."

"Ohh..." Smiling, Andy reached under the pillow and pulled out three medium-sized spoons.

Andy and Nina were in their kitchen alcove chatting like soul mates over a light breakfast. Other than her cast, they'd recovered from their jarring introduction. Andy had never felt so at home or at peace. Only the knowledge that things could get even better gave him incentive to move on.

As if reading his mind, Nina asked, "How are we going to celebrate our two-week anniversary tomorrow?"

"We'll be on the road by then." He pushed his cereal bowl aside. "Today is also a two-week anniversary of sorts and I'm not going to let it pass without taking an old friend up on his offer." He stood. "Pack up anything you want to keep that we can carry with us."

“Where are we going?”

“You’ll see.”

Three hours later, after a short walk from a nearby bus stop, Andy and Nina stepped into the front lobby of the Grand Imperial. The lovers were dressed in plain, dark clothes and carried loaded duffel bags.

“Will he be here?” Nina asked.

“He’s always here. And Turk never shows up ’til after dark.” Andy led the way to Stinky’s office, pausing to listen outside the door. He heard puffing, coughing, and a flatulent sonic boom.

“Should we knock?”

“No.” Andy worked his magic on the knob, then reared back and kicked with all his strength. The door flew open with a crash. The couple stepped through to find Stinky sitting behind his desk, eyes wide and cigar dangling limply.

“It’s been two weeks, Stinky.”

A dozen reactions raced across the little man’s face. An equal number of outbursts likely caught in his throat. He settled for saying, “Since what?”

“Since you canned me.”

“You still mad about that?” Stinky sucked his cigar back in and puffed deeply, but not nonchalantly.

“A bit. Except for three other guys, you’re the first person to ever can me. It hurts.”

“What doesn’t?” Stinky pointed. “Who’s she?”

“Nina.”

“She looks fam...oh yeah, the underwear broad.”

“Charmed,” Nina said sarcastically.

“Did Andy come up an’ see you?”

“Three times last night alone.”

Stinky’s cigar, which was just a cigar, drooped again.

“I love her,” Andy said.

“And I love him.”

“Amazing to think you had a hand in uniting us, isn’t it, Stinky?”

“That’s good, right?”

Andy dropped his duffel to the floor. “As a concept, good is like a spoon. You get different reflections depending which side you look at.”

“Sure, kid. Wh-whatever you say.”

“Remember when you fired me? Said if I didn’t find another gig in two weeks you’d eat your shorts.”

“So?”

“It’s been two weeks.”

“And you haven’t found work?”

“Haven’t looked.” Andy shrugged. “But I’m going to hold you to your promise all the same."

"Huh?"

"Get ready to chow down, Stinky. Nina?"

Nina reached into her duffel and withdrew a twelve-inch knife.

"You're gonna stab me?" Reflected in the giant blade, Stinky's face went from ruddy to pasty.

"Oh please. Now come here. Come on, move!"

Stinky warily emerged from behind his desk. Nina smoothly positioned herself behind him, pressing the knife to his neck. Her nose wrinkled, smelling Stinky's fear. Or maybe his socks.

"Wh-wh-what're you doing?" Stinky stammered, working his mouth even after he'd stopped speaking.

"Thanking you for everything." Andy stared at Stinky's brass belt buckle, concentrating until it twisted in half and dropped to the office floor.

"Ha-haven't lost your touch, eh kid?"

"Not so boring anymore, is it?" Andy pulled Stinky's pants down around his ankles. "Kick them off," he ordered.

"You're raping me?" Stinky protested, slowly removing his feet from his pant legs.

"Don't flatter yourself." Grimacing, Andy bent and removed Stinky's checkered under shorts. On the whole, he preferred Nina's unmentionables.

"Wh-what're you doing?" Stinky demanded, trembling with true fear.

Struck by how pathetic his ex-employer looked, Andy dismissed the thought. No sympathy. As Nina said, you have to look out for yourself, right?

Some of the little man's bluster returned. "You think you'll get away with this, you stupid punk? Turk's coming in early today. You better get lost while you can."

"I'll never be lost again." Holding the shorts at arm's length, Andy went to his duffel bag and removed a large pair of scissors. He set about dividing the shorts into squares, an inch to a side. "Bite-sized morsels, Stinky. Like Shreddies, only with skidmarks." Once finished, he gathered up the squares and took a spoon from his duffel.

He then nodded to Nina and she forced Stinky at knifepoint into the visitor's chair before his desk. Andy handed him the spoon and the pile of fabric squares. "Dig in, dickhead."

Seeming to realize he had no choice in the matter, Stinky tentatively tasted a spoonful of his underpants.

As soon as the spoon was far enough into the little man's quivering mouth, Andy unleashed the full force of his power. The move earned him a splitting headache, though not nearly as bad as the one he dished out.

Stinky lurched violently as the spoon warped and twisted in his mouth.

The utensil burst in a spray of stainless steel, shredding the inside of his skull with shrapnel. He collapsed to the floor, leaking blood and brains from his perforated head.

"Astounding," Nina breathed, appearing undisturbed by the bloodshed. Andy nodded. He'd finally lived up to his name.

"Why'd you kill him?"

"He thought he was better than me. Even worse, he made me believe it too. No dressing room, no promotion, no praise and no gratitude. I had to talk to his thug when I had something to say. And he knew I needed him, knew I wouldn't have been here if I had an ounce of wit or ambition. He even taunted me with you, never suspecting you'd turn my life around. I thought I was scared of the world when I was really scared of myself.

"But observe." Andy knelt in front of Stinky's small, sturdy safe, which was gathering dust in an office corner, and used his power to manipulate the lock. "Wit." The door swung open, revealing two stacks of rubber-banded bills. Twenties. Andy stuffed one stack into his duffel. "And ambition, thank you very much. Bugger must've been cheating me too."

"What about the rest of the cash?"

Andy smiled. "Consider it Turk's share. Hush money."

Nina came to his side. "We won't get caught, will we?"

"Not a chance. With Turk out of the picture, Nero Wolfe couldn't solve this crime. The cops might suspect me but I'm no one. Bending spoons? Whatever. They'll assume I'm a fraud and a waste of time. You're the only one who believes in me." He made for the door. "Time to hit the road."

"But our cars are wrecked."

Andy retrieved Stinky's pants, fished in the pockets, and came up with keys. "These are for the Chevy parked out front by the hydrant."

"I thought that was ille..." Nina broke off as Andy gave her a bitter look. "Right. No one cares."

He put his arm around her. "Not without a damn good reason."

They left the theater in silence.

EVERYTHING MUST DIE
EDWARD J. MCFADDEN III

Time is circular, and people and animals alike come and go, leaving behind their souls and that which they created. Yet in time, even these creations fade to myth, and even myth is forgotten when the circle is completed and what was, becomes what is. Only the wise see this fading and even they are helpless against it.

Wind gusts across the lake and Jacob covers his eyes, shielding them from the dust that flurries in the air. He wipes his face and the dirt leaves an ill taste in his mouth.

At first Jacob thought only the animals in Lancing Ferry were dying. Being somewhat out of the way, living many miles from any of the main roads, he thought that the people of Lancing had done something wrong.

He noticed it while skipping stones on the banks of old man Grat's pond. The long green vegetation that usually stretched upward reaching for the sky was downcast and drab. Their leaves looked somewhat brownish, their height not what it had been in prior years. Then there was the spotted turtle.

Jacob and his friends had collected the mystical creatures when they were young boys, sort of a sport really, for they were agile and smart. But now there were no spotted turtles left, a testament to the fact that the animals were dying.

Jacob lets his hand drop to his side and the wind rips into him. Clear tears are driven from his eyes, the wind gouging his eye sockets, hiding dust within. Green algae lies stagnant across the once lush pond. Glancing to his left, he sees the old crusted rope that still hangs from the great oak that rests protectively above the now still water. Dead branches hang from the tree, its leaves beginning to brown and rot away. Jacob turns away. There is nothing left for him to see here.

It has been a strange year in Lancing, recalls Jacob as he makes his way home. The wind howls with extra strength, ripping through the town, tearing down signs, keeping children indoors. Some say the wind is killing the animals, carrying some disease or poison. Yet those who know better realize that it is not possible, for it would have affected the people as well.

The horizon is no longer bright blue and filled with the freshness of sunrays. It is brown and dull, hanging like a dead thing waiting to fall and crush everything beneath it. Jacob wonders what things are like outside his little town, or over in America. He wonders if it's like this everywhere, but even as he finishes the thought he knows it is.

Entire species of animals are fading away, becoming lost in history. The blue whale, the greatest creature on Earth, almost gone. Jacob wonders how something so strong could die, be beaten.

Jacob finally arrives at home to find a beautiful red robin sitting on the gutter above his front door. The bird does not sing and when it sees Jacob approaching it flies away. He watches it fade into the distance, until it is gone.

He sees a small black ant carrying a large piece of popcorn across the sidewalk. So small, yet so strong. He can hear old man Weber's car engine racing in the driveway next door. Wisps of smoke race from the tail pipe and fill the air with a black cloud that blocks his view.

Jacob remembers his grandfather and how he had died of cancer. Pestilence brought on by the creations of man. He had loved birds, remembers Jacob as he scans the heavens for the red robin, but it is not there.

Jacob sits on his front porch and listens to Mrs. Joves' television blaring. The public service announcement for recycling brings a smile to his lips as he sees the plastic cups protruding from the ground around the tomato plants in the garden. Then the soap operas return and Jacob flees, the ultra realism of the content making him shudder.

Down the street several boys are playing stickball with an old broom handle. Behind them, off in the distance, the large red brick chimney of the glass factory stands like a sentinel over the trees. Black smoke pours continuously from its bowels, filling the air with a dark and putrid smell. The boys continue to play and Jacob can foresee them trying to explain to their mothers how they got so dirty. "We didn't play in the dirt, Mom. I swear."

Then Jacob hears his mother calling him and he turns and dashes back toward the house. He sees her standing before the screen door, staring out into the yard. She looks old to him. He can't remember her ever looking so old. He stops before the front door and looks at her. She gives him a smile and draws him inside. Lunch is waiting on the table for him.

"When will daddy be home?" asks Jacob as he bites into his sandwich of processed cheese.

"Same time as every day," she says perplexed. "You can hear the whistle and go meet him. I think he'd like that." Jacob frowns.

Jacob sees the old wooden cross on the wall and wonders why God does not help. Say a prayer and he shall answer. Jacob wonders what tomorrow will be like. He can't bring himself to pray.

Later he wanders through the woods looking for frogs. He is yet to catch one this summer. They seem to be hiding better and better every year. Last summer he had caught only one and the year before three. His father brags about how he had caught hundreds each summer when he was a boy. Jacob comes to the only logical conclusion: He is not as good at catching frogs as his father was.

Jacob grabs his nose as the horrid smell of rotting flesh pervades the air. A dead possum lies in the pathway. Flies flock around the dead animal, dive-bombing its remains. Jacob stares at the dead animal for a long time, its eyes black with death. Its fur is still smooth and clean and it shines in the thin rays of sunlight that seep through the sparse tree cover.

A crow can be heard wailing in the distance and darkness falls about the forest as a large cloud drifts before the sun. A gust of wind rips through the forest, tearing living leaves from the trees. Jacob heads for home.

As Jacob approaches his house he sees how faded and covered with dirt it is. The discoloration of ages has been great. He sees the red robin again; only this time the bird does not fly away when he approaches. It is still and lifeless and Jacob frowns as he moves closer and finds the bird lying on its side.

The newspaper lies on the stoop. The headline reads, *Seven People Killed*. Jacob picks up the paper and thumbs through its pages even though his father has told him not to. Jacob counts the murders, which total seventeen. Jacob is happy he doesn't live in the city. He thinks he would be afraid there. He reads the small headline on page thirty-four, "NASA May Fold". Jacob sighs, wondering how his children will live. He decides at that moment that he doesn't want children. He doesn't want them to be in pain or to worry.

Jacob settles into the comfortable swing on the front porch as he cradles his book of fantasy. It is a story of great darkness, evil and death. Jacob thinks that Lancing could use a wizard to help heal the blights of the land. Every place could use a little magic. In the book the death is beaten, but Jacob doesn't believe.

Jacob reads for a while, then is distracted by the factory whistle blowing. His father will be home soon and he tosses the book aside and darts up the road.

His father is covered from head to toe in soot. Only his pale white eyes stand out, glaring at the world around him. He is tired, so very tired. He coughs as Jacob approaches and tells the boy to stay away from him, he's dirty.

Jacob sits on the curb and thinks.

Jacob is only thirteen years old and yet he worries about man's improprieties. He can see and he does not understand how his elders cannot. The circle is almost complete and Jacob wonders if humans will weather the storm.

MEMORIES OF ALWAYS
BRENDON ADAMS

The town is always quiet after all the tourists leave; paper blowing like tumbleweeds, the half-fallen signs and over-filled garbage cans reminding everyone it's time to pick up the pieces and start preparing for next summer. Already a chill wind blows off the ocean and the streets are empty; except for Ray who sits in a deserted open-air café in the center of town. The once thick green vines crawling up the latticework around the tables have already begun to whither and die; Ray reaches out and pulls a leaf from the vine.

Winter is coming to the Cape.

Suddenly an old woman emerges from the building, the screen door can be heard slapping against the wood frame as she approaches Ray with a look of disgust carved in her wrinkled brow. The old woman mumbles something inaudible as she snatches the empty glass from the table.

Ray lets his head fall over the back of the chair, devouring every last ray of sunlight. Eyes tightly closed, he imagines the people on the streets; the children playing, and the giant pirate spitting clear water at the miniature golf course. Laughing, that's what I miss most, he decides. The sound of people who have escaped their responsibilities and, for a couple of days, are free. He remembers the spray of sea water on his face, the sound of waves crashing on a crowded beach. He remembers.

No one knows what really drives the male spirit. Some say food, others conjecture that peace and quiet without nagging will win any man. However, the one sure thing is a bikini.

Ray sat with mouth gaping as he watched Sheryl rubbing suntan oil on her already brown skin. Her long blonde hair gave her the appearance of striking beauty from a few paces away, but closer inspection revealed an oddly attractive young women, marred only by an imperfect nose and a crooked mouth.

"Go talk to her," pushed Jenny as she watched the blood rise into Ray's cheeks. Everything looked beautiful—the sand, the sea, Sheryl. Ray looked at Jenny with eyes that told everything of their sometimes-romantic-twenty-year friendship. He had hoped to marry her one day, but now that was long ago. Yet, he still felt uncomfortable with her seeing him ogling another woman. "Don't worry, you always worry."

Ray rose and brushed the sand from his swim trunks and looked back at Jenny. She already had her nose buried in her book, she wouldn't put pressure on him by watching.

The sun got hotter and the sea breeze seemed to die away as Ray crossed the beach. When he reached Sheryl, she was lying with her eyes closed. Ray stood for several moments, watching.

"Can I help you?" she asked. "You're blocking my sun."

Ray stood wide-eyed, lips flapping—then his hands began moving feverishly. "Yeah, of course I can understand sign language. How else would I know what you said?" She laughed. "Why don't you sit down." Ray's smile almost split his head.

Opening his eyes, Ray could see Mr. Handly slowly making his way across the deserted street toward him. It was times like these that Ray was happy he was deaf. Jenny had warned him of the endless hours of rambling one had to endure if cornered by the old man. "When I played for the Bruins there were no pads, no curved sticks…" The man waved to Ray and walked past him into the Whispering Inn.

The sun had begun to set and it was time to move on, but to where? Rising, Ray dropped a five-dollar bill on the table and headed toward the road. Pausing at the curb, he turned and looked at the Inn. He probably wouldn't be back until next summer, if at all.

The old waitress stared at him. Collecting her tip, she lifted her bony hand and waved. He remembered all the good times he had at the Inn. All the good times.

"And you, should try one of these," laughed Sheryl as she pecked Ray on the cheek. Ray still wasn't comfortable kissing Sheryl around Jenny…she always appeared hurt. Ray found that Jenny watched Sheryl more than him, and Sheryl seemed to like it.

"…and once Ray even proposed to me! We were only thirteen, of course, but it still sent my father through the roof. 'You kids are too damn serious. You should be playing with dolls.' It's no wonder I have a complex."

Ray's eyes darted with laughter as his hands and arms flailed.

"I did not! It was you. You liked the song and insisted that I dance with you. He's impossible Sheryl, how do you do it?"

"Music, how did he hear music? I thought you were always deaf." The questioning tone in Sheryl's voice was easy for Ray to read in Jenny's eyes. After a pause, his hands flew.

"Not until you were twenty-two. How did it happen?"

Counting the cracks in the sidewalk always passed the time quickly for Ray. He frowned as he remembered his friend Kent telling him how stupid his voice sounded when he attempted to talk. Best not to try.

Where to now? Back to the park? Maybe I'll go see the lake before it freezes.

"WOOOOOOOOOOW!" shouted Ray as the thick swinging rope snapped and Ray hit the water with a slap. Jenny tread water several feet away, watching, waiting, but Ray didn't come up.

"Ray! Ray!" Jenny yelled.

Ray's laughing head popped through the surface.

"Did I scare you?"

"You asshole! You scared me to death! Shithead! I'll get you for that—someday, when you least expect it, when you have long forgotten…you'll pay." Jenny laughed as she swam to him and raised her hand to smack him. Instead, she put her arms around him and began kissing his neck. Slowly their bodies floated listlessly in the blue water. Breaking the embrace, Jenny said, "I'm ready, Ray. I know last week I said I wasn't…but it feels right now somehow."

Ray lifted her in his arms and headed for the shore, Jenny kissing his neck as he walked, caressing his back. He almost fell four times.

Ray snickered as he recalled making love to Jenny. They say that ninety-year-old men remember their first time like it was yesterday, but the truth be told, men forget. It's the woman who remembers—remembers everything that has any importance, and a lot of stuff that has no importance at all. Maybe that's why Jenny gives me a look every time I kiss Sheryl, thought Ray…as though I was betraying our pact, something we shared together years ago, until the accident. The accident, everything always seemed to come back to that.

"Jenny!" screamed Ray as he darted down the green grass-covered slope toward the lake. "Jenny, where are you?" Ray's eyes darted about frantically searching for Jenny, who had disappeared under the surface of the lake only moments before. Pausing at the lake's edge, he strained his eyes, searching through the pale blue water.

Nothing.

Abruptly, Jenny burst through the surface at the far end of the lake, yelling and sputtering, "Help, help me!"

Ray turned and traversed the lake's edge as fast as his legs would carry him. Diving from the raised embankment Ray could see the placid lake thirty feet below.

He remembered the impact more clearly then anything in his life. As he brought his hands forward to create a point that would slice through the surface of the lake, Ray could vaguely see the glint of tiny stones laying on the floor of the lake and the shallow clear water lapping against the shore.

With the agility of a cat that has been dropped upside-down, Ray spun in mid-air, landing firmly on his side. Ringing engulfed Ray's head as he reached for his ears—but one arm wouldn't move.

Ray's right arm dangled like a dead tree branch. Then the shock dissipated and pain rocked every inch of Ray's body. The sun faded to a pale white and time seemed to stand still. Eyes closing, his face hit the surface of the shallow water. The last thing he remembered was Jenny's frantic face as she knelt beside him. She was yelling, he could see that—but somehow he couldn't hear her. He was dying. Everything went black.

Crossing the street, Ray headed toward the school. He could see the caged children as they stared out windows with glazed eyes. The first week back was always the hardest. He could almost feel the crowd roaring as he made his way across the old baseball field toward the playground. The swings blew in the gentle breeze, a leaf fell from a nearby tree and Ray caught it in his hand.

It was just like the county championship game all those years ago. Ray had never been good at sports—hence his being exiled to right field seemed to solve everyone's problems.

That is until Fred Grover belted his almost home run. Ray's diving catch had saved the day…my only sporting moment, smiled Ray as he sat on one of the swings. Gently he pushed himself back and forth.

"What do you want to do tomorrow?" asked Sheryl. Ray sat Indian-style on the ground before her.

"Sailing," slurred Ray, his voice distorted. Sheryl was the only one he talked to.

"Sounds good to me." Smiling, Ray began moving his hands in a slow series of shapes.

"Why do you always have to talk about her? Everywhere we go it's, 'Jenny and I did this' and 'Jenny loves this place.' Sometimes it seems like you still love her."

The slight pause in Ray's voice and the doubt in his eyes would have been visible only to Sheryl. Her eyes blazed as Ray burst into unintelligible speech.

"You're mine now, Ray. She is never going to have you again." Ray masked his worry by making a small joke, and she smirked.

It was getting harder and harder to appease her short fits of anger—he didn't remember her being like that.

"Look, I'm sorry…it's just that I love you so much and I won't let anyone take you from me." Ray threw his arms around her and with his head resting on her shoulder, he closed his eyes in doubt.

"Sir." A woman was standing before Ray. "Sir, the children are coming out for recess. Could you please leave?" Ray had become quite adept at reading lips over the years, yet he always seemed to miss a word—people talked so fast.

Rising, he motioned with his hands and the woman's face flushed; that touch of pity that everyone had for him. It never seemed to fade—neither did his anger for it. Pity would do nothing for him, he had learned that. Pity.

Ray's hands moved feverishly as he saw Jenny's concerned eyes considering him. "That's natural, Ray. Asking someone to marry is a big step."

"Itttt'sssss not that," stammered Ray. For a moment their eyes met and they looked hard at one another. Ray's voice spoke differently from his heart, "But I'm scared, Jenny." *But I still love you, Jenny.*

Putting her arms around him she pulled him close to her. "I know, marriage is a scary thing." Ray lifted his head. Years later he couldn't remember the conscious decision to kiss her—it just seemed to happen. Fate.

Ray almost fell as he bumped into Tammy. "Hi, Ray. You gotta watch where you're going, you might hurt someone."

Slowly his hands shaped, "Sorry."

"It's O.K., I'm just kidding—how have you been?" Tammy seemed to regret asking the question as soon as she asked it. Cheeks flushing, she looked away.

A hasty, "Good," from Ray and she was scrambling away yelling something out being late.

I guess this small vacation town still hasn't gotten used to what happened, thought Ray as he watched her retreat down the road. Hell, I'm not sure I believe...even after all this time. Time.

"What are you going to have?" Sheryl looked prettier than ever—her blonde, now short and tightly cropped, hair shined in the dull light of the restaurant. Her knowing eyes watching him with an almost child-like anticipation.

How do women always know what you are going to do? Ray remembered the ring in his pocket.

He moved his hands in a circular motion, signing "Steak"—but his fingers came to an abrupt stop as her gaze shifted to the doorway.

Jenny had entered the Whispering Inn, stopping to say hello to Doc Berdon and his wife. Pulling his gaze back to Sheryl, he knew what he would find there.

The child-like anticipation was gone and she looked like a cat ready to jump. She watched Jenny with cool hatred.

"Why does she show up wherever we go?"

Sheryl stared at Ray, waiting for an answer to what he thought to be a rhetorical question. She didn't back down and Ray signed, "She doesn't. There's not exactly a lot of places to eat in this town during winter."

Seeing them, Jenny waved, but did not join them.

"So you told her? Do you tell her everything?"

Ray tried to sign—Tell her what?—but she cut him off.

"Do you tell her what we do in bed? Do you tell her she was better, or that you really love her? How many times have you snuck around behind my back to meet that little tramp?" Sheryl was on fire and Ray didn't even try to stop it. "Well, I'm going to end it."

The cold wind ripped through Ray as he made his way home—his frail hands stinging with pain and arthritis. Why do I remember these things, he thought? Better to ask why I can't forget.

Turning the corner Ray could see his small yellow house nestled back among three large oak trees. The porch was empty. That's odd, she always sits on the porch and reads the paper this time of day, he thought. Perhaps it's getting too cold for her. Perhaps.

"...dust to dust. Let us remember her always and let her bask in the glory of God. Amen." Ray almost fell as he approached the coffin. Alone...all alone.

Clutching a rose so tightly that the stem snapped, he saw his reflection in the shiny black surface of the coffin. Tears dripped down his face. He could see the priest approaching from behind him...the white clouds...the blue sky.

"Why...why did this have to happen?" whimpered Ray. "Why? I will miss you. I will miss you...

"Ray, is that you?

Ray closed the door behind him and surveyed the living room. Immaculately clean, as usual. Jenny came bustling through the swinging kitchen door with a towel over her shoulder—her shiny gray hair tied back in a ponytail. Even with the age wrinkles creasing her once smooth face, she looked beautiful. He smiled.

"Where have you been? It's getting cold out there and your arthritis is going to act up."

Ray signed, "I stopped at the cemetery, then had a few drinks at the Inn. Town's dead." For an instant Ray saw shame in Jenny's eyes.

"Well, dinner will be ready soon. Why don't you get washed up." Ray nodded and headed for the bathroom.

Watching himself in the mirror he rinsed his hands. He thought he looked old. It's been so long, why can't I forget? To forget.

"It's so beautiful here. Remember when we were kids and we used to come up here and make out?" joked Jenny. The blueness of the lake stretched out before them and the winter breeze ripped across the grassy meadow, creating whirlwinds of dried grass.

"Yeah" answered Ray at last, his voice steady. He felt uncomfortable being here with her. If Sheryl found out there would be hell to pay.

"Why did you ask me up here?" she said, and Ray's face went red.

"I'll tell you why." Sheryl's cold voice snapped both of their heads around. She sat on a large rock several feet away staring into the clouds. "He still loves you, that's why. Problem is, he loves me, too." She rose and walked toward them. "Bigger problem, he thinks he loves you more."

Ray and Jenny stood opened-mouthed. "Sheryl, I never meant to…"

"Shut up! I don't care about what you meant. As soon as she saw I was more important to you than just a simple summer fling, she started to turn you against me! You're nothing but a tramp!"

Jenny crossed the space between her and Sheryl with two quick steps. Raising her arm, Jenny punched Sheryl, leaving her scrambling backward with blood dripping from her left eye.

Ray remembered laughing at the scene. When he was young he could hardly get a girl to talk to him. Now he had two brawling over him. His smile faded as the two women grabbed at each other.

Strangely frozen, Ray watched the confrontation unfold before him. Jenny had tossed Sheryl into the lake and the two women fought toe-to-toe knee deep in water. Ray couldn't help but think this would solve his problem. Now he wouldn't have to choose.

With a crashing blow, Sheryl went down, her face submerged in the shallow water. Jenny was on her, holding her head beneath the surface. Ray tried to cry out, but the look of uncontrollable rage and hate on Jenny's face rooted him silently where he stood. Sheryl's arms and legs flailed like slippery tentacles then went still.

Sheryl floated lifelessly on the surface of the lake and Jenny fell back weeping, looking at Ray who stood rooted with horror several feet away.

Returning to the present Ray could see Jenny watching him in the reflection of the bathroom mirror. She had aged over the 40 some-odd years, yet her eyes still glowed with remorse.

"Why did you cover for me?" She had asked that same question of Ray for decades, yet he never answered. He couldn't—there was no answer. Jenny frowned and Ray looked away.

For Ray it was simple—he would always remember Sheryl, her face, the way she loved him. And when the summer began to fail he would remember their times together. He would remember how his love for two women had left scars that would never heal. Memories, good and bad, that would stay with him, always.

A LIMERICK HISTORY OF SCIENCE FICTION

1926   At the start, Hugo brought out Amazing,
        In spite of some serious hazing
            From lawyers and writers.
            (It seems that the blighters
        Sought cash for their written star-gazing.)

1938   John Campbell then surveyed the field,
        And said, "Now this drivel must yield.
            I shall draw a fine line
            With writers like Heinlein
        And think of the power I'll wield!"

1949   Tony Boucher at once saw the light,
        And he said (sounding quite erudite):
            "I don't give a fig
            If the concept is big—
        My authors must know how to write!"

1950   Then Horace Gold quickly appeared,
        And he wasn't the failure we feared,
            Galaxy was a fire
            With wit and satire—
        And the poorer stuff all disappeared.

1964   The along came Mike Moorcock, who said:
        "SF is most certainly dead.
            Who wants to re-hash
            Even more of this trash?
        I'll give them the New Wave instead."

1978   Judy-Lynn del Rey said, "Lester,
        Our readers will never dig Bester,
            But with cute fuzzy robots
            There's no ifs and no buts,
        You'll be a most happy investor."

1984   A mirrorshade crowd made the scene,
          And said, looking quite lean,
            "With punks made of cyber,
            And no moral fiber,
          We'll sweep the bestseller list clean."

1996   When Lucas from college departed,
          His vision to film was imparted;
            The books have been pleasant,
            But quite adolescent—
          And now we're right back where we started.

-MIKE RESNICK

ONE SMALL STEP
MARY SOON LEE

Tiptoeing across the darkened kitchen, Anne walked over to the holo-window. A crisp black sky, punctured by pinpoint stars, stretched above the curve of the lunar dome. Brilliant floodlights at the dome's entrance picked out an arc of dirt-gray ground, scored by broad tire-treads. The scene's designer had clearly chosen aesthetics over realism: no one would waste so much power illuminating the soil.

And yet Anne held her breath, picturing herself standing there, only the hiss of the spacesuit's air pump breaking the quiet of the long lunar night.

Maybe, just maybe, it would actually happen.

One corner of her mouth quirked. True, the odds against her were about eighty thousand to one, but that was much better than yesterday. She fingered the slip of computer printout in her pocket, a letter from MediaVision certifying that she'd passed the second round of tests.

Footsteps creaked in the neighboring room. Quickly, Anne turned the kitchen lights back up, and dialed a luxury breakfast into the meal-maker: real eggs with a dollop of dairy cream. Good food always improved Peter's mood, and this was going to upset him.

As she finished setting the table, Peter strode in, his forehead creased in a stately frown, perfectly framed by his graying hair. She'd seen him practicing that frown in the mirror, the stern politician striving to help the electorate, but the effect was spoiled by his baggy red dressing gown.

"Good morning, dear." He gestured at the holo-window. "What was wrong with Niagara?"

"Nothing exactly. I wanted a change. You remember that lunar competition?"

He nodded, intent on buttering his toast. "Hmmm. Centennial celebration, back to the moon in 2069, Stars and Stripes waving frantically as America returns to her glory days."

"Well, I entered."

Peter put down his toast, and stared at her. "I thought you'd decided not to. I know the space science gimmick appeals to you, but this isn't really about science. The government provides thirty percent of MediaVision's funding. And do you know why? Certainly not to support science."

Anne bit her lip as Peter switched into lecture mode. Why did he treat her like a child? He was fifteen years older than she, and sometimes it seemed more like sixty. She made herself concentrate as Peter continued.

"Automation has concentrated resources into a few large organizations.

Only one person in eight even has a job. But it suits both MediaVision and the government to maintain the status quo. The Lunar Program is just window-dressing, designed to deflect attention from the drop in living standards."

"Fine. I agree with you. But the program does include real science."

Peter stabbed at his eggs with unnecessary force. "Go ahead then. Never mind the impact on my re-election chances if the press find out about this."

Anne silently counted to ten. "Peter, this is important to me."

"And I'm not." He shook his head, his face sagging into tired lines. "I'm sorry. You didn't deserve that. I don't want to argue any longer."

He walked into the bedroom.

Anne stared at the door, half-wanting to rush after him and apologize. But she'd spent her whole marriage putting Peter's career before every-thing else. This time she wasn't going to. So long as the Lunar Program included a radio telescope, she'd try to be part of it. Two years after she had finished her Ph.D., the government had shut down the last major tele-scope at Arecibo. Overnight, radio astronomy became a closed science, research limited to old data.

Peter had never really understood why she missed it, but at least he used to care, used to hug her when she was upset. Her hands trembled as she cleared the dishes away.

A bright yellow yolk slid into the sink, wasted, and stupidly she found herself crying. She blinked impatiently, but the tears kept coming.

Crouched in their home simulator, the bodysuit warmly slick with her sweat, Anne struggled to keep her lunch down. Not that 'down' was a clear concept anymore. Aside from her death-grip on a blistered chunk of rocket hull, the universe had been replaced by a crazy, tumbling blackness that spun endlessly around her. Vivid sparks of light laced themselves into rushing constellations, and twisted away beneath her feet.

"Stabilize," she muttered.

A fist-sized blob skidded past her shoulder: the space station, its spi-dery profile miniaturized by distance. If she wanted to get back to it, she would have to cut her momentum. And since the spacesuit's maneuvering jets didn't have enough fuel to stop both her and the rocket hull, she was going to have to let go of the hull.

Anne took a deep breath. Strange how comforting a piece of metal could become. She timed her rotations, watching for the tiny silhouette of the space station. With a grimace, she pushed clear of the wreckage, using the reaction to reduce her spin.

Better. She was even drifting in roughly the right direction.

She fired the spacesuit's thrusters, killing the last of her angular mo-mentum, and adjusted her vector toward the station. As her pulse-rate slowed, Anne sniffed the air suspiciously. Lemon, that was odd. She was almost at the docking port before she remembered cleaning the room this morning. She hadn't gotten so caught up in a simulation in years.

Anne pulled alongside the docking hatch, and turned the airlock lever. The image dissolved under her hand, fading into the matte black of the simulator walls.

"You have completed the first half of round three early. You may take a five-minute break."

Unzipping the bodysuit, Anne quickly toweled herself dry. Her arms ached, she was parched, and she was grinning like an idiot. Even if she didn't make it to the final, that program alone was worth the entry fee. Besides which, she was certain she'd done well. Anne grabbed for the water bottle, the cool liquid sweetened by anticipation. Still grinning, she gently stretched sore muscles, easing through isometric exercises.

"Thirty seconds."

Anne zipped up the bodysuit, and the room blinked into a gleaming laboratory, all smooth surfaces and polished tiles. A heterogeneous assortment of instruments and samples lined the far bench, ranging from a compound microscope to a mass spectrometer.

"You have two hours to test the instruments. Note any faults in the laboratory log."

Shrugging, Anne walked to the bench. She picked up a radio receiver, and unscrewed the casing, her tongue lodging itself between her teeth.

By the time she had worked her way down to a solidification furnace, she was entirely absorbed in the task. Half-forgotten skills resurfaced from her undergraduate days, crystallography and microbiology lectures, hours bent over graffiti-pocked lab benches, the blond-haired technician who cracked crude jokes.

Anne positioned a probe over the furnace's circuitry, locating a fused contact. Abruptly, the scene shivered into black.

"Round three ended. You will be notified of the results within twenty-four hours."

Straightening up, Anne rubbed at an ache in her neck. Slowly, she stripped out of the suit and peeled off her damp underwear. Clearing up the mess in the simulator could wait; she needed a shower. She stepped into the living room, and froze.

Peter was sitting on the sofa, a terminal on his lap. He should have been at the council session until late in the evening.

"Anne. I'm sorry about this morning." His eyes tracked her nude body speculatively.

She flushed; Peter hadn't stared at her that way for months. "What are you doing here?"

"I wanted to apologize properly. I realize you get bored, but you know how bad it would look if we both had jobs. People are jealous enough as it is." He stopped, his fingers teasing at a tear in a cushion. "This isn't coming out how I intended. Here."

He produced a tiny silver parcel, tied with red velvet ribbons.

Anne unwrapped the parcel, and lifted free a thin gold heart, strung on a chain. Something complex twisted in her stomach, and she knelt down beside him, her throat tight. "You put it on."

His hands fumbled at the nape of her neck. "I know it's not much, and I've been working too hard recently, but I still love you."

Anne closed her eyes. The pendant lay lightly against her skin, reminding her of how they used to be, little kindnesses that transformed into something vast.

"Anne? What's wrong?"

"Nothing." Her voice was husky. "Thanks for this."

He bent forward, and nuzzled her neck. "Woman, you smell dirty. You need a good scrubbing."

Wrapping his arm around her, he led her to the shower.

Anne and Peter sat at opposite ends of the kitchen table, the MediaVision brochure spread-eagled between them. Flamboyant holo-logos danced round its perimeter, scattering rainbow shadows across the imitation wood.

Congratulations! You have qualified for the Grand Final of our Centennial Lunar Contest. A Transair hypersonic shuttle will fly you to sun-soaked Florida. Enjoy a relaxing week in our luxurious Cape Canaveral complex, while a panel of experts evaluates you and our other ninety-nine finalists.

MediaVision: striving for the tomorrow you deserve.

"Congratulations," Peter said heavily. "When are you leaving?"

"Tomorrow. If I go. I haven't replied yet, "

"Don't play games with me. You've made it abundantly clear this is what you want."

Anne bit her lip. After a second, she nodded, not meeting his gaze. "The shuttle leaves at 9:30 P.M."

"I suppose I should wish you luck."

"It wouldn't hurt."

Instead of answering, Peter toyed with a napkin ring, rolling it back and forth until Anne wanted to scream. Finally, he lifted his head. "What happens if you're one of the winners? How long will you be gone?"

"The initial contract is for two years. One year training, one year on the moon." The calm in her voice was a cold lie, but anything more would fracture her control.

"Have you read the small print? Never trust a lawyer, particularly if he uses small print, and they all..."

"...use small print. The only anomaly is a clause about agreeing to minor medical procedures. I assume that means things like having appendectomies beforehand, to minimize the need for surgery."

Peter scowled. "Well don't sign until you've checked. I want you to come back in one piece."

"You can bet on it. I'll probably be home inside a week." Anne hesitated. "I'll miss you."

The napkin ring clicked as it rolled from one side of the table to the other, to and fro, to and fro. Peter stopped it with his thumb. "Miss you too. Good luck."

The project director welcomed Anne in person, ushering her into a large west-facing office. Orange sunlight glowed through tall bay windows, gilding a cut glass vase filled with cream roses. The room smelled of flowers and seasoned leather.

"Sit down, sit down." He motioned at a chair with a languid sweep of his hand.

"Thank you." Anne perched in an antique mahogany chair that belonged in a museum, or a film set, where more people could appreciate it.

"You're one of our star candidates, Anne. May I call you Anne?" He didn't wait for her nod. "I shouldn't tell you this, but I'm confident you'll be selected."

"What about the remaining tests?" Anne blurted, and then flushed, feeling like a gauche adolescent.

"Just routine health checks." He dismissed the subject with a wave of his hand. "The Lunar Program is extremely important to MediaVision. The spin-offs in the children's market alone will run into hundreds of billions of dollars."

"Most impressive." Anne forced a polite smile. Maybe she was naive, but she would have preferred more idealism and less emphasis on profits.

"To tell you the truth, we had some difficulty finding first-rate astronomers. You're almost an extinct species."

"We disappeared along with the government funding. Odd how often that happens." Anne managed another smile to soften the sting. What was she doing? The director was practically offering her the job, and she was arguing with him.

"Well now, you can't expect the government to support economically unviable fields. But let's not discuss politics. I just wanted to check you're ready to join us."

Anne nodded, not trusting herself to speak. The gold heart hung from her neck in mute reproach.

"Good, good. If you're not too tired, we could get your physical out of the way immediately. Then you can sleep on the decision, and we can sign the contracts in the morning. Well?"

Anne blinked. "I'm not tired."

"Excellent." He waved her toward the door. "I'll see that you're sent a copy of our employee benefits brochure. MediaVision is more than generous. Any questions?"

Anne followed him into a hallway, her feet sinking into the deep carpets. "How did you become involved in the Lunar Project? Are you a scientist?"

He laughed. "Nothing like that. I'm more of an image man. Before this project, I was in charge of casting actors for our various virtual reality milieus. Do you have any idea how expressive your face is? I could spot your disapproval at a hundred paces."

Anne stopped dead, her cheeks burning. "I'm sorry."

"Don't worry about it. You don't have to like me. I've studied your profile, and you'll do just fine. When we let you loose on the moon, you won't need to fake your enthusiasm."

Certain that her face was bright red; Anne marched on down the corridor. If Peter was here, he'd be smirking, telling her he'd warned her that MediaVision had no interest in science. And despite that she'd have been glad to see him.

The director led her into an empty examining room, and pointed her at the diagnostic chair.

Anne sat down gingerly, eyeing the tray of mirror-bright instruments to her left. Hooked and pointed lengths of metal winked back, their tips needle sharp.

"Relax. Stay as still as you can. This won't take a minute."

Skeptically, Anne adjusted the estimate to at least three minutes. She counted the seconds mentally, trying not to move as the robot scanners hummed into action. Angled black manipulators uncurled from the sides of the chair, tracking up and down her limbs.

Fifteen seconds: a thin probe pricked her wrist, a red drop disappearing into its tubing. Anne remembered the small print about minor medical procedures, and wondered just what 'minor' meant. Thirty seconds: to Anne's surprise, the machines finished, folding back into the chair.

The director glanced at the readouts. "According to the doctor here, you're in excellent health."

"Wait." Anne stood up, and wiped her damp palms on her skirt. "I have a question. Your contract mentioned medical procedures, what exactly is involved?"

"Minor cosmetic surgery." He tapped instructions into a panel inset in the desk.

A small holo-generator activated, sculpting a woman's head, red-gold hair cupping a complexion as pale as Anne's. The woman's cheekbones accentuated the oval of her face, lending it a delicacy that Anne's narrowly missed.

"Meet the new, improved Anne," the director said, smiling broadly. "This is my current favorite. Would you believe that hair color is called Sunset Fire?"

For a moment, Anne refused to believe what she was hearing, but the damn head hovered above the desk, its eyes an identical cloud-gray to her own. Anne's fingernails dug into her palms as she turned to the director. "You want me to undergo surgery so I can look like some fairy-tale model! Smiling sweetly from adverts to boost MediaVision's precious ratings?"

"Calm down. Cosmetic surgery is standard throughout the industry. And we're only proposing routine adjustments: minor changes to your facial structure, breast enhancements, an operation to extend your leg bones." He leaned toward her. "This is such a small thing, a detail. I know how much you want to go to the moon. Don't let this stop you."

Anne bit her lip. What difference would it really make? When she was on the far side of the moon, quarter of a million miles from MediaVision, none of this would matter. Only that wasn't quite true. She could almost hear Peter, the twist of derision in his voice: "The Lunar Program is just window-dressing, designed to deflect attention from the drop in living standards."

And she would be part of that window-dressing, right down to the Sunset Fire tints in her hair. They'd script her speeches; tailor her figure for the audience's enjoyment. No one would pay attention to the science itself. She lifted her chin, and stared straight at the director. "I withdraw my application."

His eyes widened. "Don't be foolish, at least think about it overnight, we could increase your salary."

"No." She fastened her fingers round the heart-shaped pendant, suddenly exhausted. "I'm ready to go home."

July 20, 2069. The team of astronauts soft-landed on the moon, MediaVision logos blazoned on their helmets, but Anne wasn't watching the broadcast. She stood in the simulator, the lunar landscape outstretched before her, undisturbed by any sign of man. Glancing up, she saw the broad pale band of the Milky Way, radio waves spilling from its heart in silent splendor.

And it hurt.

Not that she regretted her decision, but it still hurt. She reached backwards, and closed her hand over Peter's.

Awkwardly, he folded her into a hug.

MEESTER SMEET
TOM PICCIRILLI

Pynch swallowed his third scotch of the morning, turned to his assistant producer and said, "You're kidding me, right?"

Edgar sighed and hugged his clipboard to his chest. "Now you're asking me if I'm kidding. I've been calling you about his situation for more than a month, but you've been too busy scouting locations and trying to pick up every snow bunny in the Swiss Alps to listen to me—hey, uhm, don't they got the AIDS over there yet?" From what Pynch had been telling him there was at least one place on Earth where they weren't too paranoid to have a fun screw. "So listen, Marciello's girlfriend gets to play the seductive French maid. If you say no, he, well, if you're lucky he'll just pull his half million investment out. At worst, cripes, you know that crazy bastard."

"The French maid?" It took Pynch a while to remember the character: a small role from way back in the first draft of *A Feast of Angels.* "I thought we cut her completely out."

"We did. But Marciello liked the part for his girlfriend, so he had the script rewritten again."

Pynch's stomach tightened. "He did, huh."

"And, uh, it's kind of been significantly altered. She gets at least two full minutes of screen time now." Edgar checked his clipboard, turning pages. "You know the scene where Smith and his lady go to the little church in Tijuana for Christmas, to pray for good weather for the starving Mexican farmers? Uhm, ah, now they do Easter at St. Pat's to ask God to help little Mikey after he got hit by a bus on Eighth Avenue."

"Who?"

"Little Mikey. Marciello's got a grandson, ten-years-old, wants to do a hospital bed death scene."

"Oh Christ."

"Marciello's hoping to get a cameo from Cardinal O'Connor, too. He hates all the micks, but, you know, it's the Cardinal."

Pouring himself another scotch, Pynch gave Edgar that slow, lethal glare that expressed how disappointed he was that his assistant producer had not handled the situation much better in his absence.

Edgar wasn't taking any of it, though, and held the clipboard up and out now, aggressively, like he was getting ready to swing a hatchet. "Hey, I told him yes 'cause I figured he'd just stab you in the head if I said no, okay? You really want to argue about it?"

"Refresh my memory here," Pynch said. "This girlfriend of his—"

"Carmella."

"Yeah, with the mustache, right? Or did he get a new one?"

"No, no, the one with the mustache."

Pynch remembered her from a big set party the night before he left for Switzerland; Marciello waltzing her around, singing Italian songs, fondling her at the end of the diving board. He suppressed a shudder. "And the really squeaky voice, and big black mole that takes up half her forehead? Who got off the boat like six months ago and can barely speak English?"

"Yeah, her."

The part, as Pynch remembered it from the first draft, called for a luscious maid to try to seduce the socially conscious, working class everyman hero Christopher Smith. "We changed Smith from a real estate mogul with political aspirations to some schlep of an accountant. Why in the hell would an accountant have a French maid?"

"He's a very well-to-do accountant now," Edgar said.

Pynch tried thinking about the pudgy Carmella dressed in the slinky maid outfit, the little white hat hidden in her kinky hair, saying in grating broken English, '*I'm 'a from Phila-del-fia. I'm 'a so lonely here in Cal-i-fornia, Meester Smeet,*' and licking her lips with a dark, slug-like tongue, giving a sexy come-hither squint straight into the camera. Agh. Aw man, how that mole would look under the lights in close-up, like it weighed three pounds, alive and crawling.

Pynch winced and said, "Edgar, where's that psycho son of a bitch live again? You got it written anyplace on that freakin' clipboard?"

Pynch knew that the director, Jimmy Hale—who expected him to handle every trouble along these lines—was not going to be happy with this new turn of events. He didn't know how to tell Jimmy that Marciello was rewriting the script, casting his own people, throwing in the Cardinal, all of that. Jimmy was way too busy dealing with his own personal problems; namely the fact that the cops were just about to figure out he'd had his sister killed for her inheritance, in order to finish off his last action flick *Rearing Hell*, the one that finally made him a star.

Pynch stood out in the hall looking at Jimmy's redheaded secretary—Felicity, Chastity, something like that—thinking about how *she* would have made a perfect French maid. She had those nice juicy lips she always kept wet with Vaseline, beautifully-sized chest out to here, legs that topped off at her neck, always wearing black pumps.

He cleared his throat and said, "He in?"

She leaned forward in her seat and spoke quietly—an act of conspiracy—waving her freshly painted fingernails in the air, softly cracking gum. "Yeah," she whispered. "With the police."

"How long they been here?"

"Fifteen minutes."

Good. That meant they weren't arresting him. Just asking more questions. Pynch sat and wondered what Jimmy would do, how he would approach Marciello, exactly what he would say. Jimmy had a real genius when dealing with people. He was as good with the serious players as the actors and crew, with women and the police, with just about everybody except his sister. She'd been too much like him. Pynch found himself missing her a little now and again.

When the cops finally left they didn't even glance at Pynch. He got up and walked into the office.

Jimmy Hale, who was always cool and still looked calm even after facing off with the police again, said, "I heard you got a lot of action."

"You too. So what have they got?"

A non-committal shrug. "Nothing. You just witnessed the death throes of their investigation."

"Good. But we've got a problem with Marciello."

Jimmy froze, took a slow deep breath, and gave the same killer glare at Pynch that Pynch had given Edgar. Jimmy was much better at it, and Pynch didn't even have a clipboard to defend himself with. "How's it go?"

"It goes like this…" Pynch began, and after he'd laid it all out—the Cardinal, the accountant, the mole, and the out-of-control bus on Eighth Avenue—Jimmy leaned back and said, "You're kidding me, right?" He made lots of slow, angry gestures with his hands. "Okay, listen. I don't want to hear this. Take care of it."

"Me?" Pynch said. His voice cracked the word in half.

"You. Who else?"

Pynch felt the cool slide of sweat form on his upper lip. "I should do this? I got his address right here. I thought maybe you could go over there, smooth everything with him."

"What? You expect me to take care of *your* silent partner 'cause he's decided to throw his mutt of a woman at *my* camera. You seen her, right? You remember that act they pulled on the diving board? Turned everybody's stomach. Jesus, I'll give her a walk on, a few lines maybe, keep her in the background behind a plant or something, but he wants two minutes?" When Jimmy Hale was infuriated he spoke with a nice, humorous lilt, the kind that distracted people and made them think that things weren't so bad. Pynch did not like the lilt, and remembered Jimmy's sister warning him to watch out for it. "He's rewriting my script, throwing in his own scenes, going behind my back after all the shit I've gone through, that I've done to make this picture mine? Nuh uh."

"But Jimmy, I don't know how to handle guys like Marciello. I mean he's the head of his own outfit, you know, crazy bastard like to play with knives, always cutting himself slices of fruit and cheese and sausage. I heard he likes to take off guys' ears, too. No shit. Sometimes he throws them in the fire and sometimes he just hands them back so, if the guy's lucky, he can get it sewn back on. I mean...."

Jimmy smiled.

Good Christ. It was the whitest, most friendly and perfect smile of all time.

Pynch got the hell out of there.

He pulled up in front of Marciello's place expecting to see at least a few soldiers surrounding the front door, maybe a tomato garden in the back yard like the one Brando keeled over in at the end of *The Godfather*. Instead, Marciello's house had that southern California Spanish look, lots of tile and cacti and stone, nobody in sight. He went to the front door and rang the bell.

Marciello answered. "Pynch, good to see you! Nobody could get you on the phone this last month. I hear you had a good time porking all those Swiss blondie skiers. You bring back any of them European pornos?"

Since he hadn't talked to anybody in a month, Pynch didn't know how everybody knew about the snow bunnies. "Forgot. Next time."

They moved into Marciello's office, where he sat behind a desk with about a hundred framed photographs on it: kids, women, brothers, uncles, sons, a lot of cracked black-and-whites from a half century ago. It looked like Marciello could send a lot of people after Pynch, if he got pissed off, a bunch without necks, all of them with that insane Italian blood-bond. He wondered which was little Mikey, looking to score his death scene.

Marciello swung around in his seat. He was cutting up some pepperoni and cheese. "You hungry?"

Pynch swallowed hard, staring: a little piece of cheddar, a tiny slab of pepperoni, and a razor-sharp blade maybe a foot long. "Uh, no. Thanks."

"So what can I do for you?"

Damn Jimmy. He could have handled this like a pro, sat and out-talked Marciello and made it sound like music, and nobody would have to get mad or hurt. Pynch did not have the ability. The only reason he got laid on his vacation was because he couldn't speak the language. "It's about the film, Marciello. We've got a problem."

"Oh?"

And then the words came tumbling out of him. He sounded meaner than he meant to, more hard-ass, taking no crap. No rewriting, no Cardinal, no mustache except maybe an exterior shot behind a tree from a block away. Then he suddenly backed up, smiling, trying to make it sound like a joke between buddies, shoulder-to-shoulder, oil it up, but he didn't have the knack.

As Pynch spoke, Marciello's movements got slower and slower, like he was winding down from slicing his food, but winding up to cut into something else. "Pynch, first you take my money, and then you come into my house and lay down the law to me? I'm a major partner. You buy with my cash, you pay with my cash. I have a say on who does what in *A Feast of Angels*."

Pynch kept his eyes on the knife. He desperately wanted to hang on to his ears. If Marciello got his hands on one of them Pynch hoped the guy would hand it back, let him pack it in ice and drive off to the hospital. "You're absolutely right."

"You agree?"

"Yes."

"Then why are we having this conversation?"

Marciello took another bite of food and got up out of his seat, fast and low, the blade held lightly in his fist. Pynch slapped a palm over his left ear and cried, "Wait!"

Marciello said, "What's with you?"

And Pynch didn't know how it happened: he was so keyed-up, watching the knife, that the moment Marciello took a step toward him he sort of slung himself out of the way, in a move he hoped would be like that of a dog turning over belly up, begging for mercy. Instead he tripped and stumbled forward on the Spanish tile, moving almost directly into that knife. Marciello tried to get out of the way, a puzzled look on his face as they collided.

"Hey…"

It took nothing—not a hard lunge or a stabbing motion, Jesus, nothing, but the blade just eased through his ribs, as if no bone or muscle stood in its way. Marciello didn't make a sound as blood burst from his shirt front. He crumpled to his knees, still puzzled, kind of shaking his head, wondering what it was all about, just what in the hell had happened, and then fell over face-down with a chunk of pepperoni wadded into the side of his cheek.

Pynch said, "Oh my shit."

He looked down at the body of a serious player, a major investor in the flick, and watched the blood flowing free. He glanced at the framed photographs on the desk, all those family members who would be coming for him now.

As he turned to run he saw that she stood in the doorway staring at him. He said, "Hey, Carmella, now listen…listen, it was…" and soon noticed she wasn't looking at her dead lover on the floor. Instead she came towards him, gazing straight into his eyes, mugging for him like she wanted to do for the camera. The hint of a smile curled those lips, tip of a sluggy tongue sticking out of the corner, frizzy hair all poofed up, that mole staring at him, too. She grinned.

He thought about it again. Jimmy had said he'd give her a few lines. Let's see. *'I'm 'a from Phila-del-fia. I'm 'a so lonely here in Cal-i-fornia, Meester Smeet.'*

Hell, it was only a movie.

CONDOM CITY

special sale
welcome we've got
special bring the kids

they can blow them
up as balloons
a huge lot, ready for

delivery. Many driven
by little old ladies,
hardly used.

Immaculate condition.
Inspected. Some come
with leather. Low

mileage, clean like
new. A few, as is,
cruise. A variety

of sizes for your
special needs. Safe,
flawless, air bags.

All colors, loaded.
You can't afford
not to. Won't last.

-LYN LIFSHIN

AND THEM, TOO, I HOPE
PAUL DIFILIPPO

I saw the first of the new creatures on my way to work one Tuesday morning. Of course, I didn't know then what I was looking at, or what it all meant or portended, no more than the rest of the world did.

Having just gotten off the First Avenue bus, I was walking down the sidewalk toward my office building when something in the gutter caught my eye. At first I thought it was a discarded length of rubbery yellow garden hose, about six inches long, or some other bit of anonymous industrial debris.

But then it moved. Like a headless snake it writhed and rooted among the papers and trash, apparently questing for something good to eat. I surmised this motivation on the part of the lemon-colored hose because it was making a snuffling noise one could easily associate with hunger.

I don't remember being frightened at all, just curious. There wasn't any sense of menace emanating from the flexible yellow organ; no horror-movie shiver swept down my spine. I felt only the same sense of dispassionate interest your typical city-dweller takes from watching pigeons or squirrels feed. It all seemed surprisingly normal.

I moved to the edge of he curb and looked down. The rubbery texture of the hose was still dominant close up, but mitigated by what were plainly pores, some of which had short black hairs growing from them. As I bent down for a closer look, the hose briefly curled upward, as if sensing me. I saw two contracting and dilating nostrils sheened with moisture. Then my eyes traveled to the other end of the hose—or snout, as I was beginning to think of it.

That end vanished down a storm drain. Plainly, the snout was attached to something.

I stepped into the street and tried to make out the rest of the body hidden in the darkness of the sewer. But the snout must have been quite long, for nothing bulked immediately behind it.

On an impulse then, I grabbed it.

I still don't know why. I just did it. The first person ever to touch a New Creature.

And thank goodness it was one of the harmless ones.

The slim trunk stiffened like a board. It was warm and tough.

A pair of red eyes with black diamond-shaped pupils, set amid a swatch of gray fur, suddenly appeared behind the grating of the sewer.

I yelped and let go of the snout, and it retracted as fast as if it had been on a mechanical take-up reel. Then the eyes vanished too.

Well, of course I was stunned. I looked around to see if anyone else had witnessed my encounter with this strange new addition to urban subterranean life. But all the passersby were too busy, wrapped up in their own worlds.

So I continued onward to work.

Despite some deep reservations as to how my story would be taken, at coffee-break I told my co-workers about the incident. They all laughed, naturally. Someone mentioned the old urban myth about crocodiles in the sewers. Then we all went back to our desks.

But later on I was glad I had mentioned it. Because when all the various early sightings of the New Creatures worldwide were eventually correlated, it turned out that my encounter had been the first one!

I knew it was sheer luck and that I hadn't done anything special except to keep my eyes open and not dismiss what I saw. Still, being first did make me feel kind of special, as did all the attention from the media.

But of course, my story paled next to the New Creatures themselves. It was just a sidebar in the biggest event of historical times. But it was my personal brush with greatness, the only unique thing that ever really happened to me in my whole life.

Anyway, that evening I went home as always. As I ate supper I watched the early news, but there was nothing on it about the Yellow Snout, as I had named it in my head.

But next morning that was practically all the media could talk about.

The city was inundated with Yellow Snouts.

They seemed to like the dank darkness of the underground tunnels lacing the metropolis. But many had been seen scuttling across streets and parks, apparently from one lair to another. They were indeed gray-furred, about as big as a wild hog, but more sinuous, with short fly-whisk tails. Their snouts were a good eighteen inches long and kept coiled close to their heads when not in use, almost like a butterfly's proboscis. The Yellow Snouts appeared to be omnivorous scavengers, as they had been observed consuming an immense variety of edibles, ranging from carrion and hotdogs to lettuce, peanuts, french—fries and pretzels.

People were being advised that morning by the media not to approach the Yellow Snouts, although the animals had exhibited no hostility yet, and in fact seemed skittish around people. (It was not even certain if they possessed teeth or claws, venom or barbs.) Specimens both living and dead had been secured by Animal Control authorities, and local, national and global experts were examining them already.

When I went to work that day, I was something of a celebrity already. People who had heard of my encounter yesterday—and soon that was everyone in the building—tended to regard me as an expert on the Yellow Snouts, and asked me lots of questions about them, mainly where they could possibly have come from.

This was the main question everywhere, of course. Public opinion was about evenly split between two theories: the Yellow Snouts had been dropped by a UFO, or they had been manufactured in a secret lab.

But as things turned out, both of these theories were wrong, and much too tame.

Of course, I had no insights that anyone else didn't possess, and I was reduced to listening to the radio for further information.

Around noon, news of the Yellow Snouts was eclipsed or supplemented by a new event.

In Ohio another New Creature had surfaced.

That was what the announcer called it, and we all instantly knew that term was going to be the collective name for the Yellow Snouts and this other visitor.

The Ohio New Creature was something like a giraffe, except twice as tall. There was a troop of several thousand outside Des Moines. Its body was shaggy like a mammoth's, but striped blue and orange. It seemed specialized to browse on some crop at the height of its head, since its unjointed legs made it unable to bend and reach the ground. A local mayor had started calling it the Dali Llama, and the name seemed to stick.

This second sighting made the world sit up and really take notice. One New Creature, however odd, was an anomaly, but two were a disturbing trend.

Were we undergoing a planned invasion? Was some mad bioengineer letting loose the creations of his vats? No one knew, but everyone had an opinion.

The next sighting came from Texas. A kind of flat desert burrower like a manta-ray was sighted by hundreds of people. They were dubbed Sandfish.

Hard upon this sighting came reports from California of a kind of small centaur, six-limbed in the classical manner, with a wolf's lower body and a monkey-like torso. Some reporter christened them Lobochimps.

By now it was plain that whoever was depositing these creatures or whatever was making them appear was working westward. Ships in the Pacific were alerted to be on the watch for anything peculiar breaking the surface of the sea.

Productive work at my office, of course, and pretty much across the world, had more or less come to a halt. A group of us had adjourned to a bar with a television, where we could wait for the latest New Creature to appear.

Around six o'clock, all local programming was interrupted for a nationwide broadcast, which was also being fed by satellites around the world.

On the screen came the bearded face of a scholarly looking man. The crawl across the bottom of the image identified him as a famous Harvard naturalist who had written many books of popular science.

Basically, as best as I can recall, with only four New Creatures to work with, he had correctly devised the same theory that later scientists would confirm. He was a very smart guy.

This is what he told us.

The New Creatures were not extraterrestrial in the common sense of the word. They were carbon-based life using the same DNA as our familiar dogs and cats, spiders and snakes, with the same kinds of proteins and amino acids and other biological stuff. Their proteins even exhibited the same "chirality" as ours, whatever that was, and even interbreeding was possible. The odds against organisms from other worlds being so similar were astronomical. (The famous man smiled at his pun.)

Also, it was not likely that they were artificial, for they were too randomly complex. No sane person would have bothered to design such creatures, full of anatomical quirks and dead-end organs as they were. It was obvious from dissection that they were the result of evolution. An evolutionary track parallel to ours, but just as valid, given some unknown set of environments and circumstances.

This word "parallel" was the key, said the naturalist.

The New Creatures were from another Earth. Modern physics now permitted such alternate dimensions, he said. How they had crossed from their dimension to ours he would leave to the physicists also. But he could hazard the guess that a single crack in space, a wormhole or flaw in the continuum, was sweeping across our globe as it rotated, depositing New Creatures wherever it touched.

What was happening on the other side of the flaw, how it was managing to hoover up whole flocks of creatures from obviously radically distinct environments, was even less apparent.

It was possible, he continued, that this strange phenomenon had even happened before. The ancient explosion of life forms, some of them quite bizarre, recorded in the fossil record of the Burgess Shales, for instance, could be explained in this way.

In any case, said the naturalist, it was now up to people whether they would allow the New Creatures to take their place in the world. Many of them, such as the Dali Llamas, might be unfit for our world and starve without human aid. The New Creatures would possibly bring with them new diseases and parasites, and wreak ecological havoc, displacing native species. Yet the deliberate slaughter of so much new life, in a world that had already seen so much extinction and which was suffering from dwindling biodiversity, was not a step to be taken lightly.

And with that the naturalist concluded his speech, and we all went home, slightly tipsy or outrageously drunk, numb or wondering.

Well of course we all know now that slaughtering the New Creatures soon proved to be impossible, thanks to their sheer numbers. As the Cosmogonic Locus—for so it was dubbed—circled the globe once, twice, a dozen times, it deposited vast herds and swarms, prides and packs, flocks and schools of New Creatures in widely scattered locations. (The first amateur videotaper who caught a stampede of Gnashtusks emerging from thin air sold the tape to CNN for a cool half million.)

This parallel Earth seemed even more fecund than our own, a whole alien ecology we could only decipher in bits and pieces, host to a thousand exotic breeds which made our world look like a primitive Galapagos Island.

Nothing short of a nuclear attack could have eliminated, say, the hundreds of thousands of Snuffleupaguses in Montana or the millions of Sneetches in Mongolia, not to mention the zillions of Flutterbyes in Mexico.

To say nothing of the thankfully benign but embarrassing Polkadot Virus which took up residence in that securest of homes, the human body.

After all, look at how little success we had had trying to stem the migrations of killer bees or fire ants. There were minor successful local massacres, true, authorized and unauthorized; and some natural predator-prey pairings of New Creatures were imported intact, which helped to stabilize things. But on the whole, any human efforts to eliminate the New Creatures were like trying to bail the ocean with a spoon.

As the years went by, the arrival of more and more New Creatures became just a fact of life. People and societies and institutions and ecologies have either adjusted or failed. The NRA has disappeared: but that's because now everyone goes around armed. We don't hear much from either Hawaii or the Sierra Club these days. And Australians almost wished they could have their over-abundant rabbits back, in place of the Weaseldillos that eliminated them.

Life certainly is richer and more strange, though. That's for sure. For a while there, it was rather like inhabiting the Garden of Eden and getting to name all the animals for the first time once more.

Scientists these days seem to feel that the influx is slowing, although they're not really sure, since it's hard to pick new faces out of the crowd, so to speak. When I think back to that day when I first grasped the Yellow Snout's snout, it sometimes seems as if I personally formed the bridge that let the New Creatures cross to our world. I know it's silly, but that's just how I feel sometimes.

I guess the only big question remaining now is one that was brought up by the famous Harvard naturalist in a recent interview. None of the New Creatures to date, he noted, had exhibited anything like human intelligence. He went on to speculate whether any such intelligence had ever evolved on this parallel Earth, and whether such sapient beings were smart enough to stay out of the path of the Cosmogonic Locus, or might be caught up in it one day. The interviewer asked mightn't they even be controlling the whole process, and the naturalist admitted that might be possible, although he couldn't see why.

It made me wonder if we might get a visit someday from our smart or smarter cousins next door, and how they'll fit in. Maybe they're even tailoring our world to their own specifications before they arrive. Who knows?

I know lightning seldom strikes twice. But I'm keeping my eyes open.

Maybe I'll be the first to spot them, too, I hope.

THE 2ND COMING

The Best of Pirate Writings Vol. 2   Ed. by Edward McFadden 1-890096-13-X, $14 US

SF & fantasy collected from Pirate Writings magazine. The stories are not about Pirates, nor are they "pirated". Pirate is more indicative of the attitude & ambition that set the magazine apart from the rest & made it one of the best small press speculative fiction magazines of its day.

Featuring the talents of:
Brendon Adams • Linda D. Addison • Kathryn J. Brown • G. William Cromer • Paul DiFilippo • Steve Hamilton • J.L. Hanna • Anthony J. Howard • Brett Hudgins • Mary Soon Lee • Lyn Lifshin • Edward J. McFadden • Brian Plante • Mike Resnick • Tom Piccirilli • Arthur J. Scott • Josepha Sherman • Allen Steele • Christopher Stires • Patrick Thomas • Jeffrey Valka

PIRATE WRITINGS

Tales Of Fantasy, Mystery & Science Fiction, Vol. 1

Edited by Edward J. McFadden

Trade Paperback ISBN 1-89009604-0; US $12.95;
Some Limited Editions still available ISBN 1-890096-06-7:

Christine Beckert - David Bischoff - Carroll Brown - Jack Cady - Jennifer B. Crow - Charles de Lint - Paul Di Filippo - Alan Dean Foster - Esther M. Friesner - Ed Gorman - Geoffrey A. Landis - Sharianne Lewitt - Ardath Mayhar - Edward J. McFadden III - Bobbi Sinha-Morey - Leland Neville - Lyn Nichols - E. Jay O Connell - G.F. O Sullivan - Tom Piccirilli - Robert J . Randisi - Mike Resnick - Jessica Amanda Salmonson - A.J. Scott - Timothy S. Sedo re - Eric Sonstroem - Nancy Springer - Allen Steele - Sue Storm - and Roger Zelazny (One Of The Last Amber Stories)

PRAISE FOR PIRATE WRITINGS
"EXCELLENT." SCIENCE FICTION CHRONICLE
"FABULOUS...QUITE AN ACHIEVEMENT." DEAN R. KOONTZ
"SIGN ON UNDER THE FLAG OF MCFADDEN'S JOLLY ROGER NOW!" ASIMOV'S

ISBN 1-890096-08-3 $14.00 US

DESTINY'S DOOR
The bestselling novel from Judith Tracy

Here's to those that hope and pray.
Fate has led you here today.

Have we the power to grant you this,

Search your heart and make one wish.

Click here to Enter

Someone is attempting to break into Donald Thurman's computer. An accomplished hacker himself, Donald tries to trace the interloper -- but there is nothing to find. Not even an identifying cyber address, something that should be impossible. Impressed with the invisible hacker, he succeeds in making contact only to find he has discovered a new life form.

They are sentient beings who live in a computer environment and are searching for their creator. Donald becomes their mentor, their friend and their confidant. *They* even set up a website to help others, in order to prove themselves worthy of meeting the creator. But the world of infinite data grows smaller. Soon it becomes more of a prison than a home. *They* want to apply their newfound knowledge. *They* want to experience all life has to offer. *They* want out and unwittingly, Donald opens the door:

Destiny's Door.

"INVENTIVE, WILLING TO TAKE CHANCES... AND A CLIMACTIC TWIST."
-Paul Di Filippo, **ASIMOV'S**

"A REMARKABLE SCIENCE FICTION NOVEL."
-Leann Arndt, **BUZZ BOOK REVIEW**

"ELEGANCE, A REALLY GOOD COMMAND OF BASIC STORYTELLING... AN AUTHOR TO WATCH."   -Andrew Andrews, **TRUE REVIEW**

> ### *COMING SOON!*

VALLEY OF THE ANJELS

ISBN 1-890096-23-7, $14 US

*the first volume in a new fantasy series by best selling author **Judith Tracy***

THE STARSCAPE PROJECT

BRAD AIKEN

$14 US

BOOK 1: WELCOME TO THE WILSIDHE
Patrick Thomas
ISBN 1-890096-12-1
$7.99 US

BOOK 3: DARK PROPOSAL
Judith Tracy
ISBN 1-890096-15-6
$7.99 US

BOOK 5: THE UNDERCOVER DRAGON
Tony DiGerolamo
ISBN 1-890096-17-2
$7.99 US

THE WILDSIDHE CHRONICLES™

A Young Adult Fantasy Series For Readers Age 10-14 to Adult

In an instant, a spell by the Courtesan Asgar gets out of control and 300 kids from Pennsylvania pay the price. They are kidnaped right out of their school and dumped into a world where magic works and dragons, dwarves and pixies live. At first the Wildsidhe seemed like a world of make believe, but all too soon the kids find out the danger is all too real. The Courtesans Asgar and Queen Morna have decided to use the kids as pawns in their dark games and they don't care who gets hurt.

The only edge the kids have is that iron and steel can hurt the Courtesans and other Wildsidhers who want to hurt them. Luckily, part of their town got caught up in the spell and came over with them, even if they don't have electricity or running water. Now they have to learn how to survive far from home, with no parents or grownups to help them.

Some days it just doesn't pay to go to school.

BOOK 2: DOUBLE CROSS
Patrick Thomas
ISBN 1-890096-14-8
$7.99 US

BOOK 4: LEGACY
Judith Tracy
ISBN 1-890096-16-4
$7.99 US

BOOK 1:WELCOME TO THE WILSIDHE—The kids are kidnaped by Asgar. Justin must learn if he has what it takes to be a leader. Cindy learns she has magic powers she can't control & Terri's wheelchair gains the power to fly.

BOOK 2: DOUBLE CROSS—Back home, the FBI blocks off the town from the rest of the world. Asgar's curse will bring over the kids left behind on their 11th birthday. Tiny & Bobby try to run, but it does them no good. Morna tries to trick Bobby into volunteering to sacrifice himself to the Shadows. Now only Tina can save him.

BOOK 3: DARK PROPOSAL—Because of The Treaty of Shadows, the Courtesan king must marry into the royal bloodline. Asgar learns Cindy is of that bloodline & proposes. Justin says over his dead body. Asgar has no objections.

BOOK 4: LEGACY—Alana, Cindy's grandmother, escapes from the FBI lock up of the town. She returns to the Wildsidhe to teach Asgar a lesson—You don't mess with family.

BOOK 5: THE UNDERCOVER DRAGON—The FBI finds out that they can send 17 year old Jamel over to the Wildsidhe. Geting back is up to him. Asgar can send him home, for a price-find the Grimstone in caverns filled with dragons & dwarves. The FBI never said there'd be days like this.

BOOK 6: CAR TROUBLE—One of the kids best defenses has been their cars. A dwarf clan decides they want one and try to bully a car out of the kids. Justin says no, so the dwarves decide they have only one option left: steal one.

BOOK 6: CAR TROUBLE
Myke Cole
ISBN 1-890096-18-0
$7.99 US

THE FIX :®
THE FIX IN OVERTIME
TONY DIGEROLAMO

The world's most powerful substance
The World's worst detective
The Earth may be destroyed tonight and
the only man who can save us
Still lives in his parents basement.

ISBN 1-890096-09-1 $14.00 US

ORDER NOW!

( ) <u>MURPHY'S LORE</u>™: <u>TALES FROM BULFINCHE'S PUB</u>   Patrick Thomas   ISBN 1890096075/$14.00 US

( ) <u>MURPHY'S LORE</u>™: <u>FOOL'S DAY</u>   Patrick Thomas   ISBN 1890096113/$14.00 US

( ) <u>MURPHY'S LORE</u>™: <u>THROUGH THE DRINKING GLASS</u>   Patrick Thomas   ISBN 1890096190/$14.00 US

( ) <u>MURPHY'S LORE</u>™: <u>SHADOW OF THE WOLF</u>   Patrick Thomas   ISBN 1890096210/$14.00 US

( ) <u>DESTINY'S DOOR</u>   Judith Tracy   ISBN 1890096083/$14.00 US

( ) <u>WORLD TREE</u>™ *A roleplaying game of species and civilization*

     Bard Bloom & Victoria Borah Bloom ·   ISBN 1890096105/$29.95 US

( ) <u>THE FIX</u>®: <u>THE FIX IN OVERTIME</u>   Tony DiGerolamo   ISBN 1890096091/$14.00 US

( ) <u>THE BEST OF PIRATE WRITINGS</u>™:VOL. 1 Edited by Edward J. McFadden III   ISBN 1890096040/$12.95 US

( ) <u>THE 2ND COMING: THE BEST OF PIRATE WRITINGS</u>™:VOL. 2 Ed. by Edward J. McFadden   ISBN 1890096040/$12.95 US

( ) <u>EVERMORE</u>   Hunter Lord & Ariel Masters   ISBN 1890096016/$5.99 US

( ) <u>WOMBERS & INNUENDOES</u>   Hunter Lord & Ariel Masters   ISBN 1890096032/$9.95 US

<u>THE WILDSIDHE CHRONICLES</u>™:

( )   BOOK 1:<u>WELCOME TO THE WILSIDHE</u> Patrick Thomas   ISBN 1890096121/$5.99 US

( )   BOOK 2: <u>DOUBLE CROSS</u>   Patrick Thomas   ISBN 1890096148/$5.99 US

( )   BOOK 3: <u>DARK PROPOSAL</u>   Judith Tracy   ISBN 1890096156/$5.99 US

( )   BOOK 4: <u>LEGACY</u>   Judith Tracy   ISBN 1890096164/$5.99 US

( )   BOOK 5: <u>THE UNDERCOVER DRAGON</u> Tony DiGerolamo   ISBN 1890096172/$5.99 US

( )   BOOK 6: <u>CAR TROUBLE</u>   Myke Cole   ISBN 1890096180/$5.99 US

ORDER HOTLINE: 1-845-557-8955 OR USE PAYPAL AT PADWOLF.COM

PADWOLF PUBLISHING INC. PO Box 117, Yulan, NY 12792-0117

PLEASE SEND ME THE BOOK(S) I HAVE CHECKED ABOVE. I HAVE ENCLOSED $______ PLUS $2.00 SHIPPING & HANDLING FOR EACH BOOK. (If ordering 2-6 of The Wildsidhe Chronicles series, shipping is $3.20.) SEND CHECK OR MONEY ORDER. (NO CASH OR COD'S) NY RESIDENTS PLEASE ADD APPLICABLE SALES TAX)

CREDIT CARD___________ NUMBER_________________________________

EXP DATE __________

NAME ____

ADDRESS ____

CITY _________________________ STATE________ ZIP__________

Please allow 2-6 weeks for delivery. Prices & offer are subject to change without notice

PADWOLF PUBLISHING